Summer in the Heart

Also by John McMillan

On A Green Island

Summer in the Heart

John McMillan

iUniverse, Inc.
Bloomington

Summer in the Heart

iUniverse books may be ordered through booksellers or by contacting:

iUniverse
1663 Liberty Drive
Bloomington, IN 47403
www.iuniverse.com
1-800-Authors (1-800-288-4677)

ISBN: 978-1-4620-0974-9 (sc)
ISBN: 978-1-4620-0975-6 (ebook

Printed in the United States of America

iUniverse rev. date: 4/12/2011

"That summer in the heart which is known only in youth."

Richard Jefferies

To the memory of my mother and father

Chapter 1

A Song of the City

"I don't understand you, Jim Mitchell. You got distinctions in English Language and Literature and fail, fail, fail in everything else. Oh, except Art, that is."

The form master, Geordie Spence, wore a cream jacket of Irish linen; his long, bespectacled nose was red and peeling from refereeing cricket matches in the sun. My school report lay on his desk between us, just the two of us there in his classroom in the new redbrick Johnston Wing of the Royal School. The hot afternoon sun shone in on us through the tall windows. The open windows let in balmy breaths of summer and the light, airy sounds of a game of rounders.

"I like English the most, sir and I like drawing and painting."

"I can tell that alright," said Geordie drily. "But you need these other subjects whether you like them or not: maths, science, et cetera. You won't get anywhere without them, you know, Mitchell."

"Yes, sir," I nodded gravely. But it was the last day of the summer term and I didn't care about my report any more. There'd been a relaxed atmosphere at school all day, the teachers chatting to us, reading us stories or doing quizzes. The two long months of the summer holidays lay ahead: bliss!

When I left Geordie's room it was only ten minutes to the final bell. Instead of returning to Reverend Gilliland's Religious Instruction class I slipped away early, out the girls' gate and down the avenue to the Antrim Road.

It seemed a long, long time, an age since my first day at the grammar school in September when I'd come with Ivan Mollen in the bucketing rain. Ivan from the Top Road was the only other child from Loughside Primary School going on to the Royal School after the eleven-plus Qualifying exam. I searched anxiously for him along the crowded platform at Loughside station and found him in the waiting room with his mother.

"We're here, Jim," said Mrs Mollen, a formidable retired schoolmistress. "It's bad for Ivan's chest standing around on that platform."

I had seen her before during the summer, on the shore at Hazelbank, holding a bath towel ready for Ivan as he came shivering from the tide.

Now Ivan, wearing a sheepish half-grin, sat beside his mother on the long green wooden bench, near the coal fire. He was dressed like me in the new school uniform with the maroon badge on the cap, except he was wearing short grey trousers, beefy purplish knees poking out under the navy Burberry, while my capacious long grey flannels concertina'd around my shoes.

We boarded the busy Belfast train, Mrs Mollen ushering us along the corridor, through the sliding door, between knees in the compartment to some spaces next the window. The whistle blew, the train jerked and the platform slid away. We emerged in the rainy light, swinging, bumping over the points, straightening up and rolling above the backs of the estate houses, then galloping out across the open green fields between the mountain and the Lough, the clouds of smoke and steam from the engine whipped away in the wind and rain.

The three of us travelled in silence. I sat listening to the conversation of the middle-aged commuters who shared our carriage. I would become familiar with the same faces each day, the voices bluff and know-all with a supposed Ulster hard-headedness but leavened by polite banter; the endless discussions of business and current affairs, and the leathery impassive faces with a way of speaking out of the side of the mouth. I thought of them as the "Jimmies":

"Is thet right nowr, Jimmy?"

"Oh aye, Jimmy, indeed and I'm not tellin' ye one word of a lie nowr!"

The bigger, more important Jimmies were "Mister":

"And tell us nowr, Mr McIntyre, what have you got to say on the subject?"

"Well don't ask me, Mr Dunwoody, sure heven't we got the expert with us, over in the corner there—you're very quiet the day, Mr Mawhinney!"

Mr Mawhinney: "Well hould on nowr, Mr McIntyre, I make no claim to be any kind of authority whatsoever on the subject, but I can ectually speak from first hand experience of exectly this type of problem in my own line of business right enough and there is one thing I can tell ye for sure..."

And wise Jimmyish heads nodded approval as the Oracle held forth. I could tell Mr Mawhinney was a man whose opinions you listened to. Unlike most of the politicians up at Stormont or worse still, over the water at Westminster, Mr Mawhinney acknowledged the hard facts of economics.

Losing the thread of the important debate, I stared out the window at the black snake of the cinder track wriggling along beside the railway. We hurtled across the iron bridge over the Valley of Death, a glimpse of the full brown river away down through the treetops bringing boyhood summer memories of walking here across the fields with Davy Robinson to explore the sinister green gorge where murder most foul had occurred.

Past Bleach Green halt and Whiteabbey station the train panted through the deep cutting under one, two bridges and into the tunnel. We surfaced in the open at Greencastle with the Lough stretching away, choppy, grey and misty, to the gantries and cranes of the Belfast shipyards. A high tide washed the sloping sea wall below the railway embankment. On the other, landward side of the tracks the canal ran dark, stagnant, littered. There was a boatyard, scrap metal yard, a tract of waste ground, then the prefabs, row upon row of the dingy little bungalows off the Shore Road. Above, Cavehill reared its craggy head, Napoleon's nose among the rain clouds. We came in past the football stadium and the sunken backyards of the railway terraces. The big dusty windows of Jennymount Spinning Mill loomed over the tracks, blotting out the sky in the approach to Belfast station.

That first morning with the Mollens we caught the red double-decker bus up Duncairn Gardens. Descending at the Antrim Road in the relentless rain, we were swept along in the river of navy and grey uniforms with their maroon bits, over the pedestrian crossing with its lollipop man and up the leafy avenue past the Presbyterian church to the red sandstone walls of the school.

At the boys' entrance, the rain splashing off her raised umbrella, Mrs Mollen said, "Well, here you are then, men. Now, you'll remember the way back to the station, won't you?"

I wasn't so sure about that; Ivan's lower lip trembled but he controlled himself. With a "Cheerio then!" Mrs Mollen turned back down the avenue, stepping out briskly over the puddles in her brogues and transparent ankle-length Pakamac. Ivan and I looked up at the Victorian edifice, a castle with its towers and bumpy, sheer stone walls that seemed to tumble against the smoky racing sky. High up rows of narrow dark windows glinted evilly. Big prefects were waiting to herd us inside. Two chubby country lads, we fell in timidly with the others hurrying in out of the rain.

Our first morning at grammar school was spent sorting out timetables and textbooks. I liked my green cloth-covered copy of *The Splendid Spur* by Sir Arthur Quiller-Couch and the poetry anthology that opened with John Masefield: *"I must go down to the sea again, to the lonely sea and the sky".* There was a first French reader illustrated with jolly little cartoons of French life, all bustle and quaintness. Even the fat, grey-covered *Arithmetic* had a friendly look and feel about it like a Billy Bunter book. There were all the exciting new subjects: Latin, Biology, Physics and Chemistry, with a different teacher and room for each subject. There was Physical Training every day, in the well-equipped gym, Rugby on Wednesdays, Swimming on Thursdays. It was a fresh start, opportunities opening in every direction. I went around that morning in a glow of anticipation, a dream of all-round achievement and excellence. I would be a brilliant scholar *and* a champion sportsman.

Our form had five streams, A to E, based on our eleven-plus exam and intelligence test results. I was in C, Ivan in A, so we soon parted company that morning. After dinner in the roaring, clattering canteen I went out in the playground, casting about vaguely for Ivan.

The rain had stopped. There he was, in his element, over by one of the corner towers, smiling and talking with two other lads from the A stream—they all had that brainy look, a sort of amused eccentricity, like adults playing at being children. I knew Ivan was pretending he didn't see me so I just stood there friendless, arms folded, by the toilet block, viewing the yelling scrum of the playground with a mature sort of disdain.

An undersized fair-haired boy called Campbell came running up, snatched my school cap from my head and ran off gleefully with it. I gave chase but as I caught up with Campbell he threw my cap to Rea, an undersized dark-haired boy.

"Oi! Gimme back me cap, you nit!" I shouted, charging Rea, glad of the diversion although I feltt this was a childish game for eleven-year-olds.

I was one of the first out the school gates when the final bell went at ten-to-three but Ivan was already well ahead of me down the bottom of the avenue, running for the ten-past-three train from York Street. The red double-decker was turning down Duncairn Gardens; Ivan was already at the stop. I sprinted after the bus but the schoolbag, rock-heavy with new books, slowed me down and I saw the bus pulling away and Ivan settling himself on the long back seat staring out at me, the pale blob of his face shrinking as they accelerated.

"Och, sure what's the flippin' hurry anyway?" I told myself. "You get on home to your mammy, Ivan. I can walk to the station and buy myself a cup of tea with the fare-money I've saved, while I wait for the quarter-to-four."

The sun poured down now out of a washed blue sky, white cumulus piled around like mountains of the school canteen's mashed potato. There was a blue sheen on the wet tarmac, a dazzle of puddles. Breathing the carbon-tasting city air, I strolled down the hill taking in the strangeness and excitement of it all. Pausing to look in the window of Pat's Pet Shop, I gazed longingly at a white mouse in a cage, up on its hind legs spinning a wheel.

"Och, I want a wee mouse like that! Daddy and Mammy'd never let me but sure they needn't know! It could live in my pocket and go round everywhere with me!"

Further down the road I was pulled up suddenly by a shop window crammed with amazing old things: gilt-framed pictures and mirrors, jug, basin and chamber pot sets, oil lamps and candlesticks, clocks and books and trays and fire-screens. Like a magic window on the past! I stood there wide-eyed, transported. The little shop was shut and dark, adding to its aura of mystery. It occupied the ground floor of a dusty-windowed, lifeless Victorian terrace. In a fantasy I broke in through the back and crept around fingering the antiques. It was like stepping back in time a hundred years. The idea sent a shiver of excitement through me.

I continued on, past St Barnabas' Public Elementary, a dark Dickensian school and the Duncairn Cinema which

showed old films, a change of bill every two days. Down on the corner with York Street there was a newsagent's selling paperback cowboy novels by J.T.Edson and American pulp publications that must have come up from the docks: war and horror and space comics and fan magazines. I stopped to browse the stands and shelves and sniff the heady peppery smell of the new pages.

Out on York Street with the traffic barging to and fro it was twenty-past-three on the station clock. I waited to cross at the traffic lights, in the beery, stale smell from the mustard-coloured pub on the corner with Lower Canning Street.

Inside the station I headed for the Refreshments buffet. I had been there before with my parents, but to walk in on my own now and order a cup of tea like the complete man about town was really something.

"What can I get you, love?" enquired the wee Belfast woman behind the counter. "Cuppa tae? Right! That it? Fourpence, please, son. Thank you. Now you just sit down and I'll bring it over to you in one minute."

The buffet was quite empty. The walls were decorated gaily, incongruously, with a mural of Caribbean island scenery and figures, a design that was repeated on the Formica table-tops. I sat over in a corner with a view out the window to the platform gates and toilet block.

"Here you are now, love." The waitress placed the tea before me. Being called "love" like that affected me, piercing the shell of my strangeness here in the city and giving me a warm gooey feeling. This was a city with a heart.

I stirred in the sugar lumps, sipped the hot brown liquid, sweet and homely. Outside the window the drowsy afternoon quiet was splintered suddenly by the rattle of

trolley wheels across the station concourse and then the voice of the youthful porter soared, echoing around the high, sooty glass roof in an imitative emotional burst of song: *"Put your head on my shoulder..."*

It was nothing more than a spontaneous release of creative energy in a workingman's day, a hit song off the radio. But I would never forget that brief startling performance at the station, that September afternoon fifty years ago; it seemed to stand for something romantic and irrepressible in the soul of ordinary people.

Chapter 2

School Days

Now the school year had gone and with it the dream of fame, the applause of the whole school ringing in my ears as I stepped up to the platform at prize-giving to receive its highest academic and sporting accolades. That was not to be; the big city grammar was a different world to my old country primary school where I had been the wee star, successful and popular. The sheer size of secondary school encouraged obscurity; it was easier to keep your head down, to exist in a daydream.

My life soon settled into a strict routine, rising at seven on cold, black winter mornings to shiver into my clothes in front of the small electric fire in my bedroom. I wore hand-me-down white shirts that my big brother had owned as a sixteen-year-old in his first job back in 1952. The cuffs covered my hands and the shirt-tails hung to the backs of my knees; I stuffed them down the waistband of my first pair of long grey flannels, voluminous bags that flapped and beat like sails when I walked.

Downstairs the living room was cosy and cheerful. A big coal fire blazed out life and hope from the small fawn fireplace. The wireless was tuned to the Light Programme, an orchestral medley that managed to be spirited in a restrained fashion, as became the hour of the working day. Mum, in a heavy old brown checked dressing-gown, put my breakfast on the table under the window: cereal, boiled egg and toast, cup of tea.

"And how is the scholar today?"

"Got all my homework done anyway: Latin declensions for Robbie, fractions for Jake." The enthusiasm in my voice made me wince a little at my self-deception, but it kept my parents happy.

"You're some boy at the *amo, amas, amat!"* Mum joked.

"Aye, *amamis, amatis,* my aunt!"

"What would Mr Reid say if he heard that?"

"Prob'ly laugh; he's an awful nice wee man. Too nice for some of the ones in the class; they just take advantage, so they do."

"Och, aren't they just the wee brats, some of them!"

Bundled into my blazer and Burberry, scarf and cap and gloves, the heavy, stiff leather satchel buckled at my chest, I was ready for the off, over the doorstep into the gusty dark. Mum watched me down the garden path and with my last little wave from the pavement below I saw the door close on her kindly, intelligent face and the comfort of her small domestic world. I was on my way to the train, lowering my head like a bull to the icy blasts that met me at the corner of Coolmore Green. Up Station Road I fell in with the shadowy drift of commuters, the remorseless *click-clack* of the shorthand-typists' stiletto heels. It was like joining a procession of the damned. This was the

unstoppable machine of the working world and all you could do was say your prayers at night and put up with it.

I hardly laid eyes on Ivan Mollen after that first day at school. I travelled alone on the quieter 8.20 train up to Belfast then walked in all weathers from the station, cutting through the back streets. Lower Canning Street was wide, with gaunt, mysterious old houses, their different sizes and colours giving them a curious individuality. The road was cobbled where it ascended steeply to the intersection of North Queen Street. Then it was over into narrow Upper Canning Street with its two long facing rows of uniform small redbrick terraces dwindling away to the horizon.

Sometimes a housewife would be out scrubbing her front doorstep and the patch of pavement in front of it but that was the only life you ever saw in the strangely silent, deserted back streets. I had ventured this way with a certain trepidation at first, feeling conspicuous in my grammar school uniform but I need not have worried; the delft figurines, dancing shepherd and shepherdesses and the like, displayed in the neatly-curtained windows of front parlours signalled a working class respectability here. After a while I felt confident enough to duck down the alleys that ran behind the houses like secret passageways. I emerged near the top of Duncairn Gardens, the roar of traffic on the main road jolting me out of my morning reverie.

The fallen autumn leaves, swishing underfoot, piled the pavements of the avenue up to the school. There were bright frosty mornings with a smoky smell. I had a late pass because I lived in the country; the playground was deserted when I arrived. From assembly the one voice of the whole school was raised in a song of praise. I crept in

and drank thirstily at the fountain under the Gothic arches. It was good to go inside, exhilarated from the sharp air and golden light, and climb the big central staircase to a classroom high in the old building where you could tuck yourself away in a corner, hug the radiator pipes and daydream to your heart's content.

At the Royal School nobody forced you to work. The teachers in their swirly black gowns were relaxed and liberal and witty. There were no crook-handled thin canes in their classroom cupboards. One older teacher had been appointed to administer the cane as a last resort punishment for exceptionally bad behaviour and this was a very rare event. White-moustached Jimmy McCain—his real name!—turned out to be a decent man when I got to know him in later years in his English class, with nothing of the sadist in his character. Perhaps he'd been chosen for that very reason. A few other masters circumvented the caning policy by using a meter stick or board duster or cuffing round the ears. It was unusual however and if a pupil's parents reported a teacher he was in trouble.

Scarily, I had the Headmaster, Mr Leatherbarrow, for Geography, not one of my better subjects. Just the sight of this austere little Yorkshireman with his shiny pate, snowy hair and quick, watchful terrier head was enough to impose silence on an assembly or crowded staircase. There was nothing nasty about the Head; his simple, unquestionable authority and aura of strict duty were awe-inspiring, like God.

Geography was first period in the morning. I made a point of getting there early and then sitting near the back of the class. Being right at the back might only draw attention to you. I kept my head down, willing myself invisible, like a camel. It seemed to work; no questions were ever directed at me and I did not volunteer any answers.

The half-basement window looked out on the boys' gate, so anyone wandering in late and not looking right—maybe flouting the school uniform regulations in a duffel coat, winklepickers or drainpipe trousers—would be spotted by Leatherbarrow, who'd dash out and apprehend them. We watched from the window: there was an endearing boyish quality about the sprightly little man out there dancing on one foot on the frosty tarmac, hoiking up his trouser leg to reveal a long grey woollen sock and pointing at his 24 inch bottoms and round toecaps as an example to his errant pupil.

"So go home this evening and find something sensible to put on for school tomorrow and don't be so silly and stu-pid in future!" The Yorkshire voice lent an incontrovertible plain, no-nonsense quality to his words. I learned too that he could be light-hearted at times, joking like an affectionate uncle with Ferris, a brainy scientific boy in the class.

The dream of sporting prowess fizzled out miserably early on. Physical training and games proved a disappointment to me, just plain uncomfortable as the winter weather took hold. We rarely had use of the exciting apparatus in the gym; instead we were turned out into the playground in all weathers, shivering in our maroon singlets, white shorts and canvas gutties, to play basketball, a game I soon lost interest in. I'd hang about on the periphery, moving just enough to keep from freezing to death. The worst thing was when the two appointed captains chose their teams each day and I was left to joint-last in the line-up with Gaston, the fat freak of the class.

Then "Mitchell," they chose me indifferently. I suppose I should have been grateful to Gaston saving me from being Paddy-last.

I'd looked forward especially to swimming, a voluntary after-school activity, but never went back to the class after the first session in the Victorian municipal baths, put off by the wet squalor of the changing cubicles, the smell of chlorine, the ugly white tiles like a public lavatory and the crowded, bumping, splashing bodies, with the great mongrelish din going up under the high glass roof. I had only swum in the sea before, Belfast Lough, just Matt or Davy and me and the expanse of salt water, two boys under the sky, wild and free as the gulls.

Rugger was compulsory; every Wednesday afternoon a fleet of buses took every boy in the school out into the countryside at Ballywonard. The playing fields with their high white Rugby posts stood among wintry, misty hedged fields. Out on the pitch, insignificant among thirty players in white-collared red jerseys and navy shorts, I learned to look busy and keep my circulation going, while doing my best to avoid the slippery oval leather ball, the charging bodies and the crunch of bones as a tackle brought you down *splat!* The bodies piled on top of you, the wind knocked out of you and the studded boots milling around your head.

There was a ghostly feeling as the afternoon light failed across the mucky field and you waited for the last long trailing blast on the referee's whistle. Back in the pavilion the changing rooms were crowded with boys of every shape and size off the pitches. The senior boys, some hairy and bandy as apes, strutted like gladiators under the steaming showers. I felt small and soft and pink like a marshmallow and vulnerable as a baby. Avoiding the showers, I pulled my trousers on over numb, clay-encrusted knees and hurried out for a seat on the bus.

Going back into town through Glengormley, past the Zoo, everyone on the bus sang:

"Free beer for all the wor-kers!

When the Red Revolution comes along!"

The only good thing about Rugger practice was getting home afterwards in the five-thirty dark, chilled to the bone from the long afternoon on the pitch. Now the living room's welcome was brighter and warmer than ever, all aglow with a big blazing fire that twinkled on the mantelpiece ornaments and the gilt picture-frames on the walls. I sat down famished to Mum's lamb hot-pot with the sliced potatoes on top crispy from the oven. Dinner had never tasted so good.

There was the world of the school: of milling crowds and big classes, being one of this great uniformed mass, yet lonely inside, with lots of new acquaintances but no real friends.

And there was the world of home, Mum waiting for me in the afternoons after school with tea and biscuits by the fire. Refreshed from her afternoon nap, she was bright and quick as a bird, sitting forward attentively on her armchair, holding her cup and saucer, her shins measled with purple blotches from the heat of the fire, her feet in a pair of tan mules.

I loved these cosy chats, just the two of us. Whether to please her or delude myself, I wasn't sure, but I bummed like mad in a desperate attempt to attribute a positive identity to myself at the school.

"...Anyway, Geordie tested the class on *Ode to a Nightingale* and nobody could get much past the first two lines, *'Hail to thee, blithe spirit, Bird thou never... er...went...I mean, wet!'* Not even Felicity Price and then Geordie says, 'C'mon, Mitchell, let's hear it!' and I stood up at my desk and recited the whole poem off pat, and Geordie turns to the class and says, 'Now wasn't that easy?'"

"Well, good man, Jim! All that recitation and drama you did at Loughside Primary is standing you in good stead now. And tell us about your wee chums. What about Roy Campbell?"

"Och, he's a wee eejit, Mum, so he is, smoking fags in the bogs with the big lads and him not the height of two turf, as Dad would say. They tell you smoking stunts your growth and there's your proof!"

"I suppose he thinks it makes him big."

"He's just a wee spacer! You can hardly get a sensible word out of him. Campbell's spooly! I've met some nicer fellas now that you can have a decent laugh with, like big Cyril Breakey. Honest, he's twelve years old and six feet tall! Still in short pants, and goes round mimicking Charlie Drake in a high wee cockney voice, *'Hi-lo my dahlings!'* He calls me *Skiboo,*" I announced proudly—a nickname conferred a degree of popularity.

"Why *Skiboo?"* Mum didn't look so sure about this. "Isn't that one of Dad's characters?"

"Think I told people it was my middle name! Anyway, that's just one of my nicknames; some of the lads call me *Beatnik* or just *Mitch*."

"Well, well, it's never a dull moment at that school!"

After our chat, with a couple of hours free till teatime, I changed into jeans and jerkin and met up with Matt Connaughton to wander the estate and its environs. We drifted like phantoms in the cold dregs of the daylight with the foghorns blasting away mournfully out on the Lough. We'd encounter other little groups of lads and sundry adventures along the way.

Matt remained firmly my best friend; an older boy, from Knockshanagh Park up by the railway, he went to the Catholic school in Carrickfergus. We both came from Great Northern Railway families out of County Fermanagh, a fact that had seemed to bond us from the word go. My new life at the Belfast grammar had not come between us yet; I'd found nobody there to compare with him: mature, sensitive Matt, with his Teddy-boy quiff of fairish hair and mild, shy green eyes. Steady and loyal, he was always there waiting for me after school and at the weekends and school holidays.

Inseparable, the two of us ranged the small universe of Loughside, between the mountain and the Lough. The sprawl of the new housing estate where we lived had eaten into the meadows bordering the old country village with the single mile of Station Road between the Top Road and Shore Road. We wandered the cinder track that followed the railway above the estate, out into the fields towards Jordanstown; explored the old goods line that curved inland to Mossley; hid in the jungle of the cuttin' under the railway bridge. There were the shortcut tunnels of the green loanings that burrowed down to the shore; we'd come to know the trees along the way individually, like friends, had climbed every one, sheltered under them.

The winter evenings drew in. A campfire flared behind the laurels deep in the churchyard, shadowy gang-figures gathered about it under the big cedar of Lebanon. There was the glow of a communal Woodbine fag passed in the dark; spuds baked in the red heart of the fire. From that secret rendezvous there were thrilling forays out in a big gang, stealthy, invincible in the early dark, to "rob an orkie" down Station Road.

The black dark and biting winter cold sent us home gratefully to our tea, smelling the night air and smoke and frosty leaves on your hair and clothes as you entered the luxurious warmth of the house with the sizzle of chops frying from the scullery, the table laid beneath the curtained window of the living room, Dad home from work:

"You've been smoking?"

"Me? No."

He nodded. "You've been smoking." That was as far as it went, with nothing more needing to be said.

After tea a slouch on the sofa in front of the fire, cup of tea and biscuits, watching the news with Dad. Ensconced in his chimney-corner armchair by the bookcase for the night, he watched telly, read the *Belfast News Letter* and the *Daily Express*, dozed fitfully. Mum read her magazines on the sofa, *Woman* and *Woman's Own, Women's Realm* and *Woman's Weekly.* She wasn't much interested in the telly unless it was a handsome cowboy, *Maverick* or *Bronco,* or the boyish charm of Reginald Bosanquet reading the News. I sat on through the after-six news programmes in a stupor of procrastination, reluctant to tear myself away from the company of the fireside to school homework in the barrenness of the front room.

I shut myself away there across the hall from seven. A square bay window overlooked the green; there was the piano and china cabinet and the uncomfortable stiff armchairs that seemed to have been designed for non-use in drawing rooms. The open fire was only lit here on special occasions; a squat, smelly oil heater roasted my shins while I stewed over my textbooks at the little wobbly folding table put there for me, ticking off the tasks listed in

my school diary. At nine I cleared away my books, packed my bag ready for the morning and returned to the fireside and telly. Sandwiches and tea were served on a tray at half-nine. Maybe there was a play to watch on the telly before bedtime.

I saved up and got the white mouse from Pat's Pet Shop, travelled home with it in my gabardine pocket. It kept crawling out onto the train seat but I had a compartment to myself. I named him Beppo, stroking his soft little white back with my thumb and feeding him grains from the bag of mouse-food I'd bought. He deposited a tiny black dropping with every step he took.

At our house the Yale key was in the front door as usual; I let myself in quietly and hung my coat with Beppo in the pocket in the cloakroom under the stairs. I knew Mum and Dad didn't want pets. Beppo was to be my secret. I thought it'd be easy to keep something so tiny hidden. But of course he was an animal, with a mind of his own and legs. It was a Friday night and we were watching a TV film in the dark, just the light of the screen and the fire, when there was a scampering and scuttling the length of the wainscoting behind us.

"Och, it's not a mouse!" Mum craned over her shoulder into the flickering darkness, gave a mock shudder. "We had plenty of them at Creenagh where you were born, Jim, but never since we've been living in these new houses!"

Dad wielded his big shoe, tiptoeing to the light switch, turning on the light. "There it is in the corner!" He advanced stealthily in his carpet slippers.

"Dad, don't! That's Beppo, my pet white mouse!" I gulped.

I was surprised when they weren't cross about it, maybe because it was such a tiny, harmless and undemanding creature. Or a cute wee-boyish thing for me to have done. Instead, they found a cardboard box for Beppo to live in, in a corner of the room and agreed that I could join Pat's Pet Shop's Christmas Club and save for a proper mouse cage with a wheel. In the meantime Beppo proceeded to eat his way out of a series of cardboard boxes and race round the wainscoting all day.

I ended up getting quite friendly with Roy Campbell at school. We were both jokers and a bit indolent, wasting time together at the back of the class, although I thought he was just too silly sometimes, a queer little runt with the Charlie Chaplin walk he cultivated. Embarrassing. There was no stillness or depth to Campbell; his mind jumped around like a flea, making any real conversation with him impossible. But he was company nevertheless, somebody to sit next to in class or be with in the playground. Nobody else wanted him.

When June brought the good weather and the approach of the end of term Campbell invited me over to his house at Cherryvalley one Saturday. It sounded nice, like a place out of an Enid Blyton book. It was out the far side of Belfast, two bus journeys from the station on one of the first glorious Saturdays of summer. I changed buses at City Hall. The flower sellers were busy by the railings in the bright sunshine. Flocks of noisy pigeons on the lookout for passing grain lorries lined the long ledges of the domed municipal edifice; they swooped down insolently and perched on the heads of the green Victorian statues. The traffic raced the circuit of Donegall Square. Red double-deckers pulled up at the stops; I watched anxiously for my number. I'd never travelled this far from home on my own before.

A tramp—at least he looked like one—was standing beside me at the railings. He spoke to me and I answered politely, thinking of him as a poor well-meaning crathure deserving of my Christian sympathies.

"Ye're a real wee gentleman, I can tell," he was saying in a hoarse, cracked voice. That was how I saw myself, in the sturdy Christian tradition of *Tom Brown's Schooldays*. This tramp was another human being after all. I relaxed and talked to him about my summer holidays, going to my uncle's farm at Bushmills. I asked, "Do you know that part of the world?"

"I know they make a very nice wee drap o' whusky there all right!" he said. I guessed he was a drunk; all tramps were. I smiled indulgently. Then suddenly his bristly mug was shoved up close to mine: runny pink slits for eyes, sour boozy breath and teeth like rusty nails as he mouthed lewdnesses at me.

"Excuse me," I said, polite to the bitter end and made a dash for my bus which had just come. I sat upstairs with my heart banging in terror, feeling contaminated and sickened by the man's words which kept repeating in my head like a disgusting refrain, "*...rub my belly against your belly...*" When I dared to look out the window I saw he hadn't moved from the railings. He looked so insignificant waiting there, just an ould fellow watching the crowds of shoppers go by in a kind of dream. Did he even remember what he'd said to me?

Fear turned to boiling anger in me. How dare he speak to me like that? I blamed myself too for being so naïve, like a willing victim, trusting a filthy old drunk like that. Had I not eyes to see that scum was scum? The bus with the upper deck where I sat half-empty took off Cherryvalley bound, the wind blowing through the open windows raking my hair excitingly. But the day had lost its innocent sense of Enid Blyton adventure and the unfolding, unfamiliar streets of the east side of the city pressed about me like a malignant fist. The incident at the bus stop had left my mind in turmoil. Suddenly the world seemed a vile, fearful place. I couldn't wait to see Campbell and tell him about the man, to share the crawling predatory horror of it with someone I knew.

The grey industrial streets gave way to semi-detached suburbia, small front gardens, trees growing out of the pavement, everything basking in the peaceful early afternoon sunshine, as if nothing could ever be wrong in this world. I got down at the parade of small shops indicated on Campbell's spidery directions and walked up a short curving hill to his address. The house was behind a tall privet hedge; gates opened on a short drive, garage, and the front door with its bell-push.

Campbell answered the door, wee-boyish in khaki shorts and a loud patterned sun-shirt. He was quite a handsome boy, with wiry, wavy fair hair and pale skin, light blue eyes that regarded me now without feeling, just a habitual vacancy like the sky.

"You didn't get lost then?" he said. "Country bumpkin! Ha-ha-ha!"

"I met a dirty old man outside the City Hall," I blurted straight out but somehow I was making light of it with my voice, as if it were all a joke. Of course it was impossible to tell Campbell anything. Nothing was to be taken seriously.

Now he just laughed his odd humourless laugh and said, "We're in the dining room."

I followed him through to where two other boys not at our school and not my type were sitting at the long polished table in the narrow room, looking up at me suspiciously with no greeting. I'd wondered if maybe I could get a bit closer to Campbell on this visit, get him on his own and find out what really made him tick, but I realised there was no possibility of this now.

They were playing with a tape recorder on the table, recording themselves speaking into it. I thought that fun and when they handed me the mike I sang my favourite song at the time, Bobby Vee's *Devil or Angel?* The others looked on, deadpan; with a sinking of the heart I could see they weren't musical. Now one thing I'd shared with all my best pals—Rusty Meekin, Davy Robinson, Matt—was a passion for music, which provided a sort of soundtrack to our young days, picked up from Luxembourg or the Light and sung on our wanderings and adventures until the songs became an integral part of them.

The afternoon went downhill fast after that. I was obliged to join Campbell and friends in a game of soldiers over the fields behind his house. I had played cowboys and Indians back in Ormagh till the age of nine but never soldiers; comics and films about the War, all that modern, mechanical, dehumanised destruction, left me cold. It was the six-gun, bow and arrow and tomahawk for me. I had no choice but to fake some enthusiasm now, running for cover or lying on my belly in the grass and firing a stick cut from a tree for a make-believe gun. The game with its ponderous manoeuvres that I found boring and difficult to follow dragged on through an afternoon that clouded over grey and muggy.

Campbell took me indoors for tea at half-five, seated at the long table again with his family. The brother Philip was a dark, more serious teenaged version of Roy, with a reputation for delinquency at school that had on one occasion earned him the rare penalty of the cane from Jimmy McCain for vandalising toilet seats with acid—fortunately nobody had sat on them. Mr and Mrs Campbell were stiffly respectable, unsmiling and uncommunicative, ignoring me or giving me funny looks. I imagined they must have me down for another tearaway like their sons. Then whose fault was that? I felt uncomfortable at their table, like a bit of dirt trod inside after our afternoon up the fields.

In the evening the rain came on, cooling the streets and raising whiffs of dust, drains and gardens. Campbell and I took the bus in the direction of town to a local ABC cinema that was showing *Payroll,* starring Michael Craig and Billie Whitelaw. The British black and white film about gangsters and a robbery gone wrong wasn't up to much, as usual, but it was atmospheric in a B-movie way and it was the first time I took any interest in an actress. She was blonde but different, with striking features and I liked the name Billie—tomboyish, not sissy. Until then I'd only had eyes for John Wayne, Lee Marvin, the tough guys. It was good anyway after the long day to lose yourself in the dark and plush of the big comfortable cinema, the giant life unfolding up on the silver screen.

It was a double bill, the other film totally unmemorable; three hours on we emerged in the long evening light and I took my leave of Campbell. I was glad to be going home and seeing Matt again tomorrow. There was the quiet warmth of invincible friendship we shared together and even if his family didn't have much, they always made me feel welcome and special.

So I came through that long first year at grammar school; disappointing to begin with then somehow neither good nor bad, the main point was that I had survived it. I was ecstatic as I walked away from school on the sunny final afternoon of term, with July and August stretching out ahead of me like a long, happy lifetime. The trees lining Duncairn Gardens were bright green in the hot sunshine; the breeze coming up from the docks smelt of freedom. The streets grew hotter as I walked; out on York Street the traffic glared and fumed. The big grey station building waited, cool and cavernous. Then it was goodbye to the city for two months.

All summer long, two, three times a day, Matt and I went swimming at the tide. We accessed the Lough shore through the shady, tall-treed, mysterious grounds of one of the big houses that backed on to the water. Only once some posh old doll popped up and shouted, "You are trespassing on Mr Villier-Stuart's garden!"

The shoreline ran clear to Carrickfergus castle standing out mightily on its rock. We swam off the sloping sea wall or a short stretch of sandy beach, no one else around, Crusoe and Man Friday. If the ebb tide was too low for bathing we walked out across the exposed grey muddy expanse of the bottom of the sea towards the facing County Down coast. There were shells you could hold to your ear and hear the sea in them, flat stones to skim, miniscule mounds of worm-casts, scattered pools and barnacled rocks, a vegetation of green slime and shiny brown sea-rods with pods to pop, and a jetsam of bottles and cans and planks. With the creatures of the deep left stranded in our human element now, we got our own back bashing the limpets off the rocks, stoning the stranded

jellyfish and teasing with a toecap or stick the sideways-scuttling ugly pincered crabs.

Chapter 3

The Tower

The easy, good-natured liberal regime I had experienced In Form 1 changed abruptly in the second year when I found myself demoted to the D-stream for maths following my poor report and placed under the instruction of Cheyenne Bodie.

My heart sank as I entered the classroom high in the old building, smelt the rotten eggs stink of the adjacent chemistry lab and saw the tall malignant figure of the master standing at the front, arms folded across his broad chest like an emperor, statuesque, observing our arrival with a curious impersonal distaste.

You buttoned your lip, bowed your head and slunk to your desk, hurried to get your books out, ready. A couple of obtuse idiots didn't seem to cotton and went on blithely chattering away till they suddenly realised theirs were the only voices in the room and looking up met the cold-eyed stare of the master.

"What's your name, sonny?" The voice had a peculiar soft menace. "Aye, I'm talking to you, sonny: the one with the big mouth."

"Chambers, sir."

"And tell us now, Chambers, do the rest of us have to wait here all day while you finish your conversation with your fat friend there? Your name, sonny?"

"McElwaine, sir."

"Well, Chambers?"

"No, sir."

"Well now, that's awfully considerate of you, Chambers...*just a minute, sonny!"* Cheyenne broke off in a bark at a senior boy cutting through to the lab next door, a minute after the rest of his class had gone ahead and shut the brown inner door. "Where do you think you're going? You don't come barging through here late for your class! You can just take yourself back out that door, down the main stairs, across the playground and up the tower to the far door of the lab."

The senior boy's face darkened with chagrin as he retreated. It would take him another five minutes, including an exhausting vertical climb of spiral stone stairs, to get to his class—but he knew better than to protest.

Cheyenne was well over six feet tall with a lean athletic build. There was a boyish quality about his comparatively small head with its side-parted chestnut hair that grew low and thick on the brow, but the yellow-skinned cowboy's face with its impersonal grey eyes—a face that older girls considered handsome—betrayed no trace of the redeeming kindness or humour you would normally expect to find in a teacher.

For such a big man he had rather a small, high voice which he tried to force down to a deeper, manlier tone. The

Malone Road accent, clipped and precise, had a crooning sort of malevolence.

"I don't know what you've all heard about me," he addressed the class now. It was widely rumoured that he had broken a boy's arm at Down Grammar, the school where he'd taught previously. He seemed to be referring to this as he continued, "It is true that I once had occasion to punish a boy with especial severity. Yet some years later, after he had left school, that same boy, who had become a young man by then, stopped me in the street one day *and thanked me for it!*"

This little anecdote did nothing to reassure me and I began to live in an almost constant neurotic terror of Cheyenne Bodie. To make matters worse I found him an awful teacher, the kind who is doubtlessly clever and knows all the answers but is unable to clearly explain the process by which you arrive at them. He had an arrogant way of talking over our heads in a monotone and you were afraid to ask any questions. His method was to chalk a theorem up on the board and make us work through it together, calling out the answers to him at each stage while he tapped them up on the board, his back to us in a wide bat-winged fall of black gown. Whenever we got stuck he prompted us with grudging clues, but if these still failed to elicit the required response he went off into a long sulk. Propping his backside on his table, arms folded resolutely, face set in a wounded, morose expression as he looked from us to the blackboard and back, he waited in silence like that for the remainder of the period if necessary and then sent us off to stew over it for our homework.

A small group at the front of the class who responded to his questions became the focus of his attention, as if the rest of us did not exist, except when he rounded on us occasionally, upbraiding us for our stupidity.

"What are you all going to do when you leave school?" he barked in exasperation. "What about you, Campbell?"

"I want to be a vet, sir."

"Humph. Galbraith?"

"A marine engineer, sir."

No comment. "Mitchell?"

"A writer, sir."

I half expected him to burst out in derisory laughter at that but he seemed vaguely intrigued, taken aback perhaps, and responded in an almost sympathetic tone,"You do realise you will need your Senior Certificate for that, Mitchell?"

"Yes, sir," I said, not daring to contradict him although I believed that writers were a special breed who existed outside the normal constraints of society.

Terrified of Cheyenne, I sweated over the maths homeworks, neglecting my other subjects and still getting nowhere near the answers. In bed at night I curled into the foetal position with the covers over my head and imagined I might stay cocooned in darkness like this forever. But morning always came, the crashing, glaring horror of the bedside lamp Mum switched on, bringing my cup of tea, her grating cheeriness, and my one thought, like a man waking to the day of his execution, that I would soon be facing Cheyenne with my homework not done.

I went on desperately poring over the homework on the train, to no avail. Maths came in double periods daily, after break or after lunch. I didn't wait with friends but hung around on my own outside the boys' entrance where the schoolbags were piled against the wall, my nose in my books as I struggled with the figures to the very last minute, in desperate hope of a eureka moment that never came.

When the bell went for class I could at least be one of the first up the stairs and into D17, creeping self-effacingly over the grimy floorboards to my desk. Cheyenne would be writing up Pythagoras on the board; there was the tap and squeak of his chalk and the faint rumble of traffic from the avenue far below. The stink from the adjacent chemistry lab was like the smell of fear itself. The cramped, old, claustrophobic classroom was stuffy and dusty like Cheyenne's mathematics.

The very moment he finished writing on the board and turned to face the class we had to be on our marks, ready to call out answers. And now it was all really happening, the nightmare become reality, it wasn't so bad any more somehow. The hollow sick dread in the pit of my stomach eased, a numbness anaesthetised me; Cheyenne paid no attention to me whatsoever. He didn't even look that bad any more; you could almost imagine liking him.

The double maths class that fell after lunch twice a week, occupying the whole afternoon, was the worst as I had to get through the long morning first, just wanting to go and sit on the toilet with my nerves. When I could take no more I started to truant, mitching off Tuesday afternoon. I'd had permission previously to leave school early for an appointment with the orthodontist up by Queen's University. Now I got the Basildon Bond from the sideboard drawer and Mum's notebook where she wrote her daily shopping lists. Copying her neat rounded hand and employing an appropriate formal, concise style on to the thick blue watermarked paper, I forged a letter from her to the Headmaster, inventing another appointment with the orthodontist that meant I had to leave school directly after lunch and before Cheyenne's class.

I went about the whole business with a cool, deadly sort of professionalism, I imagined, drawing on a confidence in my artistic and literary skills. I imagined a living for myself in white collar crime maybe, if all else failed. I caught my breath as I handed in the letter at the office first thing in the morning and watched the secretary read it. But she issued me with a chit straight away, excusing me the afternoon's classes. What a feeling, tucking that slip of paper into my wallet, to hold there cosy against my heart, my ticket to freedom.

Instead of climbing the stairs to Cheyenne's class, I walked out the school gates at half-one, "A free man," I told myself and acted it, swaggering a bit and whistling *The Gipsy Rover.* I jumped on the first bus into town, clattering up the stairs and settling myself in the front seat for a leisurely panoramic view of the wider world.

My meticulous plan of deception allowed for the possibility that *someone might follow me* so when I got to the city centre I caught the connecting bus to University Road as I'd done for my previous bona fide appointment. I got off at the old university building and crossed into Elmwood Avenue. The orthodontist's was down the far end of the elegant tree-lined street of tall terraces. As I approached his number, I looked over my shoulder. Nobody was following me. I passed the surgery and dived into the alley that ran behind the houses. I felt at home now in these Belfast back alleys that seemed designed for fugitives. I walked up the alley the length of the street and re-emerged in the open at University Road. Mission complete, I was back on safe ground, returning from the orthodontist's. There was time to kill so I crossed into the

Botanic Gardens. The weak, pale winter sun was shining on the glass dome of the conservatory and the black, gnarled, frozen shapes of the trees.

My mitching went off so well the first time that I did it again, and again. Cheyenne was perfectly happy with the chits I submitted—I don't suppose my absences registered much with him; I made myself invisible in his class anyway. Grown in confidence and daring, I abandoned the charade of going all the way to Elmwood Avenue and hung about the city centre. I wandered uneasily round the covered Smithfield Market stalls that sold books and records. Or slipped into a matinee at the Regent Cinema, a cheap ticket to the front stalls to sit self-consciously, a whole row to myself, gawking up at the giant figures on the screen, worried that a dirty old man might come and sit next me. I emerged afterwards with a headache in the sick grey vacancy of the afternoon light.

This went on for several weeks. At first it was enough for me to get out of Cheyenne's classes one afternoon a week, simply to know freedom in those moments of my life. The absence chits could only provide a brief respite however; the joy of Cheyenne-free hours soon faded and the sick nervous feeling in my guts came back. It lived there now like a cancer eating me, blotting out all hope for the future. Till one morning I couldn't get out of bed.

"I've a pain in m'stummick, Mum!" I groaned.

She got Dr Conroy to me. "Where's the pain?" He poked about for a minute, "There," I said and he wrote a prescription. As Mum showed him out I lay back on the pillows with an enormous sense of relief, feeling the pain dissolve and the day open up before me all shining and lovely. Then it was reading *Wind in the Willows* in bed, with Mum bringing milky coffee and Marie biscuits for elevenses, chicken noodle soup for lunch; going downstairs before Children's Television at four, with tea and fresh-baked, buttered currant bread by the fire. Not a bad day for a boy at home with a sick tummy.

The whole purpose of my life now was to escape Cheyenne. I'd look at the other students who weren't in his class and long to be them, or stare after the other maths teachers, Jake and Charlie, in the corridor, experiencing something like love for their baggy, creased, homely geniality. I'd have given anything for a place in either's class.

When my morning sickness returned Mum was unsympathetic. "Ach, Jim, ye can't be sick again! What's wrong with ye in the name of goodness?"

She stormed out of my bedroom. Dad appeared shortly afterwards, a calming patriarchal presence, treating me in a grown-up way. "Now Jim, your mother is very concerned about you having days off like this." And suddenly I was telling him straight out about Cheyenne Bodie and how I was scared sick of going in his class every day and could learn nothing from him anyway. I said the other maths teachers were really good and I wanted to be in Charlie Bonner's E-stream instead. Dad was completely sympathetic; he asked a few questions to clarify some points and concluded, "I'll write to Leatherbarrow and ask him to take you out of Bodie's class."

The sense of relief that Dad was on my side and the thing would get sorted now and I wouldn't have to stay in Cheyenne's class was mixed with apprehension about the transitional period: Cheyenne would doubtless hear what I was saying about him and would not be pleased. The question was how promptly they would move me now.

There was light at the end of the tunnel but still the fear and, added to this, new tortures of embarrassment to endure on the way. I had an interview with Mr Leatherbarrow and Pop Jarvis, the head of maths, another Yorkshireman, white-haired and professorial, who taught the top sets. Pop was indignant that I should cast aspersions on Cheyenne's teaching—"Mr Bodie is one of our finest teachers!" he blustered. "Are you aware, Mitchell, that we have pu-pils asking to be put into his class?"

I didn't doubt that; it was a mad world, but I stubbornly insisted, "I can't understand Mr Bodie's teaching method. It'll be easier for me in Mr Bonner's E group." I had carefully considered what I would say about it all and decided not to mention Cheyenne's bullying and my terror of him. When you thought about it, he had never laid a finger on me or anyone else in the class; indeed he scarcely raised his voice to us now. Nothing as wholesome as a clip on the ear or a bawling out; Cheyenne's method of control was purely psychological, an insidious, psychopathic, deadly instilling of terror in his victims

"Depends if Mr Bonner will have you," Pop rejoindered bluffly.

I'd already taken to hanging around Charlie Bonner's class just along the D corridor before the bell went, sitting with a friend who was in it and who assured me it was great. The E group were the eleven-plus failures whose parents paid the full school fees; a less competitive, more affable crowd it was hard to imagine. Charlie Bonner came in with no fuss, no threat, a plump, avuncular figure with a heavy, florid, kindly face and an accent lilting as the rain of his native Clare.

"I t'ought you had joined us," he remarked in that dear brogue as I got up to go to Cheyenne's room. It was the distance between heaven and hell.

A letter came home from the Head agreeing to transfer me to Charlie Bonner after the Easter break. This was my worst fear realised: the purgatory of several more weeks with Cheyenne. I was painfully conscious of my position now under the man I feared most in the world, whose very ability to teach I had rubbished to his superiors. I could only presume they'd passed my comments on to him. Yet maybe not, for he gave not the least sign of anything amiss or untoward in his attitude to me, to the point where I wondered if they'd decided to spare his feelings and keep him in the dark about me. I began to relax a little and just count the days to the end of term.

"Mitchell, stay behind and see me," he said quietly after dismissing the class one afternoon the week before Easter.

He was marking our homework books at his desk. With just the two of us left in the room, I stood there looking over his shoulder, petrified. My exercise was open in front of him. The big hand turned the pages with a casual contempt. The calculations I'd entered in blue fountain pen ink were sparse and exaggeratedly neat, a pretence at work; Cheyenne's marking in red ink was faint and cursory, disinterested.

Without looking up he addressed me in his mournful soft voice, "I've been teaching for a good many years, Mitchell, but I don't believe I've ever seen anything quite so pitiful as this before." Then I nearly jumped out of my skin as he let out a murderous bellow that darkened his face and throat,*"It's just plain atrocious, sonny, isn't it?"*

I had a momentary image of the boy at Down Grammar with his broken arm dangling uselessly at his side.

"Well, what have you got to say for yourself, Mitchell?"

I was staring at my feet in a self-defensive show of contrition. Cheyenne turned his big yellow face on me. "Look at me when I speak to you, Mitchell! I don't like a boy who won't look me in the eye!"

Then I looked up into the narrowed grey eyes that were cold and angry yet detached and impersonal. The effort made my eyes water. I struggled to stop my body shaking. I felt my bowels loosen.

"Tell us, Mitchell, when are you going to stop all your whinging and whining and buckle down to some hard work for a change?" The big fist came up and the huge forefinger prodded my belly on the alliterative "w"s, making me fart, and unaccountably I almost let off a crazy peal of laughter too.

"Go on, get out of my sight, sonny!" Cheyenne growled.

I hastened away on hollow legs, down the deserted cavernous staircase in the silent building, everyone else gone home. A strange thing was happening to me. Tears were in my eyes. But they were not tears of hurt or fear. No, they were tears of *gratitude.* I paused for a minute, my hand on the banister. For a minute—that was all—I wanted to go back and apologise to Cheyenne for everything I had done and beg him to let me stay on in his class. I thought of the boy with the broken arm again. "*That boy came up to me in the street one day and thanked me for it.*"

And I knew now that story was true.

Chapter 4

The Family

Sometimes on the way home from school I called in on Dad at the office. It was next the station, on hammering York Road. A long, low, grimy redbrick block with bars on the opaque windows, it looked more like an engine shed. The sign on the narrow green door announced *Railway Accounts*. Inside it took a minute for my eyes to adjust to the greenish gloom. The place had its own peculiar smell, a mix of tea, tobacco smoke and polish. Dim long corridors that seemed underground stretched away in different directions; the one in front led to a hatch in the wall, through which I could spot Dad's distinctive smooth bush of wavy grey hair and hornrims bowed over his desk.

I entered the wide, low-ceilinged office with its clerks and secretaries burrowing away in a confusion of horrible dry-looking paperwork under the olive-shaded electric lights that burned through the brightest summer's day. I prayed that I should never end up working in an office.

"Och, look who it is, Mr Mitchell!" the kindly young secretary Margaret called out and I loved to see my dad look up in surprise and his face light up with that proud-father affectionate smile I only got from him whenever we chanced to meet up away from home like this.

"Ach, Jimmy!" he greeted me coddingly. "Come and have a Spangle!" He kept the packet of little square, wrapped boiled sweets in his desk drawer. I associated Spangles with earlier childhood trips to the cinema with Dad.

Everyone was looking up from their desks at me now, smiling. I was a celebrity here, my father's son.

I always felt sorry for the old man caged in this office after the prestige and independence of his former job as district audit inspector on the Great Northern Railway, his own boss, travelling the north-west region every day. That was before closures had forced his move east to the Ulster Transport Authority and this clerk's job to see him through to retirement.

He worked under the eagle eye of the accounts boss Mr McGarrigle. "I dropped off to sleep the other day and he pounced. He was raging with me," Dad had told us and I felt the humiliation of it for him. Not that he seemed too bothered; he viewed the world generally with a sort of sleepy resignation these days, past caring too much. He was on a lot of medication now for asthma, chronic bronchitis and angina.

Continuing the relaxed routine of a working lifetime, he took the train home for lunch, catching the nap he called his "cheepy-cheeps" in his armchair by the fire afterwards, before heading back to work in the afternoon.

He found constant amusement in all the little idiosyncrasies of the people around him, wherever he was. At the office there was the tiny girl with enormous glasses who protested in a surprisingly large voice too, *"Hey, stop messing about with those lights!"*

Or the two colleagues who talked TV programmes.

"Have you seen Harry Worth?"

"Good crack, is he? Okay, *I'll give that a bash* tonight!"

Dad would adopt those random expressions, trotting them out at every opportunity: "Will you *give that a bash?"* He found them oddly endearing and reassuring in some way.

It was like the nicknames he liberally bestowed on neighbours. In Ormagh there was "Miss Mann" opposite us—Billy Mann, an effeminate man who lived with his mother and went in for Irish dancing in the traditional narrow green kilt.

The "Dog Faces" were two young brothers down the same street: "Ah'm a dog-face!" Dad would proclaim as they passed our window and he'd bay like a hound. The tone was always affectionate, never intolerant and sneering. It was more a celebration of the infinite variety of humankind.

On Loughside estate there was "Catso" with all her cats; "Trews" who often wore trousers, still not universal on women then and something Dad didn't entirely approve of; and "the Big Eyes", the three teenage Coyne sisters.

The nicknames and expressions stretched away back over half a century to his Edwardian childhood, like the chant of an Indian boy he boarded with at Navan College: *"Ry-ba Mazu-zack, Be-num Bas-sum,"* a sort of roll-call of Indian boys' names, accompanied by a counting forefinger. And so *Ryba Mazuzack* became a catch-all nickname Dad applied to sundry characters across the island of Ireland.

A popular evangelical hymn of his childhood was sent up regularly by him:

"Shall we gather at the ri-ver?
The beau-ti-ful, the beau-ti-ful ri-ver!"

Then there was the tight-lipped, crushing pronouncement of a "saved" woman of his young man days: *"The lips that touch liquor shall never touch mine!"*

I loved to hear Dad's talk of the old days, growing up in a family of eleven children on a farm in Meath at the start of the century. The children went barefoot all summer and seemed to terrorise the roads around Rockfield. As the oldest of the eight brothers Dad was the ringleader. A favourite trick was to lie down in the road when he heard one of the new motor cars coming. When it stopped for him he jumped up and ran away.

Or they would harass a passing bearded Edwardian with shouts of *"Beaver!Beaver!"* In truth it sounded much naughtier behaviour than I would ever get away with. And it got worse as Dad got older, with him running away from Navan College and walking to Dundalk. He seemed proud of the number of beatings he incurred from his father—*if he could catch hold of him* that was. On one occasion Dad had climbed to safety up a tree and yelled down every swear word under the heavens on his poor father's head.

One way his father managed to keep control was to mete out random punishment to his sons. *"That was your brother's beating,"* he'd explain drily in a Dungannon accent. Yet he could be unaccountably humane at times, simply shaking his head fatalistically on one occasion when Dad burnt and ruined a brand new pair of leather boots by leaving them to dry too near the fire.

There was a photo of grandfather Edward Mitchell in the sideboard: a youngish man with a clean-shaven, handsome, expressionless face, black hair parted dead-centre, soft dark eyes. He managed the farm at Rockfield and also served as a butler—Mum preferred "gentleman's gentleman"— to the Rothwells at the big house. Imported from County Tyrone, with a reference from the Lord Lieutenant of Ireland no less, Grandfather was an Orangeman, a lifelong teetotaller and non-smoker.

"You don't drink, you don't smoke—what do you do?" the other men teased him at Kells fair and thinking of his eleven children he just smiled.

"What was your mum like?" I asked Dad. She seemed a bit of a non-person; it was the father who had loomed large.

"She was alright," said Dad vaguely. "She used to go off into a brown study."

I could well imagine that, from the strain of all the childbearing. I knew the two older sisters, my aunts Kitty and Charlotte, had taken a lot of responsibility for the younger ones.

My paternal grandparents both came from farming stock in Tyrone. Between finishing at Navan College and starting his career on the Great Northern Railway, Dad had a halcyon year staying on his maternal Uncle Joe McCandless's farm at Coalisland. He worked on the farm, zipped around the country roads on a motorbike, went to dances and courted girls for the first time. It was during the Irish war of independence; Dad recalled a single image of that conflict: a crowd obstructing a Black and Tan officer making an arrest in the main street of Coalisland.

A priest weighed in, laying about the Tan's shoulders with his walking stick.

Dad started courting Mum while he was working in his first job at the booking office at Drogheda station. She was living with her sister Kathleen and my granny Girvan in the clergy widows' house in St Peter's Place. Mum and Dad both attended the Church of Ireland and she would make sure she was out in her small front garden whenever he passed by on his way to church. The ploy worked wonders, they were soon courting; however, Mum would have to wait another ten years before he married her. First he had to see his younger siblings through school and in the case of the twins Jimmy and Ernie, through Trinity College Dublin.

"Och, me lov-elly brodthers!" Mum would mimic him still in a sort of sentimental country bumpkin voice, her throat flushing with rancour as she recalled the years of self-sacrifice, waiting to be wed. "It's a wonder you were able to tear yourself away from them at all!"

"I don't speak like that!" was all he said, coldly.

Maybe it was all that frustration that had given her a wild temper in their courting days. "I called her a 'red-haired vixen' once," Dad liked to recall with amusement, no hint of any grievance, for that was just how women could be.

Mum had been educated with the clergy daughters at Alexandra College, Dublin. She came from "quality," Church of Ireland clergy and major-generals, with blood links to Ffortescues and Lytes, Wallop Brabazon, Lady McCreagh, Josias Dupre and the Reverend Blackhall Vincent. It was Dad who was proud of this lineage; he regarded a clergy daughter as quite a catch for a farmer's son like himself.

"The working class are good looking," she said in reference to his background. "And your father is a good business man. The one thing he's not is musical."

That was her one mild, implied criticism of him. She'd studied piano and knew classical music and the Irish traditional airs. Lady Gregory had been a regular visitor to Alexandra College, promoting Irish culture and awarding an annual prize. All that great culture seemed very much in Mum's past now, just vague memories. Marriage and children and moving house every few years with Dad's successive promotions on the GNR had all taken its toll and left her fit for nothing but a little light music—Russ Conway's piano, *Side Saddle,* was a favourite—and the romances in women's magazines, squeezed in with the half-cups of weak tea she drank to get her through her long day's chores.

Dad hadn't read a book since Edgar Wallace in the thirties but he devoured the daily newspapers, local and national, every column inch. He retained a fondness for Shakespeare, occasionally dipping into the *Complete Works* to quote some gem of wisdom—a favourite was Polonius's *"Neither a borrower nor a lender be..."* There was a fascination too with the dark legend of D.H. Lawrence and with a banned book he had read once, *The Life and Loves of Frank Harris.* All this came out only as I grew a little older and he began to talk to me "man to man" and also because I was an avid book reader with advanced tastes by the age of fourteen.

Both Mum and Dad kept diaries faithfully, just a brief entry for every day of the year: the weather, the repetitive but quietly satisfying daily activities, the domestic temperature: *"Ma in a wax."* Bundles of the Letts' pocket diaries going back years, tied in rubber bands, occupied a sizeable corner of the bookcase. Sometimes Dad would look through them and read extracts aloud. The past was always a living source of wonderment to him as it was to me, so he had a ready audience. He also liked to root out old snaps from a green hessian pouch in the sideboard.

"Ach, ye're not getting out those dosey ould snaps again!" Mum protested. "I look a show in them!" She didn't set much store by memories, the old dead days with all the little indignities and funny mixed feelings of the past. She preferred to be centred in the present with its smooth routine and unconscious tasks, humming contentedly to herself as she went about her chores, or curled up in her bed for a rest with her magazine.

"M' nerves!" she'd exclaim, hand to brow, at any sudden loud noise or minor mishap about the house, as if her whole small domestic world threatened to come crashing down around her. Dorothy and I liked to mimic her, till *"M'nerves!"* became one of those humorous family expressions, but I knew Mum meant it.

There were little old brown photos of the Mitchell family all gathered together, Grandmother in the centre slumped in a chair, looking half-dead long before her time, her grown-up sons and daughters around her, crowded into the frame, two photos to get them all in. The big successful family, eight brothers and three sisters, was a source of immense pride to Dad, as celebrated in his poem "The Mitchell Family" (Creenagh, 1946):

"Dad and Mum have passed away
But the family I am glad to say
All look well and are well fed
None have died and all have wed."
What more could you want in this life?

Of course Mum's background could not have been more different. She had lost her father, the Reverend Jim, at five, and her family, her younger sister Kathleen and her widowed mother, our granny, just annoyed her more than anything else.

There were advantages for me being the youngest child of older parents. They had made all their mistakes with the other two, so I enjoyed a civilised upbringing, no rows or beatings. I was quieter, easier than my brother and sister.

"Sure I only beat the badness into Ned," Dad would lament of my elder brother, whose mixture of cleverness and personal inadequacy was a sort of legend in our family. Everything he attempted in life seemed dogged by his own wilful perversity: dropping out of art college, then throwing up the job in Irish Linen that an uncle's influence had secured for him—he said he couldn't stand clocking in and out; subsequently going missing in London for two years, then turning up out of the blue speaking with an upper crust English accent and living at home on the dole, painting his pictures, drinking and smoking his "buroo" money and memorising opinions and book reviews from the *Sunday Times* and *Observer* as men once memorised the scriptures, until in desperation Dad had packed him off to the College of Art for the second time and paid his fees.

Now Ned had cheap digs in a terraced house down by the shipyards. He liked to sketch and paint the back streets with their ornamental wrought iron lamp posts and the gantries looming above the wet slate roofs, the headscarved women pushing prams in the rain and the big, stolid, bullnecked dockers in their duncher caps swilling Guinness down the pub.

"Ey'm a Seocialist,"he announced primly.

"Aye, that'll get you far," was Dad's jaded response.

"Lend us a quid, Da, would you?"

Ned shoved the pound note carelessly into the front breast pocket of his brown corduroy jacket as if he was doing Da a favour borrowing it.

"Mind you don't lose that," said Da, ever the auditor. "Have you not got a wallet?"

"Nah."

"Would you use one if I got you it?"

Ned's nose curved in disdain: all this fuss about money! For a moment he looked like Lee Van Cleef, dark baddie in the Saturday matinee. "Ach, skip it!"

He had the money now and he was off out the door heading for the Belfast train and the boozer, stepping up the road with his exaggerated stride, long stick legs, winklepickers flung out, his expression fixed in its habitual rebel-scowl, jaw pulsing, eyes flashing daggers under their lowered brows. It was awful having to live in a society like this with parents like that. Petty-petty-bourgeois philistines they were. Come the revolution they'd be the first to have to go.

"I hate that!" Dad complained softly in the charged quiet after Ned's rude exit. "*'Skip it, hop it!'* He'd look after his money better if he had to work for it."

I enjoyed having Mum and Dad to myself, all quiet reflectiveness and cosy chats. My big sister Dorothy had started teacher training at Stranmillis and was in a student flat. Our house was a peaceful haven without siblings' egos crashing about the place.

That summer Dad hired a caravan at Balbriggan for a week's holiday, Mum and Dad and me. He saw it advertised in the *Belfast News Letter.* The idea seemed exciting, different. Usually our holidays were confined to short stays with my aunts and uncles in North Antrim, Tyrone or Wicklow. Once we stayed in a converted railway carriage where Ballycastle station had been, under the green sweep of Knocklayde; Dorothy only lasted a day there and had to be sent to Granny at White Park Bay. Further back I had vague memories of a momentous trip *across the water* to Blackpool, a week in a boarding house. I retained vague images of the Tower, donkey rides on the rain-wet sand and Dad arguing with a bus conductor who asked me to give up my seat to an adult, it was the rule, while I sat there between them, mortified. It seemed that *something* always had to go wrong on holidays, but you started out eager and hopeful.

Balbriggan was to be a trip back in time for my parents to their young courting days on that stretch of the Irish coast. The caravan was by the sea, it said in the ad. I liked the name Balbriggan, smacking of Robert Louis Stevenson adventure.

We went early In July, soon after school had broken up, catching the Dublin line from Great Victoria Street station down through the Mourne mountains, *across the border* which was always exciting.

We shared our compartment with the McCruddys, a Belfast family coincidentally heading for the same caravan site. Their only child Raymond was too young to be a companion for me. Mr McCruddy's swag belly fascinated me grotesquely, like a beach ball down his trousers, resting on his lap. He talked non-stop all the way down on the train, that obsessional dry, one-way

grown-up talk and I watched Dad, always such a friendly, interested man, struggling to keep his eyes open, till finally his neck drooped as he nodded off. Not the least put out, McCruddy kept up the verbal barrage unabated at Mum, the perfect polite listener, trained in the rectory, but even her agreeable, attentive nods grew weary, her face flushed and perspiring under the strain. The motormouth was making me feel a bit sick now and I had to go out in the train corridor and stand at an open window taking deep breaths.

The train was bowling down the east coast of Ireland: Dundalk, Drogheda. The July Irish weather was dry at least. Sunlight filtered through the greyness here and there in pools on the green and yellow summer fields, the dark green trees and white farms of Counties Louth and Dublin.

The train braked for Balbriggan. Dad was awake again, fetching the suitcases down from the rack. We'd arrived! A handful of us left the train, wandering out from the station in the early afternoon siesta quiet of the small town with its whitewashed buildings, bookies and pubs. It was just how I thought of the South, its traditional character well preserved.

The caravan site wasn't accessible by road transport so we had to walk there lugging our suitcases, following the McCruddys up long steep steps by a railway bridge and in single file along the cinder track by the railway line. Eventually we emerged on a field with four well-spaced caravans parked on the grass. The site overlooked the shore, dark jagged rocks beaten by a mud-green sullen sea. There was a gaunt weather-beaten farmhouse where the owner lived, hens pecking around the back door. It

was everything the ad had claimed for it, but there was something desolate and godforsaken about the place.

The caravan was small, cramped and stuffy inside, but we were free of McCruddy at last.

"Phew! Your man would talk the hind legs off a donkey," said Dad. "And the poor wife browbeaten."

Mum bustled around making the place homely, preparing a lunch with some provisions we had picked up in the town. Funny to think we'd be living here for a week. Like gypsies! We ate outside on a blanket on the warm grass with the sun coming and going between the clouds.

The third caravan was occupied by more northerners. There was a brother and sister close in age, too young for me, and a dog called Paddy. The father was one of those vigorous middle-aged men, what my father called "a Daddy-man," who joined in the ball games with the kids and the dog, calling out in a Malone Road voice, "C'morn, Peddy-Pawrs, fetch the bawrl!" Watching their game as we ate our sandwiches, I vaguely envied their self-sufficient company, the sibling companionship and the pet, the organised activities that came with a younger father; never being lonely. Though I knew in my heart it would get on my nerves after five minutes.

McCruddy called by to check we had settled in all right. "It's a grand private wee spot!" he enthused. " Sure there's iverythin' a bodie needs in them wee cyaravans though ye'd niver think it lukkin' at them and ye can sit outside and ate yer dinner on the grass like a pic-nic and the sea right on your duerstep!"

His son was with him, a ten-year-old talked into submissive silence like his mother but physically resembling his father with a long head and heavy, lumpy body like a sack of spuds.

"Raymond and me are off over the rocks to gather limpets for bait. Are ye comin'?" he invited me.

To be polite and try the shore, I followed them on to the sharp, awkward shapes of the rocks, the waves washing below with a dull, menacing rhythm. We dislodged the limpets from the rocks with blows of a stone and tossed them in the bucket.

"We'll get ye fixed up wi' a fishin' rod next, son," McCruddy told me kindly but I was getting bored already and when they weren't looking I slipped away back to the caravan to read a book.

In the evening we walked into the quiet little town, melancholy oblique sunshine on the limewashed walls. We found the bit of seaside by the harbour, old men on benches, couples parked in cars. They eyed us strangers warily.

"They never got over the Black and Tans here," Dad explained grimly.

On the second day, the Sunday, we took the train to the next station south, Skerries, another of those place-names Dad seemed to enjoy saying, which turned out a proper little seaside holiday resort with fish and chip shops and amusements, a promenade and shiny sands with the tide receding under the clouding sky. We had afternoon tea in a café with a wide window looking out on the prom, the Sunday drifters hurrying past with their heads down in a slanting shower. Another dull, wet afternoon but it wasn't bad to be on holiday; the slight boredom and feeling of aimlessness threw you back on your inner reserves. I felt important sitting there with my parents who had come back to their roots here in the south and seemed very much at home. The years had flown, their children were nearly raised.

With the rain blotting out activity, falling steadily that evening on the caravan field and the sea, there was nothing for it but to stay inside and read, have supper and go to bed early, me on the divan under the window, my parents in the tiny bedroom at the back. I lay awake for a long time listening to the tattoo of the rain on the roof and the fainter background rhythm of the tide washing the rocks darkly. It was strange being in the middle of a field by the shore, far from home. It would have been scary but Mum and Dad were only a few feet away in the bedroom.

I was woken by a disturbance in the strange pitch-dark of the dead of night. Dad was having an asthmatic attack; Mum was cross. I could picture him groping for his "whiffy" inhaler, puffing on it for dear life.

"The walls keep closing in on me!" he gasped. "I can't breathe!"

Then Mum, fit to be tied: "What in the divil's name possessed you to bring us to a caravan? Sure you might o' known it'd disagree with you! Could we not have paid for a decent boarding-house for once, where I could have a break from the chores?" Her voice, spitting like a cat, grated on me. Had she no pity on the poor man?

I lay there with my heart thumping in the close darkness. I hated it when they rowed—it was a rare event and would pass over quick as a gust of wind, but momentarily it made life go all dark and sad and futile and I wanted to curl up and die. It was just "Ma giving out the pay" as he called it—expressing the cumulative small frustrations of their long years together. He remained stoical; he knew it was the way of women and they didn't mean a word they said.

It was a relief to me in the morning when they apologetically announced that we were cutting short the holiday and going home because of Dad's asthma. I tried not to look too pleased though it was a bit sad in a way. So often, it seemed, family life could be like this. Faintly, indefinably tragic.

Chapter 5

Mr In-Between

On the radio Burl Ives sang *Mr In-Between.* I used to think how that title summed up my life as I moved into my teens.

Back from the abortive holiday in Balbriggan, I passed the long summer vacation in contentment with Matt. This was to be the last year we spent together; he would turn fifteen in the autumn and leave school at Christmas to start work. I was thirteen.

We resumed our holiday routine of swimming every day when the tide was in, regardless of the weather. The long hot July days had come; we walked with towel and togs rolled under our oxters, cutting down the cool green tunnel of the old country loaning that passed Lonegan's. I liked to pause at the gate and admire the manorial white house set back across its spacious lawns in a sort of time bubble. Sometimes we'd catch a glimpse through the bushes and trees of the rarefied aristocratic existence you imagined being lived there. Two small boys, apparently brothers with the same startling shocks of platinum hair, played together in a shouty quarrelsome fashion you wouldn't have expected. If they saw us looking they'd stop and stare back at us like animals in a compound. There was a strange worlds-apart feeling between us, illusory no doubt. Sure weren't my maternal Girvan ancestors "quality" too? I carried this fabulous secret of my aristocratic blood next my heart as I ran with the rough boys; it was part of the romantic book-adventure of my life that I was always writing in my head.

Matt and I collected the little coloured picture cards of early Elvis from the ball gum machine in front of the estate's parade of shops. Elvis was King; Loughside, County Antrim a loyal province of his realm. You could tell us, his subjects, by our sweptback hair anointed with Brylcreem or Brilliantine and secured with regular strokes of the battered plastic "bebop" brush we carried in a hip pocket of our jeans. I had even ingratiated us for life with the local bucktoothed bully Mouse McTaig with my uncannily authentic impersonation of Elvis singing *I Don't Care if the Sun Don't Shine*, complete with the echoey Sun Studio sound I replicated with my adenoids.

It wasn't just Elvis of course; our ears were glued to all the latest records on Radio Luxembourg: Brian Hyland, Tommy Roe, Johnny Burnett, Del Shannon and Ricky Nelson. Then there were the great black voices like Clyde McPhatter, Lloyd Price and Jimmy Jones. And the English stable we could readily identify with: Billy Fury, Marty Wilde, Adam Faith and Vince Eager.

Pop music, rock and roll, led ultimately to girls. The lyrics were all about falling in love, weren't they? *Peggy Sue* and *Sweet Little Sheila.* I'd been a fan since hearing *Earth Angel* on the radio when I was five; it took a long time for the penny to drop about girls and love, however. Now Matt produced teenage girls' magazines and comics borrowed from his three older sisters. There were fanzines full of all kinds of riveting trivia about pop stars like Dion and Fabian, David Macbeth and Johnny Gentle, while the romantic comics opened up a new world of girls' emotions to us. Matt was already pro-active in the field of girls but I was stunted; I'd have died if a real girl even spoke to me. True, there was wee June McGreevy upcountry at my Aunt Kitty's; we'd even kissed once but she was more of a tomboy, a chum like Matt.

Now Roy Campbell could keep his *Commando* and *Roy of the Rovers.* I was hooked on *Mirabelle, Romeo, Valentine* and *Roxy.* One comic strip serial in particular caught my newly adolescent imagination. Teenage Sue falls madly in love with moody Steve who is bad boy, self-obsessed and indifferent to her, going off to play his jazz trumpet at his bedroom window when he is "blue," leaving her to pine for him on the pavement below, but his indifference to Sue only seems to make her love him ever more desperately. Each episode finished with a hook like *"Next week Sue goes down on her knees to Steve!"* The question was how much more Sue was prepared to take in the name of love. It was wrong but thrilling that a girl could love a boy so slavishly. I thought it was meant to be the other way round but reckoned there must be some truth in it, with all those girl readers avid as I was for the next instalment. If girls wanted us as much as we wanted them it was quite a different story.

"Go on and ask Muriel out," Matt encouraged me after Muriel's friend Alice had shouted across the street, "Hi Jim, Muriel fancies you!" Muriel offered no protest at her friend's revelation; she was smiling pleasantly when I looked back at them. Muriel Ryan from Kenbane Avenue, a fairish, rosy-cheeked, gentle girl in white ankle socks, had been a year ahead of me at primary school.

"Out where?" I asked Matt.

"Walk up the cinder track. Hould her hand. When you get out of sight o' the houses, put your arm round her and give her a kiss."

Matt was totally confident; it was the most natural thing in the world to him. For a moment I overcame the nervous constriction around my heart and could picture the happy scene, me and Muriel. It was exciting, yes—but I'd never do it. Well, I was two years younger than Matt; the problem was I could seem mature for my age but didn't feel it inside.

Then there was the Swedish film Matt took me to see at the Carrick *Ideal*. It was X-rated but they didn't challenge me at the box office with Matt getting the tickets and custom very slack on a Tuesday night. Foreign language with subtitles, it promised a real taste of the forbidden. The blonde, curvy Swedish actress Ulga Hurgel—who Matt was already well acquainted with, the foreign name slipping as naturally from his lips as "Muriel Ryan"—oozed an earthy, all-woman sex appeal for the camera and the same kind of love slave quality that had appealed to me about Sue in the comic strip story. The more her man ignored her, the more Ulga was willing to die for him. Aside from that thrilling emotional undertow and Ulga's physical presence, sometimes only in her slip, lounging voluptuously on the bed or sofa, it was a ponderous, dull film really, promising much but delivering very little in the end.

"She *is* good!" I agreed with Matt afterwards, feeling very daring as we surfaced into the blue dark and the fish and chips smell of a Carrick summer's night.

Autumn came; Matt was back at school in Carrick for his final term and suddenly he was fading from my life. I missed his predictable knock at the front door, the danders and yarns together. It soon transpired that he was courting a girl in Carrick. He turned up one Saturday afternoon and the two of us were walking in the fallen leaves on Shore Road.

"Me 'n' Theresa's goin' steady." He told me what I had already guessed.

"I'm pleased for you, Matt." I was too, though I knew it spelt the end of our boyhood friendship.

"I can fix you up with her friend Colette," Matt said. "We could go on a double date to the pitchers."

I felt the old faintheartedness overcome me, the conviction that I wasn't ready for this yet, *kissing in the back seats of the cinema.* A *Catholic* girl too. That was even scarier, touching on a powerful social taboo.

I blustered and mumbled pathetic excuses.

"No money."

"Och, sure the girls don't mind goin' dutch. Theresa and I always do," said Matt.

"Too much homework, Matt, getting ready for Junior soon," I protested finally, my heart fluttering away in a sick panic. Matt didn't push it any further; I suppose he could see I wasn't ready yet. I felt such a dreariness in myself then, *afraid of girls!* He'd tried his best to coax me out of my shell, not leave me out; a good friend to the end.

My father wrote a character reference to get Matt a job as an engine cleaner on the Transport Authority, who preferred Protestants usually and he started at York Road

station in the New Year. I'd catch a glimpse of him once in a while from my carriage window, fair-haired and cocky down by the engine sheds with blackened face and blue overalls. A working man now.

The last time I spoke to him was outside the phone box on the corner of Coolmore Green. The estate lads tended to grow sullen and lumpish as they got older, chip on the shoulder, but Matt was more self-confident than ever, brimful of positive life and talkative, delighted to see me.

"I've got hould of a load of Cliff Richard records if you want to come round and listen to them sometime," he said brightly.

"Cliff not Elvis?" I said. "Yeah, I'd like," I mumbled awkwardly like a Method actor.

I could only admire my old friend's easy social skills; I'd drifted into a solitary, inward adolescent state. It was a nice idea, some real teenage life, maybe like those romance comics we used to read, but I knew I'd never make it round to Matt's. We'd travelled too far in different directions now, grammar school boy and labourer.

The last I heard of Matt he was married at sixteen with a baby and living in Eden, a village the other side of Carrick.

At school I'd struck up a sort of friendship with Norman Jameson, a tallish, heavy-boned lad with protuberant front teeth and blue eyes close-set to a long, tip-tilted nose. We were in the same class for most subjects and walked home together every afternoon as far as the station where he caught the bus to Rathcoole. Apart from that, I felt we didn't have much in common. He was scientific, which I scorned, but he had more sense than Roy Campbell and you could rely on him.

After school we stopped off at the shop top of Duncairn Gardens for Norman's fag, a Gallaher's *Green* purchased single over the counter, two pence. Further down the Gardens we made a right turn into Edlingham Street, the Tiger's Bay side of the road, then a left down the long straight blank back alleyway, where Norman lit up from a penny book of matches. I didn't smoke any more but liked the sociable ritual of it and the sense of conspiracy there between the high brick walls and yard doors, the blue smoke curling off the fag, sweetening the sour ashy smell of the alley.

A right-angle turn at the bottom of the alley and we emerged at the foot of Hillman Street by the barber's shop, its window filled with large posters of men modelling hairstyles, elaborate, improbable jobs: high-sweptback, side-swept, crossover. I had been tempted in there once for a crew cut and singe, and came out so scaldy that I hid it for a week under my school cap.

We were on the intersection of North Queen Street now. Crossing the main road we dropped down Meadow Street, a dark gully of grimy wee terraces huddled in the great icy shadow of Gallaher's tobacco mill, its sheer cliff wall of red brick topped by the dizzy soaring chimney, towering the length of one side of the street.

Sometimes we encountered the wee millies coming off their shift, walking arm-in-arm, six abreast up Meadow Street, singing in a raucously defiant manner and shouting out coarse suggestions at Norman and me, *"Hi, wee fellas, wud ye risk it for a biscuit?"*

And worse. We concealed our terror behind faint, patronizing smiles. Out on York Street we came to the faded façade of the Ridgeway Café where we turned in gratefully off the roaring road and walked between the two

short rows of empty tobacco-coloured wooden booths, a narrow and vinegar-smelling space, up to the speckled-red Formica counter with its Vincent de la Salle collection box. In a minute Mamma would appear from the back with her sallow, delicate-boned face and soft brown eyes, a gentle motherly smile for the two nice schoolboys.

"Ice-a creama lemonada?" Our order was unvarying..

"Yes, please," we smiled back; it never varied.

We sat in one of the window booths and Mamma brought the drinks: tall fluted glasses, a scoop of vanilla ice-cream topped up with lemonade, served with a straw and dessert spoon. It was chilly refreshment on winter afternoons, cold on cold, making us shudder a little as we sucked our straws and chatted there, face to face across the cold Formica. No-one else ever came in the place that time of day.

We made the drinks last, spun out the conversation; it was a welcome respite between the tediums of the school day and homework. Norman talked a lot about himself. He was an only child; he hero-worshiped his engineer father who had seen action in the war at sea. "Fell thirty feet on to a hot plate, took the skin off his back."

Dad drove a prestigious Alvis and allowed Norman to smoke. "Bought me twenty Benson's the other weekend." There was a "ya't" they sailed at Portstewart, lots of "messin' about in boats" and holidays on an uncle's farm at Ballymoney: "Uncle Sammy lets me drive the 'trector'."

"My Uncle Archie at Bushmills hasn't got a tractor," I said. "Horse and cart there still." That sort of summed up the difference between Norman and me: a romantic even then, I preferred the horse and cart.

Nevertheless I was grateful for the company; there was some shared humour too. But somehow I could never

quite get away from the feeling of how different we were. When Norman asked to come back to my house after school one day I put him off with some excuse. That would have been too much.

Norman was quite forward with the girls. Watching the school first fifteen in the cup final at Ravenhill one interminable blowy wet Saturday afternoon, Norman and Faulkner, a skinny, stooping, studious boy, got their arms round two girls in the crowd. An arm across the shoulders, that was all, but it seemed an enormous step to me. I saw one of the girls, a little jolly one, make the "square" sign and pull a face at her friend afterwards. Even so, she had not seemed to mind that too much.

My shyness of the opposite sex was becoming a problem. That autumn we had dancing lessons with the girls in the gym: the Gay Gordons, Military Two-step, that kind of thing, in preparation for our first school dance that Christmas. We were lined up against the wall bars, boys and girls on opposite sides of the gym, then the boys had to cross the expanse of white-dusted boards and ask a girl to dance. I hung back with a small group of boys each time until Alec the gym master enquired: "Is there any boy who hasn't asked a girl to dance yet?"

I was the only one who put his hand up. I then received a very public counselling on my aberrant behaviour.

"Okay, Mitchell, look at all these other lads here: Gillespie, Wilson, Forsythe, Pratley. They've all asked a girl to dance. So why can't you?"

I tried to look nonchalant with a hundred people staring at me. Why not indeed? Then Eileen the PT mistress announced "Ladies' Choice" and I was saved by a lively girl I sat near in French, Patsy McNulty, who bore down on me compassionately and yanked me after her on to the dance floor like her baby brother.

After all that I was up for the Christmas dance, which was on a Friday night before the end of term. I had counted on moral support from Norman but he pulled out at the last minute. It turned out that less than half the boys from our year, and nobody I was friendly with, were going. I persevered however, feeling that maybe here was a chance to prove myself.

The butterflies were so bad on the night of the dance that I couldn't touch my tea. On the train the inky dark at the carriage window, holding my reflection, seemed like all the darkness of the world pressing around me. Past Whitehouse the night lights of the city sprang up, a diabolical glitter. From York Street station I chose the well-lit route up Duncairn Gardens. In the dark of night-time the street had shed its busy familiarity, with a queue at the cinema and the cold light of shop windows spilling onto the pavement which sparkled with frost. I bowled along desperately up the hill, frightened of the street but conscious that every step was taking me nearer something worse, the moment of my great shame.

The dark-towered Gothic silhouette of the school loomed out in the moon glow. The sight of some girls alighting from a car ahead of me, a waft of their perfume on the night air, filled me with horror as of some invading alien species. In the toilets the boys were combing their hair in the mirrors above the long row of wash-hand basins. Sure enough there was no-one I knew there at all. I tagged on behind a random group of lads down the long, windowless corridor to the assembly hall. As we got nearer you could hear old Miss Milne banging on the piano and Eileen Crozier calling out hearty instructions to the dancers. Inside the packed hall strung with coloured Christmas streamers I tried to hide in the crowd of lads by the wall, but I felt completely alone and totally exposed.

I spotted Patsy McNulty in the distance, animated and gabbling at the centre of a crowd of girls and boys. She might as well have been at the end of a telescope focused on Mars. But there was Sonia Dowling from my section: quiet, dumpy and plain but with a little girl quality and nice long shiny chestnut hair down her back. Just waiting there alone like me.

"Dance?" I mumbled, presenting myself to her, but the word stuck in my throat as I witnessed her facial expression, a mix of hot anger flushing her cheeks and cold disgust chilling her eyeballs and curling her upper lip.

All through that torturous dance her little hand stayed limp and soggy in mine, her eyes averted crossly from me. As soon as the music stopped Sonia departed abruptly, without as much as a look, leaving me standing there foolishly, smarting with rejection now, more terribly exposed than ever.

With my fragile wee bit of self-confidence dashed, I backed off into a corner where I remained for the rest of the evening, arms folded, sweating profusely, my face burning like a beacon. I felt humiliated and lost, but rooted to the spot, mesmerised by the clumping circular procession of the dancers. At first I imagined everyone was staring critically at me; then with the dawning recognition that nobody had the slightest interest in me anyway, it seemed I was something even less than a pathetic eejit: I was a non-person, a phantom.

It was my fourteenth birthday that February. It fell on a Saturday and I woke with an excited, Christmassy sort of feeling. Downstairs the fire burned brightly; there was the sizzle and smell of bacon from the scullery, for a slap-up fry. I sat round in my pyjamas opening the little pile of cards and small gifts from Mum and Dad and Dorothy, Aunt Kitty, and my godfather Uncle Eric in Dungannon. There were ten-bob notes, *Photoplay* film annual and exercise books and pens for my writing.

Mum and Dad were smiling at me. Dorothy, home from Stran for the weekend, appeared in her pink quilted dressing gown singing, *"Happy birthday, wee fourteen!"* to the tune of the Neil Sedaka song. Everyone was being nice to me for a day.

The crisp, bright winter's morning at the windows lifted my mood; I could feel the clarity and radiance of the new birth-day inside me. After breakfast I dressed and stepped out for a circuit of the block. Frost was slowly melting on the front gardens and the big green in the flooding, dazzling sunshine. The brilliance of the light, sharpening every detail, heightened my senses with an almost hallucinatory effect. A squealy infantile joy welled in my throat. I just let my feet carry me briskly in the glad morning, enjoying the mist of my breath on the cold air and the fresh smell, the tang of coal-smoke, the peaceful rows of houses with their solid sense of plain living, the modern brick church among the tall frosted firs. I was fourteen! The number had such a satisfying rounded, important ring about it. Today the streets were mine.

I circled back to 5 Coolmore Green, exhilarated, for elevenses' milky coffee round the fire, with slabs of freshly baked soda bread and butter. After lunch I travelled up to town, to Mullan's bookshop to spend part of my accumulated ten-bob notes on a new hardback book I'd seen reviewed in the Sunday paper. Stopping for a trim at the barber's in Whitla Street opposite the station on the way back, the kindly middle-aged man who cut my hair saw my book and showed an interest..

"What have ye got there?" he enthused affectionately. "*Franny and Zooey*. What kinda names is them? What's it about? Is it good?"

"It's American—the new one by my favourite writer," I explained. "He wrote *Catcher in the Rye*."

"Sure that was your Scotchman Burns?"

"No, that was *Comin' through the rye!*"

My fourteenth proved to be a turning point. The numinous sensations of that day lingered on in me through the succeeding spell of cold, bright weather. A new life had woken in me that seemed connected to the magical late winter sunlight. I felt it most going to school in Belfast in the mornings, with the sun firing the brick and glass of mill and terrace. Upper Canning Street was transformed into a channel of resplendent light, its frosty heights like a mountainside. The little group of girls from Carrick who got off the train walked in front of me absorbed in eager girl-talk, in a marching swing of pleated navy serge gymslips and pony-tails, haloed with puffs of breath-mist in the invigorating rosy air.

I loved the old school building on these sunny winter days, glimpses of blue sky and the crooked black fingers of branches through narrow mullioned windows, the dark wooden rooms sunk in time. I sat at the back against the radiator in a dream, imagining myself a young Romantic poet, Shelley at Eton. Soon after milk-break the warm, mouth-watering smells of dinner cooking—pie and mash and gravy, apple tart and custard—began to waft through the building. There was Geography with Boozer Bunting about this time of day and the lists of crops and produce we entered on regional sketch-maps registered in my mouth and made me want to eat them, *steel* and *coal* and *iron* as well as *barley* and *cocoa* and *yams.* The boy who would eat the world.

I was to be confirmed into the Church of Ireland that year and went one weekday evening a week to Reverend Jackson's confirmation class in the church hall. We were a group of half-a-dozen or so Loughside boys, that was all, sat in a circle on the hard Sunday school chairs around Jacko who did all the talking. A decent wee man as you got to know him, he had the warm, homely touch I liked, not stuck up somewhere in the clouds.

The classes ran through the spring and we were confirmed by the Bishop of Down and Connor at St George's on York Road in the early summer. We were warned, "No hair oil, the water will run off it." It was the idea of this that made me want to laugh inappropriately when the bishop laid his hand on my head. I managed to suppress my mirth, imploding painfully. Well I was sure God had a sense of humour.

I had entered a lonely stretch in my life with Matt gone and no other real friend to take his place. I dreaded the school holidays now as chasms of alienation and boredom. To counter this, I cultivated a kind of fantasy world. I dreamt of becoming a famous actor, in the James Dean mould. I went through old piles of sepia *Picturegoer*s that were stored in the coal shed, finding articles about Dean, staring at his photo, studying the look. I got his biography, *Rebel*, which I read and re-read. His death at 24 meaning he would stay forever young was a large part of his appeal. You could reincarnate him in your own person and for a time I tried to model myself on him: intense, moody, misunderstood, angry, but also sensitive, charming, playful, funny. It was a way of dramatising my uneventful young life, lending some kind of meaning to it. I could go for a walk in the dark on my own and *be* James Dean. In a few years I would be famous like him. *The new James Dean.*

I took to hanging around the Gibsons at this stage. I'd been going to Michael, my old primary school teacher, for maths tuition for the Junior Certificate exam. The Gibsons' first-floor flat in Kenbane Crescent on the estate presented an exciting new world of sophistication and modernity to me with its smell of new furnishings and Italian cooking, its rush matting and contemporary low, angular navy three-piece suite. A big window framed rooftops and the summer evening sky; there was an airy, uncluttered feel about the place that allowed your thoughts to expand.

After my hour's grinds Leila would bring in a supper tray of hot chocolate, sandwiches and biccies and we'd sit round in the slowly waining spring light talking about everything under the sun. There was the cultural chat of books and paintings, music, plays and films, and then the amusing self-revelations as we all took turns to tell our own story. I learned that Michael, a very good teacher, had often been in trouble as a schoolboy in Ormagh.

"I'd be up in the Head's office every day for a taste of the cane over some devilment or other," he laughed.

"Like what?"

"Oh, like kicking a Rugby ball from one end of the town to the other."

As the talk flowed on it grew dark, until Leila turned on a table lamp and drew the curtains, and we were cocooned in the soft golden room above the late, quiet street. Was this really a house on Loughside estate? It felt like *Cheyne Walk,* the title of a novel in our bookcase.

"More hot chocolate anyone?" Michael enquired.

"Aye, please."

This offer was always music to my ears, meaning another good hour of sitting there yarning. As the clock hands marched towards midnight Michael and Leila regaled me with ghost stories, always scary fun. and, what was far more shocking, their dark tales of the city: of famous hard men and bloody brawls, or the secret worlds of pros and queers that lurked behind Belfast's respectable façade. After hearing these I came away filled with a fabulous sense of this underworld that existed, not in the pages of a novel, in London, Paris or St Petersburg, but no more than ten miles away, in the city where I went to school each day.

Going home after midnight across the big dark green with the enclosing long rows of white estate houses in darkness too, I felt suddenly more grown up, privy now to the seedy intrigues and vice of adult society. In bed I lay for a long time staring into the dark, my thoughts churning excitedly, in awe of this lurid real life drama. I felt sure that my good parents, fast asleep in their bedroom across the landing, had no inkling of the bad hidden things that went on in the world.

Chapter 6

Down Through

The Gibsons disappeared off for the school summer vacation, though I continued to hang around their place for a while trying to cut the overgrown grass in their front garden with a pair of blunt shears in the hot sun, a job I had promised them. After that I was at a loose end. The two months of the school holiday, once such a joy, felt like a long illness stretching ahead of me.

But while part of me feared the loneliness of my days, another side of me enjoyed the kind of freedom that the uneventful monotony of it afforded to daydream and imagine, to create. Inspired by Salinger and James Leo Herlihy, I postponed my fantasy of becoming the next James Dean and turned to writing a novel.

I wrote in a school jotter on an atlas on my knee, sitting on the side of my bed:

The Sixteenth Summer of Eugene Shannon

by

James Girvan Mitchell

The title was brilliant but then what? From the start I wanted to express my own life and the people and places I knew in a fictional form. But where to begin? Ideas and phrases whirled in my brain like windblown scraps of paper, refusing to be pinned down on the lined page that stared blankly back at me. I must have sat there an hour like that.

At least I had made a start; I had the title page, a damn good one at that. I went back every day for more tries, my nib pointed at the lined page, just me and my thoughts in the back bedroom, the sparrows twittering on the coal shed roof below my window in the peaceful afternoon. It was exciting to be poised there on the brink of the creative process, to feel it gestating, moving inside me.

I was running out of ideas and hope, however, by the time I came down late as usual from my bed one morning and got the brown postcard of Duncraigan harbour with its awkward writing in pencil:

Dear Jim,

Mrs McQuillan was wondring when are you coming to see us again. She says if your Mammy and Daddy aren't coming this summer then maybe you'd come on your own, you'd be no trouble to her. I hope you can come, so we can have some more good times at Duncraigan harbour. Archibald's leg is very sore and sometimes he has to lie in bed.

Love,
June

I told my parents, "It's from wee June. Aunt Kitty says I could go up there on my own this summer."

"Aye surely, you go on, y' boy!" they enthused. "It'll be a nice run for you down through."

"Down through" was Dad's contradictory name for that remote north coast.

I wrote to Kitty confirming my arrival later that week. I packed the little grey cardboard suitcase out of the attic and was off when the day came, taking a mid-morning train into Belfast to make the connection for Portrush.

At the bookstall in York Street station the illustration of a young blonde girl's pale, snubby face on the front of a paperback was pressed against the window. It was a drawing of Hayley Mills and the novel was *Whistle Down The Wind.* I bought it to read on the train and because something about Hayley's face in that drawing—her girlness—obsessed me suddenly.

On the slow train that took me north and inland through County Antrim, I felt my spirits start to sink horribly. Maybe it was the overcast, heavy summer's day, drained of colour and vitality, the monotonous patchwork fields fanning past under a dirty white void of sky. Through the carriage window the telegraph wires along the track sank and jerked up again as they met the poles. I had the feeling of travelling farther and farther from all life and hope. The deserted stillness of the country stations we stopped at was unnerving. An elderly man got on at Ballymoney and sat opposite me. I took an instant dislike to his rustic appearance and long, dour, shut face, his ramrod back and the horrible way he had of whistling under his breath, *"the green, grassy slopes of the Boyne"* or something like that. *Wouldn't you just love to kick him one up the backside?* I said to myself.

This was too much of a journey back in time. I decided I'd stick out three days at Aunt Kitty's then make my

excuses and return home. I had outgrown these holidays with an elderly aunt and uncle on their remote farm and the two lonely McGreevy kids from down the road hanging on to me, desperate for a bit of company in their North Antrim fastness.

Sitting at the front top deck of the bus from Portrush out the coast road, my gloom started to lift, miraculously it seemed. The wind bumped the windows and the sun struggled out shining on the white horses the waves made and the backs of the gulls sailing above their shadows in the small bays below. I felt myself raised up into light and space in the panoramic immensity of ocean and sky, the green headlands running away before us towards Scotland.

By the time the bus turned inland and began its ponderous climb up the long, steep, winding road to McQuillan's Cross, I was feeling something of the old childhood excitement of this holiday journey. Past the row of white council houses I could see the chimneys of the farm above the windbreak line of trees. I clattered down the spiral steel stairs and dragged my case from the luggage compartment. Two figures, the girl and the wee boy, were waiting at the orchard gate.

The elfin boy with his flaxen hair and pink cheeks ran forward to hug me, bouncing up like an affectionate puppy. "Jim! Jim! Ye're back! I cannae believe it ! Och, Jim, it's great, so tis!"

"Hiya, Charlie!"

Big sis hung back with her country girl's shy, modest reserve, a small, slight figure. She looked more grown up, a touch sophisticated even, in her High School uniform of navy gymslip and cardigan and white blouse.

"And how's June?"

"The best, thanks," she replied politely, hot colour suffusing her cheeks prettily. Charlie chattered away at me as we went in the wide double gates, past the orchard to the farmyard. We seemed to float in the heavy stillness after the bus had gone, the fragrance of wet fields and turf smoke drugging my senses. Then there was the richer, rank odour of manure from the outbuildings. The farmhouse was a substantial long, two-storey building with brown pebbledash walls. A collection of feral-looking farmyard cats with reptilian grey fur meowed about the back door waiting for scraps.

We passed through a low lintel into a new scullery extension. Aunt Kitty's small, lame figure emerged from the inner door to greet me.

"Jim! You're bigger than your old auntie now!" she exclaimed. "Sure you're nearly a grown man!" She wore her grey hair in a bun; her smile lit up her round face sweetly like a girl. Her clear, intelligent brow and the frank level gaze of her grey-blue eyes reminded you she had been the mistress at Duncraigan Elementary School for long years.

"At least I'm a teenager!" I said proudly.

"Do you like Cliff Richards?" she asked brightly. "One day you'll teach the young ones of your own!"

I nodded. "Cliff is good but not as good as Elvis, mind!"

"Mrs McQuillan's one of Cliff's biggest fans," said June. "Daddy's going to drive her intae Portrush to see him in *The Young Ones*."

"Will you scream, Auntie?"

"Och, go on with you—at my age!"

June and Charlie helped Kitty get the afternoon tea while I rested from the long journey, occupying Archie's armchair by the living room fire. This room had been the "kitchen" before; now a grey-tiled fireplace had replaced the blackleaded range, while the cooking was done in the scullery extension, on the new cooker powered by Kosangas containers.

Orange tongues of flame licked around brown peat briquettes on the fire in the sunken room. A tall sash window looked out on the high garden wall with the main road above. Lounging back in the low-slung, worn brown leather upholstery, sipping tea, I let myself be waited on like a young lord, plied with triangles of fresh soda and wheaten farls, with butter and honey from the honeycomb, fresh from Archie's beehives, another innovation here on the farm. .

June was a real help to Kitty; the girl cut a capable wee figure, working with deft movements and a brisk swing of hips in pleated serge, a grounded, physical self-assurance about her for all her shy looks. The heat of the cooker and the fire made her cheeks burn and her blue eyes glow, while the soft, shiny pony-tail danced at her nape.

Kitty eased her stiff old frame painfully into the round-backed green wooden kitchen chair. Accepting a cup of tea from June and fixing me with her girlish smile, she said, "Well now, Jim, tell us all the news from home!"

I felt like somebody who mattered here, a sort of celebrity and with such an appreciative audience for once I discovered I had a tongue in my head after all. Kitty drew me out with her teacher's knack of Socratic questioning. "So Mammy and Daddy are well? And tell us about Edward and Dorothy."

"Ned brought a girlfriend back from the College of Art. Long dark hair and a duffel coat and she hardly spoke a word. I thought she was ugly too!"

"Maybe he likes to get all the attention and doesn't want any competition from his girlfriend?"

"Aye, he's always looking at himself in the mirror right enough, posing!"

"He should have been an actor maybe?"

"Aye, he likes to do Heathcliff, all dark and brooding. Stands with his backside warming at the fire and barks at me, *'Sleep with the servants!'* Like Sir Laurence Olivier."

"And Dorothy, what's she up to these days/"

"She's in England with a crowd of students from Belfast, canning peas at Smedley's in Wisbech. She earns a packet working all the hours God sends, on the assembly line. She has to carry heavy boxes and says she's getting biceps like a man now!"

"She'll come back hame and bate ye up, Jim!"

"Aye, ye're not kiddin' me, Charlie, I'll be black and blue!"

Uncle Archie McQuillan wandered in later. In his mid-seventies now, he still pottered about the farm all day, dressed in my dad's cast-off three-piece suits. He'd come in and smoke his pipe by the fire, lying back in the leather armchair with the foot of his good leg propped boyishly on the mantelpiece.

The piercing gaze of blue eyes in the bald chieftain's head circled the room as he puffed for a minute, till it came to rest on me and taking the pipe out of his mouth he said: "Ye've grown, Jim, ye boy Whaat age are ye noo? Four-teen! Boys-a-boys!" Pause. "And how's Mammy and Daddy, are they kapin' weel? Aye, she's a gid wee lass, yer mammy!" Pause. "And your da's a gid mon. Aye, your faither and I, *we know each other,"* he added significantly." Pause. "And there's another quare gid wee lass sittin' there pretty as a picture: wee June! She's a quare help tae us in our ould age. Ainly she's gettin' too big noo tae sit on Archibald's knee, aren't ye, Miss?"

I immediately forgot all about my unsociable plan to stay just a short time with my aunt and uncle. The country life soon had its hold on me as the old routine of childhood summer holidays at Duncraigan was re-established. There were the walks with June and Charlie to Duncraigan harbour or Port Gobbin. We'd stop off at one of the farm shops on the way for sweets and lemonade. Down on the shore we swam in the Slough pool on the rocks or round the headland on the long curving yellow strand of the bay.

There was a run of good weather, every morning a waking dream of heavenly peaceful beauty under the vast clear blue sky that met the deeper blue band of the ocean. Rathlin Island seemed to have sailed in and attached itself to the coastline, the white church and white cliffs standing out clearly. Farther out across the hazy Moyle waters, Islay and the Mull of Kintyre looked near enough to be Irish islands.

By afternoon the road to the shore was sticky underfoot, with the hot smell of tar. The grasshoppers raised their chorus along the grass banks and heat shadow smoked above the bends as we trudged to the tide with our rolled towels and togs under our oxters. Charlie clashed the thistles along the ditch with a stick and June, conscientious as a mother, yelled, "Kape in!" whenever traffic approached.

There was the clear freshness and glad new life of morning then after lunch the time seemed to stand still as you luxuriated in the long sunny holiday afternoon. Each phase of the day had its own special appeal. But evening was the magically beautiful time, when the sun cast its most powerful spell of oblique, pouring mellow light. Seashore and cliff, peat-moss and woods, field and farm, church and castle: all was steeped in the golden radiance, suspended in an ancient peace.

June and Charlie stayed over at Kitty's for dinner, taken in the sunken musty dining room with its damp, rose-patterned wallpaper and old framed print of *Little Lord Fauntleroy.* A mysterious old door was set in the back wall, that I had never seen open. Ranged along the dark old sideboard and the long dining table were steaming serving dishes: potatoes boiled in their skins, peas, turnip, stew.

We were a family there—the family Kitty and Archie had never had. I liked to imagine I was a farmer's son. Feeling the tiredness in my muscles and the glow of the long day in the sun and air on my skin, it wasn't hard to pretend to myself I'd been out working the fields.

Only this was better than a regular family in a way; we were free of all that rivalry and petty conflict. Kitty, presiding at one end of the table, smiled round at us with happy, bright eyes and gently curving cheekbones. She asked her questions and listened attentively as we told her and Archie about our day's wanderings. Archie urged me, "Jim, hae mair praties! Ate up noo and dinnae be hungry!" June and Charlie sat there a little formally, on their best behaviour.

There was time for a dander out in the glory of the summer's evening. June, Charlie and I would take the farm track down the fields to Port Gobbin and come back by the road through Muckera. Honeysuckle and wild rose grew along the hedgerow. From a sunken field came the loud, rasping *krek-krek* of a corncrake hiding in the barley. The sun was sinking away beyond the headlands, over

Donegal, the colour fading coldly from the ocean below as we arrived at the McGreevys' bungalow.

The kitchen-living room was at the back, its long window looking down over the shadowing fields to the metallic sea. The room was bright into every corner with the incandescent light of the Tilly lamp. The turf-burning range dispelled the evening chill; there was the sweet smell of soda bread or fairy cakes baking in the oven. Jessie McGreevy, a handsome woman in her thirties, welcomed us cheerily, giving me a charming smile, while the dark wee da, Rab, jet black hair and black bristled face, frowned at the youngsters and regarded me with wide brown watchful eyes, never a word escaping his lips.

We slumped into armchairs in a satisfied stupor; Charlie read *The Topper,* June and I flicked through piles of *Weekly News, Red Letter* and *The People's Friend.* Jessie put the kettle on and cut sandwiches for supper. The only sounds were the steady hissing of the Tilly, the rustle of pages, the kettle rising slowly to the boil. I felt my face burning and a dead weight in my limbs from all the swimming and walking of the long day.

The cups of tea and sandwiches were passed out and although it wasn't very long since a big dinner I wolfed them gratefully, relishing every morsel, pan loaf, butter, meat paste, and sucking on the hot sweet tea.

"Ye'll sleep weel the nicht, Jim!" said Jessie.

"It's all this fresh sea air!" I exclaimed. Though strangely I was having some trouble sleeping.

June saw me to the gable-end for the walk back to Kitty's. We looked at each other with the funny shy feeling that came over us now whenever it was just the two of us. We stood there a moment as if waiting for something more to happen.

"Cheerio then," I said at last with a sinking feeling, as if I had failed us both in some way.

"Bye-bye," she said faintly as I turned away and struck out along the lonely dark road.

In the ghostly moonlight I could discern the long, low, savage shape of the craig hill. On the other side of the road Archie's fields ran down to the ocean churning invisibly below. The strokes of the Rathlin lighthouse beam swept the night fields and water faintly, momentarily.

Reaching Kitty's a shiver ran down my back as I descended the steps from the road to the front door, putting the dark spirits of the night-time ditches behind me.

In the hard little brass bed with its stiff covers, in the boxlike room above the landing, Kitty came to tuck me in as she'd always done, fixing a blanket across the sash window to stop the draught and snuffing out the candle. I lay there in the pitch-dark and candle fumes listening to the creaks and bumps of my aunt and uncle's preparations for bed down the other end of the passage. I winced and felt my heart beating up as they began saying their prayers together, a scary wordless chanting as it reached my ears.

In the ensuing silence, deep and hissing, I lay awake for a very long time staring into the dark. After a while I could make out the shapes of the furniture, the little old wardrobe, the tallboy and the chair with my clothes on it. There was nothing to be afraid of really. Periodically a late car would roar past along the road below, its headlights sweeping my tiny room.

Gradually my thoughts turned away from childish supernatural terrors to a new kind of anxiety as troublesome

images of June, suppressed in the activities of the daylight hours, came to haunt me in the dark.

Chapter 7

The Summer Wind

There was the shock of seeing her in her red bathing costume that first time we went swimming on the strand, her figure transformed with the first soft curves of womanhood.

We'd changed and spread our towels, the three of us, in a sun-warmed nook on top of the highest sand dune. Ready for the water, we plunged over the edge and down the steep side of the dune in a landslide of soft sand, whooping and turning head-over-heels—what the McGreevys called *"coping carly."* At the bottom we picked ourselves up and raced out across the open, windy, wide strand for the distant tide that came charging to meet us in long ranks of white horses that broke and crashed with a continuous deep-throated rhythmical roar. Reaching the ocean's edge we splashed through the hissing shallows into the blattering icy foam with wild shrieks of elation.

The long days close to the pretty girl took on a torturous quality. We could no longer play at being brother and sister or tender, unspoken childhood sweethearts. I found myself staring at her in an uncharacteristic bold fashion, willing her eyes to meet mine, to understand and reciprocate. But no, she was too young still perhaps, with the sea wind in her light brown hair and cotton frock, the sun-freckles dotting the bridge of her nose, her blue eyes as vacant and pure as the vault of summer sky.

In my adolescent frustration I felt a bit of a devil get into me, to provoke a reaction of some kind from June. On the road to the shore we regularly passed a mother and daughter, English, over on holiday, exchanging simple hellos with them. The girl was June's age, slim and sun-browned, not as pretty as June but attractive in a plain way.

"She's not bad looking!" The comment slipped mischievously from my lips, to make June jealous. But she said nothing and her face betrayed no emotion.

Another day June met them on her own. "The English woman and girl stopped in the road to talk today," she said. "The woman said she liked you, that you have an open face."

I liked the sound of that but where was June's jealousy? She'd be matchmaking me with that skinny little girl next if I wasn't careful!

The day out in Derry was the turning point. June was playing in the Duncraigan girls' accordion band on the Apprentice Boys' march. I'd watched her rehearsing in the barren chill of the McGreevys' front room, marvelling at the sounds she squeezed out of the shiny, cumbersome instrument that she wielded with such delicacy. Charlie and I went with her in the back of an old van borrowed and driven by her dad. It was quite an event to be leaving our small, remote world of Duncraigan for the crowds and excitement of the city.

It was a grey, showery August afternoon. June went off with her band to join the parade and we waited to view it from a spot beneath the hallowed old city walls which the Protestant apprentice boys had gloriously defended in the siege of Derry—eating rats to stay alive!—against James's besieging Catholic army nearly three centuries ago and we weren't going to forget that in a hurry, were we?

The quaint folksy pageant of the traditional Orange Order parades with their fluttery silk banners and stirring bands had a real excitement and entertainment value provided you could turn a blind eye to its sectarianism, as even some Catholics did, coming along for the show. However that day the weather grew wetter, it was sticky under the plastic Pakamacs we'd brought and I soon began to feel a bit saturated also by the endless mesmerising procession, the marching Orangemen in their black suits and bowlers, orange sashes and white gloves, and the succession of bands, pipe, flute, accordion, the music of each rising then fading off into the one coming up behind.

The redeeming moment was the sight of June marching past with the other Duncraigan girls in a swing of kilts and blaze of accordions, the pretty smile she shot us lifting my heart in joy and hope and pain, in that order.

We travelled home in a weary silence. The journey back felt twice as long, the damp country roads swishing and bumping beneath our wheels in the wet blue evening light. June sat opposite me in the back of the van, her hands clasping her knees below the hem of her kilt falling away in pleats. She caught me staring at her in the cover of the half-light and stared back at me this time, her gaze soft and level and mysterious, till all I could see was the whites of her eyes in the gloaming.

*

The white bungalow stood on a lonely open stretch of the Antrim coast road against the backdrop of fields and headlands and ocean. A kid goat tethered at the back rattled its chain and emitted plaintive bleats like a lost child. The golden evening air was redolent of the fragrance of peat-smoke that curled up from the chimney under the peaceful height of light blue summer evening sky. The purifying cold breeze blew stiffly off the sea, as ever, quivering the shining, upright yellow stubble and green blades of grass and rattling the leaves of the birches that sheltered one side of the house.

The oblique sunlight of half-seven shone warmly into the old Austin car body that stood in the lee of the turf-ricked gable end. The back seat of the car had been removed and straw put there for the goat. The boy and girl sat beside each other on the scuffed leather of the front seats, looking out the missing window at the stacked turf. There was a strained silence between them until the girl turned her face to his profile and reading his mind with deadly accuracy, spoke in a quiet voice without a trace of nervousness, as if she were simply acknowledging an obvious fact.

“Do you want to kiss me?”

When I turned my head her face was tilted to mine, her eyes half-shut. My heart thumped like a fist in my chest and before I should have any more time to think I fastened my mouth down on hers. For a moment I felt I was going into a swoon. The blood pounded in my ears and I struggled for breath as if I was drowning in the terrible dark sweetness of her kiss.

"Somebody might come!" I gulped, pulling back from her in terror.

"We can go in the front room," she said. "Nobody comes there." She was calm and practical, not to be put off now we'd started.

We got out of the car and I followed her indoors. I felt nauseous, consumed by dread. We turned past the closed kitchen door, her parents and Charlie inside, along the draughty hall with its residual warm odours of fried food, through to the gloomy, lifeless front room.

With the door shut behind us here we were secluded from the rest of the house. Charlie's toys and June's accordion lived here. There was a sofa in front of the dead fireplace; we sank down on it and I lay back with my eyes shut, shivering and clutching at my stomach to try and still the butterflies. The chill room made my teeth chatter comically.

"Aw, you're could!" June sighed, motherly. "Here, putt this o'er us." She tucked a plaid blanket around us and nestled in against me with her head on my shoulder.

"Got a sore stomach!" I moaned.

"Where's it hurt?" she murmured. "I'll rub it for you." She slipped her hand down and massaged gently. The knot of anxiety in my guts began to ease a little. Then, pressing the warm, moist O of her mouth against my ear she whispered, "I—love— you!"

Her perfect words, the three most wonderful words ever spoken, shocked and thrilled me to the core of my being; I was too overcome to respond.

"Did you hear what I said?" she whispered. "I—love— you!"

Words failing me still, I turned to her in gratitude and we clung to each other in long famished kisses, till our wet faces skidded together.

The room was growing dark when we stood up to go. I felt frail and shivery, hollow-legged, as if I was sickening for a dose. June walked me along the road, our arms round each other, she supporting me.

"Ye're no' weel!" she said tenderly.

Dusk was settling over the ragged hedgetops and the bushy, rocky outline of the craig. We stopped at the bend in the road to kiss goodnight, the way young lovers do.

"Will ye be a'richt the rest of the way on your own?" she asked.

"It's only a hundred yards," I said.

"I'll be over in the morning," she said. "I'll nurse ye if ye're no weel."

When I looked back after a minute she was still waiting there at the bend, watching me, her pale summer frock glimmering ghostly in the last faint glow of the day's end.. She waved faintly and then she had turned back and was gone from my sight. I pressed on towards the dark silhouette of the house on the crossroads. My feverish thoughts kept turning obsessively on the incredible momentous events of that evening: the fervent kisses, the girl's gentle touch and her words of love.

I spent the next few days confined to bed. They thought I must have caught a chill swimming in the Slough. I was moved into the guest double bedroom at the end of the passage, where my parents slept whenever they stayed. Kitty lit a fire in the small cast iron fireplace and let me have the big battery wireless from the kitchen window here by my bed.

From the high brass double bed I had a view out the back window to the headlands and sea. The August weather had turned wet and wild, gusting at the windows, rattling them in their sashes and juddering the gable end. It was cosy and I felt content to lie there and listen to the wind and be waited upon with trays by Kitty, June and Charlie. At some point in the day Archie would stick his gaunt bald eagle head round the door and enquire after my state of health.

"Lie doon under the claes, ye boy, or ye'll no' get weel," he advised me and I'd lie back flat with the covers drawn up to my chin to please him until he'd gone.

June and Charlie spent the day by my bedside. I read to them or told them stories, or we listened to pop tunes and traditional music on Athlone. If a good lively number came on, the girl and her wee brother would jig madly round the room till they collapsed at the foot of the bed, all of us in mad fits of laughter, the effect of being cooped up for hours.

June and I held hands while she sat on the side of the bed, not speaking but looking deeply into each other's eyes for long minutes on end. The firelight flickered in her irises and her cheeks were flushed, her brown hair loose about her face. When Charlie went out of the room I drew her down to me on the bed for a kiss. There was a lovely homely feeling like being married.

After the McGreevys were sent home at night, I read Kitty's *Whiteoaks of Jalna* paperbacks by the light of the oil lamp. There was Eden Whiteoak, a consumptive failed poet I could identify with and a big country house with horses and thunderstorms and people falling madly in love. It wasn't hard to imagine Kitty and Archie's as my

Jalna. One day, I fantasised, I would be the master of Duncraigan—and June the mistress of the house.

Kitty brought my supper tray of hot milk and pan loaf and butter, and tucked me up afterwards and put out the lamp. I lay awake for a while listening to the steady patter of the rain and watching the flickering play of the firelight on the ceiling shrink and fade to darkness. I drifted into warm dreams of my love and woke in the morning as she entered my room, lithe and bonny, leaning over the bed to kiss me, with the smell of the country air on her soft hair and fresh skin.

On the Sunday afternoon I was allowed downstairs again.

"Och, it's bye-bye to summer, I do believe!" said Kitty. "Three days' solid rain and still no let-up."

A fire was lit for me in the fusty, formal drawing room with its grey three-piece suite and ancient pedal-organ. Archie's silver cups for horse-ploughmanship lined the top of the bookcase; the shelves contained Kitty's brightly coloured paperbacks—the whole series of *Jalna* and Betty Macdonald's *The Egg and I* books—and the McQuillans' Sunday School attendance prizes dating from the 1870s, evangelical children's novels that were perfectly preserved relics of the Victorian age.

Wee Charlie had gone with his parents to visit cousins over the moss. Across the hallway Kitty was listening to *Your Hundred Best Tunes* on the wireless. June and I cuddled under a blanket on the grey moquette sofa. Rain drummed on the windows, the evening shadows filled the room and the flames danced in the hearth. We pulled apart from a kiss and pretended to be reading a book when we heard Kitty's hirpling approach across the hall.

"All right, Master Jim!" cried Kitty, entering the room behind us. "That's long enough for you to be up today!"

The weather cleared for a last few days of real summer with the sun pouring down at intervals. It was warm enough for us to go swimming at the strand on the Tuesday. There were a few visitors, families down on the sand under the cliffs at the Port Gobbin end where there was some shelter from the endless wind and better access to the tide. June and I spread our towels together a little way apart from the others. She was wearing her pretty red frilled costume; the sun was hot on the ground and soon we were lying on our sides facing each other and kissing. We were oblivious of anyone else, together in our own warm little love-bubble. The immensity of sky and sea around us seemed to offer a kind of anonymity until we heard people laughing.

"What are they laughing at?"

"Us maybe," said June.

"Why?"

"Because we're young."

That put the wind up me and I couldn't wait to get out of there. We must hide, keep it a secret, this love of ours; we were too young in the eyes of the world for this sort of thing. I had a fearful, catastrophising mindset. *What if it got back to Kitty? And she told my parents? My mum'd faint! Maybe, even, we were breaking a law of some kind!*

We slipped away, across the stream in the sand where some cows paddled and over the tumbled boulders beneath the cliffs. We passed the narrow mouth of the cave where a hermit had dwelt in Archie's young days and rounded the headland to the quiet recess of the little harbour with its white cottages and green lawns in the warm sun, fishing boats pulled up on the pebbles and the nets hung out to

dry. We followed the rough path that wound round the base of the high grassy headlands sprinkled with bright yellow birdsfoot trefoil and other little flowers, past small islands of jagged dark limestone in the choppy sea, and climbed to the archway in the cliffs.

Once you passed through the eye of the low, dark, dripping arch in the grass-covered rock of the headland, you emerged in the strange prehistoric otherness of the first of a series of deep coves where the tide boomed in and rattled out over big smooth round stones and there were large boulders and curious high grassy mounds like tumuli. It was to one of these that we repaired now, holding hands as we struggled up its side on the little paths that seemed worn by fairy feet. We clutched at tussocks of wiry grass to steady ourselves. At the top we were rewarded with a saucer-shaped, sun-filled bed of long grass, smoothed flat by the wind and sprung like a mattress, where we collapsed together, laughing in gratitude to the ingenuity of Mother Nature. It was our own eyrie, raised up under the vault of blue and white sky, with only the prying eyes of passing seagulls, beady and accusing.

The weather broke again, it poured and we were cooped up indoors all day under the eye of one adult or another, denied the freedom that the great outdoors afforded to young lovers. At last the rain had stopped in the evening after dinner and we made our way up the craig among the tough, dense whin bushes and rocky outcrops like miniature cliffs. Behind the low hill we were out of sight of the road and the houses. The small fields ran back bleak and desolate under chasing smoky clouds towards the boggy hinterland. The untamed hill, home to foxes and

badgers, preserved there among the cultivated fields, had always struck me as a savage, sinister place, but now its wildness suited our purpose.

"Here's a good spot!" said June and spread her navy Burberry with the tartan lining down on a clearing of rabbit-cropped grass. She lay down flat on her back on the coat, like a patient, or somebody knocked down in the road, angling her face to me and holding her arms out stiffly.

"It's warmer on the ground," she said.

I lay down half on top of her, as if I was trying to keep her warm. The wind rushed over us, moaning and shaking the bushes.

Back at the bungalow her daddy glanced up sourly from his *Chronicle* by the range as we came in the kitchen. Mammy Jessie was often "no weel" these days with splitting headaches and went to bed early, while Rab looked listlessly at the paper or stared moodily into space—*thinking long,* as they said—and smoked a *Blue*, his eyes narrowing sometimes to malevolent black slits that glittered like coal. June had told me how he began his working life as a blacksmith, sleeping in the straw in the stables, before he became a motor mechanic. I liked that story and liked to think of June as "the blacksmith's daughter," earthily romantic.

These days Rab was quick to lose his temper with June. He turned on her once after she told Charlie to "Dry up!"

"What kind of dirty ta'k is that?" The black eyes flashed murderously and he showed strong yellow teeth in a grizzly bear snarl as he blattered her mercilessly around the head. It sickened my heart to see it but she took her punishment with a dazed sort of submission, never a sound or a tear out of her. I thought what a stoical little person she was.

Rab saw us holding hands in the road and when June didn't let go of my hand he just took a long look at us and said nothing. I'd become part of this family too, going with them to the Presbyterian church at Billy on Sunday mornings and sitting up in the front pews under the great wooden pulpit. It was different to the Anglican service of the Church of Ireland; I liked the minister's down to earth philosophical sermon running through the whole service, knitting it all together and drawing you into a wholesome strong sense of community.

The rain began to fall heavily just as the two of us were setting out from Kitty's to the shore after the midday meal on the Thursday of that last week of the holiday. We had no option but to retreat indoors. There was the strange dead afternoon quiet in the gloomy, deserted kitchen with Archie gone to Ballymoney market and Kitty upstairs taking her nap. The fire was banked with slack behind the wire mesh guard, a row of socks drying on the line strung under the mantelpiece.

Here we were with the room to ourselves. June came on my knee in Archie's deep leather armchair. But as we kissed I was nervous, conscious of every little sound: the ticking of the mantelpiece clock, the slack shifting on the fire. The rain drumming down outside intensified intermittently to a deep rushing roar that seemed to engulf the whole house, as if we would be washed away at any moment.

Over June's shoulder my eyes fixated on the smoke-stained cream board ceiling with its central gas mantle: I could feel Kitty's presence in the bedroom directly above.

She had heard us come back in and then go silent. I could feel her listening as she lay there in her bed, wide awake, no more than a few yards away from where we were busy courting in Archie's chair.

"What's the matter?" June whispered.

"Kitty—there!" I nodded to the ceiling.

"We can go in the barn," said June. "Up the ladder to our secret hidey place!"

Out the back door the rain was plumping down in the deserted farmyard, hopping on the puddles and running in rivulets. As we made our splashing run for the barn door I was conscious of the line of sycamores that sheltered the farmyard tossing, swirling and swaying in a kind of majestic, mesmeric dance that seemed to accompany our own movements. It was as if the storm, the trees and us, the two young lovers, were united in the one exuberant elemental choreography.

In the gloom of the barn June led the way gamely up the ladder on the partition wall, swinging her hips boldly in the navy skirt as I came up behind her with my heart in my mouth. Atop the ladder we crawled through the hatch in the wall on to the hay piled under the roof in the dark. This was our old hang-out where we'd shelter on wet days and I'd tell June and Charlie books I'd read.

It was dark here, only the long slit of daylight under the big bolted doors. Bales of straw ascended like giant steps, the loose hay spread on top. The rain battered on the tin roof close above our heads. The hay made a soft bed for us, warm and scented of the summer meadows. I smelt the rain on my girl's hair and skin and woollen cardigan as she came into my arms.

After our courting it was good to just sit there together and talk, happy and secure in one another. Outside the rain had stopped, the birds were singing. Now we plotted and dreamed together.

"D'ye think we'll be married wan day, Jim?"

"Aye, soon as you're sixteen. Matt and his girl got married at sixteen and they have a baby now in Eden."

"Oh, that's beauty-full!" she said. "We can live here when Archibald and Mrs McQuillan are gone!"

"Imagine having the house all to ourselves!" It *would* be like Jalna!

"We'd have babies too," she said. "Lots!"

Her words thrilled my blood with a hot masterful feeling. "How many?" I wanted to hear more of this.

"I want six!"

"I'd like that too, we'll have a big family."

"Mammy and Daddy are takin' Charlie tae Portrush tomorrow. You can come over to me and we'll have the house to ourselves all day. It'll be just like we're married already!"

It was then we heard the footsteps outside the barn, saw the shadow move beneath the door. Quick-witted, I raised my voice, pretending to be telling a story, *"And then George shoots Lennie in the back of the head before the other men can get to him..."*

We jumped up and dusted bits of straw from our clothes.

"Mrs McQuillan!"June whispered. The footsteps receded faintly.

"She's gone on. C'mon, let's get outta here! D'ye think she heard what we were saying?"

I could just see it all: Kitty coming downstairs to the empty kitchen, suspicious, wondering where we could have gone in that rain, then coming out after the shower to listen at the barn door, hearing,"...*It'll be just like we're married already!"*

The fear had hold of me again, the guilt that we were doing something terribly wrong in the eyes of society. But when we went indoors Kitty was busy with her preparations for the evening meal, smiling up at us and enquiring pleasantly, "Did you get wet?"

"We sheltered in the barn and told stories, like we used to do!" A bit of me wanted those days of innocence back again.

But I got a shock the folowing morning after breakfast when I announced brightly, "I'm off over to McGreevy's, Auntie!"

"Oh no, you're not!" said Kitty sharply. "You can just wait for June to come over here! I don't want the two of you alone in that house!"

Her words mortified me. I'd guessed right, she had overheard our plotting yesterday. The game was up. I slunk away hopelessly to wait for June in the drawing room. I tried to read my book, to no avail; my mind was in turmoil. I felt humiliated, sickened of the whole risky, shameful business. I made up my mind to tell June we had to stop now before we got in real trouble.

After an hour I heard the snib go on the gate and glancing up at the window saw June come tripping down the steps by the dripping scarlet and pink fuchsia bells. I hurried to open the door. She looked lovely, all morning fresh with her hair tied back and white ankle socks and shiny black shoes completing her new school uniform, her smartest outfit.

"You didn't come?"

I put my forefinger to my lips and once we were safe in the drawing room I told her, *"Kitty knows!"*

We walked out together in the mid-morning, turning down the road to the shore. As soon as we were clear of the house June slipped her hand firmly into mine.

"We can still be together. We'll find somewhere!" she said

"We'd better not, June," I said, sick with nerves. "It's got too risky. I'm scared!" I was chickening out of the whole thing now, wanting desperately to be good and have Kitty's approval again.

"Och, it'll be all right," June insisted. "We'll find somewhere nobody can see us, up by the castle. Ye're goin' hame tomorrow and we're not going to see each other for ages."

As we walked on, hand in hand, down the winding road to the shining sea below, I felt less fearful. We were a couple, two in one, a law unto ourselves. June's unwavering sense of the rightness of it all carried the day; I wasn't hard to persuade.

We kept straight along the main road, past Dan the fisherman's bleak little grey house and the turning for the harbour, on through the village above the rocky cove. We passed a cottage with its thatch going to seed. There was sun-splash on limewashed walls, a donkey in a paddock. A *Players Please* tin sign creakied in the wind outside Effie Lyle's wee shop. Then we were out the long road to O'Cahan's castle and the Giant's Causeway. Cloud shadow ran on the open fields and white farms; to our right was the coastline, grassy headlands sloping to the rocky shore.

We came to the long, low stone wall of a bridge where we paused to watch a rushing burn, watered by the August rains, run out under our feet and down to the sea. Leaning on the coping we spotted the shelf of dry ground under the bridge and looked at each other. We climbed the fence and picked our way down through nettle beds to the water. The dry spot under the bridge looked inviting, clean and pleasant enough to sit there. Bent double, we ducked under the low arch and settled ourselves, kneeling up on the fine white pebbles, embracing.

Over June's shoulder I could see, framed in the arch of the bridge, a distant patch of sunlit, windy fields, glittery green and gold. The stream purled past close to our knees. I looked down, my eyes and hands savouring the lovely details of my girl, the delicate brown nape and the shiny chestnut pony-tail down her back, the narrowing to the waist and the soft swell of her hips. The upturned smooth bare calves above the short white socks were splayed and vulnerable looking, her head bowed, like a girl saying her prayers.

It was then, in disbelief and incredulous horror, that I felt the force of nature rising in me, unstoppable as a volcano. I pulled away from the girl in haste and rolled over on my side in a vain attempt to hold it back or release it into the water but it was too late The overpowering sensation, like a hot needle drawn through the quick of me, passed over and I lay there on my side, my back to June, like a wounded animal. My face was close to the gliding stream, brown and flecked with spittles of foam. I waited while the pulsing waves of sensation subsided in me.

"What happened?" said June.

It was then I heard voices raised, from the direction of the shore.

"Someone's coming!" I panicked.

We crawled out under the sky again. The voices grew closer, shouting and laughing.

"Hurry, June, it's a gang headed this way!" I imagined bumpkins, hooligans crashing through the long grass and nettles, in on us, laughing and pointing, jeering obscenely.

June knelt by the stream wetting her hankie and dabbing at the spots on her new skirt.

Gaining the road again we had sight of the harmless Wandervogel in big shorts and rucksacks crossing the rapids where the stream poured into the sea. Hikers from the youth hostel: there was my belligerent gang!

The sun had gone out leaving a cold desolation on the fields and sea, the flat feeling of summer's end.. All the blinding passion had run out of me leaving me hollow and chill. It was a relief to be going home on the morrow, out of harm's way with this girl and the strange force we'd unleashed together, that was as powerful and wayward as the wind and sea. I just wanted to be a child again, with a child's innocence, knowing nothing of any of this.

I had a cruel instinct to shun the girl walking by my side on the lonely stretch of country road but, "You're thinking long," she said and as she linked my arm, natural as a wife, something warm and irresistible pierced the shell of my guilty introspection.

"I get scared, that's all," I blurted. "We're too young."

"Sure what does it matter if we love each other?"

"I suppose," I conceded.

"And next summer we'll be older. If you dinna meet some Belfast lassie first."

"No, there's only you."

"Do you love me?"

"Aye."

"I love you too."

Suddenly it was all so simple really. And throwing care to the wind that blew hard and cold now, with the first droplets of an approaching shower, we stopped a minute to kiss there by the side of the road—till we heard a car coming over the hill by the castle above.

Chapter 8

The Lads

Through the winter that followed I cleaved to the memory of my summer love. Burrowing into my pillow in the dark before sleep and school, I would call up the images and sensations of those ecstatic moments with my girl.

I fantasised that I was living with my aunt and uncle on a permanent basis. June and I caught the bus together to and from school in Bushmills every day. In the early dark of evening we did our homework together under the oil lamp at the kitchen table. I helped June with her English exercises and Kitty helped me with my maths. Intermittently the winter wind shrieked like a banshee in the chimney and rain lashed the windows, intensifying the cosiness of the setting. Uncle Archie smoked his pipe by the fire, his gaze circling the room.

In this fantasy June and I existed in a perfect world of our own, boy and girl embracing at the centre of the front cover illustration of my novel. The backdrop to our picture showed the long farmhouse outlined starkly on its hilltop against the black scribble of stormy winter sky. Below the house the wind-blasted twilight fields sloped to the snarling, lashed monster of the winter sea.

Duncraigan
by
James Girvan Mitchell.

The fantasy sustained me through the dark and lonely schooldays of that winter. I turned fifteen In February and thought seriously about leaving school and taking a job. I went so far as an interview for trainee manager with a timber firm down on the docks but one look at the poky office and the other trainee managers, old before their time with their work talk and office suits, and maybe school didn't seem so bad after all.

Then out of the blue, things began to change in my life. It was the Fourth Form year, there was the school trip to Paris in the spring and, out of this, new friendships formed and I began to be drawn into the social life of Belfast city. I was growing away from the boyhood years of holidays on my uncle's farm and my childhood country sweetheart. In reality, I told myself now with the crassness of youth, June was just a wee girl. I guessed my sophisticated new city friends would laugh at her dialect. *"Culchie!"* was the common Irish put-down for a country or "agricultural" person.

After school each day we caught the bus downtown, loafing on the top deck with a lordly view of the streets opening out to us, down through Carlisle Circus to the city centre, where the tall commercial buildings and big shop windows closed in. Alighting from the bus in Royal Avenue we negotiated the throng on the pavement, dived conspiratorially down Rosemary Street and ducked into quiet Lombard Street, narrow and overhung by warehouses and offices.

The Lombard was tucked away discreetly up a long flight of stairs, like our own gentlemen's club. The brass plaque on the landing announced that the restaurant had been founded by the Ulster Temperance Society. Through the glass double doors we entered a spacious, red-carpeted lounge. No daylight, just warm, low lighting, permanent night. There were red armchairs around tables in the middle of the floor, cosy booths along the walls. Smart uniformed waitresses served afternoon tea.

The buzz of good talk, like the sound of the city's heartbeat, greeted you as you gained the top of the stairs and washed over you as you entered the restaurant. A bit of a loner for so long, I felt the kudos of being one of the gang now, the mates; I imagined heads turning, registering our entry approvingly: *"The Royal School lads!"*

Our group varied in numbers but the unfailing regulars were Stuarty, Hugh and me. Stuarty and Hugh were real Belfastmen, born and bred, not country like me. Hugh Boyd had come recently to the school after passing the Review, the second chance to gain a scholarship to grammar school. He was a year older than the rest of our form. Hugh stood out in a crowd with his thatch of fair hair and wide shoulders. In conversation he had a mature quality, with a soft-spoken refinement.

Hugh had befriended me in the back of a geography lesson. I took to him straight away, the relaxed quality that had time for you, all day if you liked, and the ironic humour bubbling away just under the surface. Hugh was already hanging round with Stuarty Rea who I'd come up through the school with—never close to him before but we'd performed Everly Brothers harmonies together in the acoustics of the bogs. He'd always been wee Stuarty who everybody knew, the class clown. A risible runt, he'd recently spurted to my average sort of height now, a dark, good looking boy, with a hapless tendency to get into trouble.

The Lombard mid-afternoon clientele was chiefly a mix of senior grammar school students, trainee managers and secretaries. We had the heady feeling of having arrived on the scene at last. The waitresses got to know us and our unvarying order of cups of tea all round—a lot cheaper than coffee.

Among the big crowd who sat together down the back a girl's wild laughter erupted. It was Gwen in her light blue Methodist College uniform, showing small white teeth in her little, heart-shaped, creamy face that peeped out from a bush of curly black hair. Momentarily every head in the place turned to stare at her. A curtain billowed in a sudden summer breeze through an open window. There was a feeling of the glamour and freedom of youth.

Our teas waited steaming in the straight white cups and saucers on the table before us. It was the high point of the day, our couple of hours' freedom between school and home. You sat there at the hub of the city's youthful life, bathing in the wonder and excitement of it, wanting time to stand still. We stretched out the magic minutes, talking through the rest of the afternoon, finding our voices for the first time. All the promise of our young lives just beginning to open out seemed contained in that eager talk around the table in the Lombard in the early summer of 1963.

Soon we were meeting up at weekends too and moving on from the Lombard to crawl the city centre coffee bars: the Ulster Milk Bar, White's, the Wimpy Bar, the Mayfair and the Lido, the Piccolo and Isibeal's. The summer holidays came round again; with time to kill we explored the city's free cultural offerings: the Arts Council gallery in Chichester Street, the Ulster Museum, the Linen Hall and Central libraries, the bookshops. Or we nosed round Smithfield covered market looking at LP records, books and guitars. If we had money there was the cinema—half a dozen of them in the city centre—and a little further out, the theatre, *The Importance of Being Earnest* at the Arts, *Under Milk Wood* at the Grove.

The streets offered their own entertainment as we wandered round in the long summer evenings. There was the Donegall Square busker who ingeniously wrung tunes out of a saw he played with a fiddler's bow, *Beautiful Dreamer*, the saw bent further for the higher notes.

The young East Belfast evangelist with a pitch in Fountain Street plied us with pamphlets in a vain attempt to save our souls. We'd stop as if genuinely interested, then mercilessly take the mick out of the poor fellow.

Once in the High Street we saw a policeman chase and Rugby-tackle a fugitive who was wielding a docker's hook.

It was exciting to cut through Amelia Street, a name synonymous with prostitution. We watched the blank windows of the sullen, mysterious wee houses for a glimpse of a pro at a curtain maybe, but never saw the slightest movement in the curiously dead little street there smack in the heart of town. We emerged by the classic Victorian *Crown* pub, beloved of Betjeman, that had featured in the novel and film *Odd Man Out,* opposite Great Victoria Street station. We were no wiser than before regarding the ladies of the night but uplifted by a sense of our own daring now.

Then there was the shock of one lovely effulgent summer's evening when the city filled up with the strange pageant of American sailors off a ship in their bell-bottom blues, strolling arm in arm with what appeared to be every prostitute in the city, all clacking stilettos, swing of bunchy petticoats and high, lacquered beehive hair.

When we tired of the streets we met up at Hugh's or Stuarty's to play poker and listen to records in front rooms; and later on to play the acoustic guitars we bought at Smithfield Market—Stuarty and I on the guitars, Hugh on a basic drum kit he'd got from the classified ads in the *Belfast Telegraph.* We played a mixture of the Liverpool sound—The Big Three, Billy J Kramer, the Beatles of course, and American folk—the Kingston Trio and Peter, Paul and Mary.

Once the excitement of new friendship had spent itself the feeling of boredom could creep in, irritation with each other sometimes as we grew desperate waiting for something to happen. Something was missing for sure—girls, to be precise. We sat over our teas in the coffee bar and watched the street door, as if they were likely to walk in at any moment: three girls, one each. But the nearest we ever got to a girl was chatting with some friendly wee waitress too old for us.

As autumn came on we tried the Saturday night Inst school hop, our nerves anaesthetised by neat Scotch drunk in the bogs, the flat quarter-bottle passed along the floor under the partition walls of the three adjoining cubicles we occupied.

I hated those dances, stood around in a gormless group of lads eyeing up the wallflowers. When you finally picked up the courage to ask one to dance—the Twist was in that year and I liked it—it was an awful anticlimax with the girl doing her best to ignore you through the dance and going straight back to her seat when the music stopped, leaving you higher and drier than ever, stripped of even your dignity now. Any attempt at conversation with a dance partner was a terrible stilted effort quickly drowned out by the Clipper Carlton showband.

We had the idea to throw a party one Saturday night at Hugh's when his parents had gone out till late. The girls were lined up: Gwynneth and Susan from school were old flames of Hugh and Stuarty; Gwyneth was supposed to bring a friend for me. It was an exciting prospect: we would effectively have trapped three girls. But in the event the girls never turned up and we got drunk on our own again on the flagon of scrumpy we'd procured specially from the Spanish Rooms.

Was it adolescent emotional frustration that turned us to mischief next? For a while it seemed we were never out of trouble of one kind or another, creating a nuisance and extra worries for our teachers and parents. After a drunken episode on a school trip the Head drove out to Loughside to visit my parents.

"Jim is not a bad boy," Leatherbarrow pronounced upon my character, "but he is easily led."

My parents took it well in the circumstances, Mum leaving it to Dad to speak to me afterwards, which he did in his quiet, tolerant fashion that left me feeling very guilty, swearing to myself that I'd always be good in future. My resolve lasted till the next bit of mindless minor delinquency. We were all intelligent, nice, middle class, grammar school boys from good, caring homes. So what had gone wrong? Just the boredom, awkwardness and frustration of youth, I suppose. It required the girl factor to exert some kind of civilising influence.

It wasn't till the Easter of 64, after I'd turned sixteen that we met up with Katie and her gang. We had come to Portrush for the bank holiday weekend: Hugh, Stuarty and I, and Ronnie Kernoghan and Malcolm Allen. It was a tradition, this Belfast exodus to the North Antrim coastal resort at Easter weekend. The other lads booked into a boarding house. I would sneak into their room and kip on the floor in a borrowed sleeping bag. I didn't dare ask my parents to pay for this trip after all the trouble I'd been in recently and told them I was staying with friends in Belfast.

Arriving Saturday afternoon, we set out to explore the town. The streets swarmed with school students like us, in our out of school, unisex uniforms of navy reefer jackets and blue jeans. There was a sense of regeneration after the long winter months and the rare, heady feeling that youth had taken over here, like some proto-pop festival.

We turned along the seafront hunching into our coat collars. Down on the sand a football match was in progress; there were even some hearty types bathing, charging into the icy Atlantic breakers. The bitter wind whipping off the crashing bilious sea made our eyes water. In a minute dark clouds were massing, swirling and spitting. We retreated to the shelter of the narrow streets and Forte's restaurant.

The large café with its yellow wooden tables and chairs was loud and smoky and packed with youth but we found a table by the big window. You had the sensation of drowning in the roar of animated conversation that rose from the crowded tables. A girl's wild laughter pealed out over the din, turning heads. It wasn't Gwen from the Lombard. This time a beatnik-looking girl sat facing out from a corner table, tossing her shiny black mane from her face, rolling her big eyes and showing her pretty white teeth and pink gums, while a group of lads in scruffy denim pressed eagerly about her.

"Looks like the same old story here," said Stuarty bleakly, "with the guys outnumbering the dolls ten to one."

It was only a throwaway remark but I felt my heart sink. The five of us sat there with a feeling of anticlimax. So here we were in Portrush—so what? There was desultory conversation over cups of tea, the ashtray filled up with butts. We stared out at the gusting rain, the passers-by blown along on it. Later we ate some chips, lining for the stomach and went out to find an off-licence.

The rain had ceased, leaving a dank blue vacancy in the evening air. Scouring blasts of the sea wind jumped us at the corners. When Hugh and Ronnie, the two oldest, had purchased the quarter-bottle of Scotch, we walked up out of the town to a headland shelter that stood deserted in the miserable spectral twilight.

Ensconced in the shelter in a row on the long bench, slouching into our coat collars, feet stuck out, we passed the bottle up and down the line. The tide boomed away below the cliffs; fag-ends glowed companionably in the gathering dark. The whisky tasted vile as ever but its firewater quickly brought warmth and forgetfulness in the cold shelter and soon we were talking away and laughing easily as if we were in the comfort of a snug.

"This is good as the pub!" someone said.

"Bit parky but."

"We could invite some birds up, have a party." We wished.

"What birds?" said Malcolm gloomily. "This place is Boytown."

"*Where the boys are.* Connie Francis song, a film, remember?"

"I'd rather not."

"What are you on about anyway, Malcolm? Sure you've got your wee Babs waitin' for you back home!"

Malcolm and Ronnie had steady girls, Barbara and Hilary; they went on double dates. That was why we didn't see so much of them usually.

"Ah shut up about the bag!" said Malcolm cruelly. "Ah'm supposed to be havin' a break from her this weekend."

"There's true love for you," Ronnie teased. "Only last week he was talkin' about marryin' her!"

"Crap," said Malcolm coldly. This contempt for the girl, a vivacious and wholesome blonde we'd all have given our eye teeth for, made us feel better. *Who needs birds anyway?* The clandestine ritual in the darkened shelter, the fiery potion from the thin flat bottle, bonded us in male self-sufficiency.

Till the last drops were shaken down our throats and Stuarty got up and hurled the empty bottle out into the windy booming black void beyond the clifftop where it disappeared soundlessly. And we all stood up, stiff with the cold suddenly and trooped back down the path to the lights of the town.

We gravitated to Barry's amusement arcade, watching the dizzying rides. There was no spare talent anywhere in sight. The camaraderie of the shelter faded along with the hope generated by the whisky; we stood round like spare parts in the noise and cold. Would it always be like this?

Malcolm, still the worse for drink, seemed to undergo a change of heart now towards the girl he'd left behind.

"I wish I'd my wee Babs right beside me here now!" he declaimed. "I love that wee girl, Ah'm tellin' ye, lads and Ah'm not ashamed to admit it! I love my Babs!" It was a declaration from the rooftops alright.

The arcade lights shone stars in the thick Buddy Holly glasses on Malcolm's pale, earnest, handsome face. He was hard to get to know, a funny moody guy. Was this what a girlfriend did for you? I wondered. All highs and lows and weird contradictions.

"He's off again!" said Ronnie. "What did I tell yous? Still, I don't blame you, Malcolm, there's nobody here to share our sleeping bags tonight, that's for sure. Shall we hit the hay, lads?"

There were grunts of assent, a sense of general disillusionment, headaches, cold feet and dampened spirits. It was a relief to give up and go to bed. I had to wait across the road from the boarding house by the station palings till Stuarty came back to the front door to signal the coast was clear. I followed him up long flights of stairs to the attic room the four of them shared, its twin beds supplemented by two camp beds. There was just enough space on the floor for my sleeping bag too.

We all got into bed and lay there chatting for a while. This was the best part of the day with the world shut out and nobody to impress but each other. The cosiness of it revived our spirits; we batted witticisms to and fro and felt glad we'd come away together after all. Then people began to drop off to sleep, one by one, and someone turned the light off after midnight. I'd set the alarum clock for five, to get out before anyone in the house was up.

I stepped out from the sleeping house with my rolled sleeping bag under my arm and shut the door softly behind me. The only person in the world out on the streets in the blowy grey dawn, my one thought was to get my head down on a bench in a shelter and return to the oblivion of sleep for another couple of hours. As I turned along the seafront the wind swooped at me and boxed my ears. Down on the sand the waves broke with a timeless, indifferent rhythm. I found the shelters full up with figures in sleeping bags stretched out on the benches. I walked the length of the promenade before I found a space right in the last cosy corner of the last shelter before the sand dunes.

I curled up gratefully inside my bag, shut my eyes tight. The wind whistled around the wood and glass structure. The surf thundered below. It was romantic alright. But the bench grew harder, the sleeping bag colder. I could have done with some of the puppy fat I'd shed over the past two years. The draughts blowing from every direction just grew colder and more persistent. It didn't take long to come to the conclusion that there was no hope of sleep for me here.

Someone was snoring in one of the other bags; I guessed they were all too far gone in drink to wake up. At last I got up stiffly, rolled up my bag and like a man sleepwalking, stumbled away for the inland shelter of the town centre streets. There I chose the narrow, deep recess of a shoe shop entrance and curled up on the tiles by the door like a dog. It was more sheltered than the seafront and there were no other guests but I was too wide awake by now and couldn't get back to sleep.

I was the first customer when Forte's opened its doors at eight. It was a blessing to sit inside in the warmth and breakfast smells, cradling a hot cup of char in my frozen fingers. I felt a mindless contentment now in just *being.* I sat there observing the street gradually come to life

the other side of the big windows, the first customers dribbling in. I didn't want to be with the others in the boarding-house; I was having an adventure, liberated from the stultification of home comforts. I'd broken away; I was Colin Wilson adrift in Soho, Jack Kerouac on the road. Anything could happen now I had opened myself up to experience.

Chapter 9

An Easter Girl

The mates rolled in after their cooked breakfast in the boarding house and ordered hot drinks. It was Easter Saturday; the café and the streets outside soon filled up with the young holiday crowd. We ventured out mid-morning to look at the sea and the girls—a few more of them here today, we concluded happily. Showers drove us back to Forte's; there was nothing to do other than sit there drugged with cups of tea and fags and the café warmth and crowd chatter and in my case the lack of sleep. The normal sense of time had vanished; I felt suspended in one eternal moment. I wasn't even sure who I was any more: just a being of some kind observing the flow of life around me.

It was mid-afternoon, the café heaving and squalid, when a couple of girls landed at the table right next us, a fantastic stroke of luck. Stuarty was quick off the mark with the chat up; the girls giggled and bubbled. How did he do that? I could never think of chat up lines—it was all so fraught and painful somehow with the horror of rejection. Why couldn't you just talk normally to girls, like to another bloke? I wondered. But that didn't feel right. Too dry. It was easy with June because we'd been friends for a long time growing up together. But that wasn't going to happen again, was it?

Stuarty had turned right round to face the girls, straddling his chair backwards Alan Ladd style, chin resting on his folded arms on top of the chair as he fixed them with an intent quizzical stare that emphasised his wit and handsomeness.

"Do I look like a second-hand car dealer?" he was quipping about his Saturday morning job at the garage his father managed. He had the girls in fits. "What do you say, Jim?" he drew me in expertly.

I half-turned my chair to the girls, tentative, grinning, being the nice quiet guy. "I don't know!" I gulped.

Stuarty came to the rescue. "By the way, this is my best mate Jim. People even take us for brothers."

"Oh, look at his eyes!" the small girl swooned. "Where'd you get those peepers?" Long, straight brown hair curtained a round, pretty face, the features mobile, little eyes full of fun. "Hiya, Jim! I'm Katie!"she said cutely.

"I'm Helen." The other girl was taller, slim, with short dark-fair hair, flushed high cheekbones and slightly bulging blue eyes.

"Where you from?" Stuarty asked them.

"Cavehill Road, Sunningdale We go to the Girls' Model—or rather we did—we've just left!" said Helen.

"Hip-hooray!" Katie cheered. "Free-dom!"

"We're starting secretarial jobs next week," Helen explained. The girls looked at each other and burst out laughing at the idea.

"Oh, you're from *Sunningdale*—posh!" Stuarty teased. "I'm just round the corner from you with the plebs on the Oldpark. All us here go to BRS."

"Ooo-ooh, the Belfast Royal School*!* Now who's posh?"

"We're staying at the Beach View Hotel," said Katie, "with Mummy and Daddy. We come every Easter. Are you all sleeping rough?"

"Charming!" said Stuarty. "Do we look—rough?" Up went the neat eyebrows like question marks, making the girls laugh again. "Ectually we're staying at a rether well-appointed B 'n' B next the station. Mrs Ferguson's. Five of us stuffed in the attic with the engines shunting below. You can't see out the window for the steam from the funnels."

"I'm sleeping rough!"

There, I'd said something! It was meant to impress but then I blushed, worried it might do just the opposite. "Well, sort of," I mumbled. The faintly smiling girls' curious stares turned on me made my words dry up.

"Are you from the Oldpark too?" Katie enquired.

I shook my head. "Ahm, near Carrickfergus." I didn't say Loughside because it sounded such a non-place.

Next thing Stuarty and Helen were standing up, scraping back their chairs, looking at Katie and me. We got up too and followed them out of the cafe. I was last out the door; Katie waited for me, zipping up the blue anorak above her tight blue jeans; then we walked together into the wind after the other two who'd gone charging ahead through the holiday crowds.

Katie's five feet came up to my shoulder; she walked by my side with the graceful locomotion of a full feminine figure, turning her face up to mine, shaking back the curtains of her hair and smiling sweet and delightful while she talked nonstop in a soft, breathy, genteel voice. All I had to do was listen and be carried headlong on the charming spontaneity and suddenness of it all. What a difference a day and a girl made: the futility, boredom and discomfort of the holiday weekend banished in an instant, replaced by a shining magical *now* that filled the whole universe.

We came out on the promenade. Ahead of us Stuarty hurried Helen along, waving his arms and gabbling at her while she looked up at him and smiled.

"My shelter!" I pointed. "Where I slept this morning—or tried to."

"Oh, you poor thing!" The concern in Katie's voice thrilled me: *she cared!*

We passed the storm-battered, faded dance hall at the end of the prom and dropped down the steps on to the rain-wet strand. A sunny interval had brought out desperate little family groups, huddled behind canvas windbreaks, building sandcastles, paddling. Stuarty was holding Helen's hand, pulling her up the dunes. They disappeared over the top. Katie's hand burrowed into mine and we climbed after them.

At the top there was no sign of the other two. Not a soul in sight. Just the wind blowing over the undulant tufted dunes, like the desert. Beyond them, the golf links. Descending to a hollow we sat down on the sand out of the wind, like our own flying saucer.

"Portrush must be the windiest place on earth!" cried Katie above the moaning of the air, smoothing her hair off her face. The wind had whipped fresh childlike colour into her cheeks. She looked a bit like June. She sat with her rounded legs crossed in their tight denim, back straight, breasts pushing out under the nylon anorak. She stopped talking and turned her face to me, a half-smile left on her pretty lips, her eyes meeting mine level and candid.

There was nothing else for it then; I pressed my lips to hers, shutting my eyes tight and feeling her soft response. The drumroll of my heartbeat accompanied the music of the wind soughing in the brittle, bleached dune-grass, the cackle of gulls and the humble, powerful sound of the surf breaking on the shore below.

With our lips still touching I opened my eyes and was looking straight into hers, catlike chinks of green dancing with a sense of wicked fun.

"You have fab'lous long lashes!" she exclaimed. "It's not fair! Hi, you look like one of the Beatles—Paul or George!"

"I play the guitar and all. Stuarty and I play together." Why not blow my own trumpet a bit?

"Oh, that's fab! Stuarty's such a laugh, isn't he? What age are you?"

"Sixteen."

"That's young for me for a fella. I'm fifteen but I look a lot older when I'm dressed up to go out."

"People tell me I'm old for my age."

"Aye, there's something about you that's older. Do you read a lot?"

"I love books. How can you tell?"

"You remind me of a fella I used to go with. He's at university now. It's cold sittin' here!" She shivered. "Look at the time. I need to be headin' back for our tea at the hotel. Wonder where Helen's got to?"

We stood up stiffly and made our way back, holding hands, down the dunes and along the beach, back up the steps to the promenade. The kiss on the dunes had sealed it and we walked in a nimbus of joy, not separate any more but a couple, while everything around us continued the same, the wind, the sea, the holiday crowds—only distanced now, less real, like a painted cardboard backdrop to the drama of us.

This was love all right, sudden, straight off, the way love should be! A spell cast over a boy and a girl who only two hours previously had been totally unaware of each other's existence on earth. But I had a desperate sinking sensation as we drew near her hotel and our parting, the fear that she would skip off with a blithe cheerio and I'd never see her again. I'd necked with a girl once at a youth hostel and that was what she did.

"Are you coming to the dance here tonight?" she said outside the hotel.

"What, in my jeans?" I looked down at my faded denim knees, discoloured from grovelling in the shop doorway that morning.

"I can ask if they hire out suits," she said. "I'll come to Fortes after tea."

She bounced up and gave me a quick kiss and was gone. I wandered off in a glow of self-satisfaction, as if I'd just won the pools. I was *seeing her again!* I felt sorry for the ordinary mortals I passed in the street now, who weren't me.

The lads were in the café, slouched around the mess of dirty teacups and overflowing ashtray.

"Yay, Mitch! Ye scored!"

"Wee Katie! Tell us, is she a good court?"

"Aye—brill kisser!" I wanted to tell the world.

Stuarty was back. "How was Helen?" I enquired.

"Good wee court alright but it was founderin' on those dunes." I could tell straight away it wasn't the real thing with him and Helen, not like Katie and me.

Katie came at seven, sailing in wearing a black leather overcoat, stockings and high heels; she had applied heavy dark eye make-up, almost panda-like. She was immediately at ease in the all-male company, vivacious and chatty, her face shining with openness and sociability, life and laughter.

But hi, she was *mine!* I wanted her to myself. After a decent lapse of time I ushered her out into the gathering spring twilight. Taking her hand, I walked her towards the shelter on the headland, the surf rumbling below us, spectral in the blue light.

The shelter was waiting there for us, empty, private. We sat on the bench and kissed for a few minutes, close and warm, lipstick and leather, in the dark and cold. Then we cuddled together for warmth more than anything else, with the draughts sifting litter around our feet and the waves thumping the rocks below. Even with Katie in my arms there was no denying the bleak forlornness of the place.

"I came here with the lads last night to drink Scotch," I told her. "Like a gentlemen's club and tonight you're the lady guest."

"I'm honoured. Your friends are fab," she said. "Stuarty's mad. Hugh's dead nice in a shy-guy way. Ronnie's funny too. And moody Malcolm's so good looking."

"Mean, moody and magnificent, like James Dean."

She laughed.

"And what about Jim?" I acted jealous. "Is he not good looking?"

"Oh, he's the cutest!"

"Well, I'm glad to hear it!. And what's Katie's secret?"

"My secret?"

"How do you do it? Be so happy all the time? Life and soul of the party girl."

"My mummy says I'm blessed with a sociable disposition. I have my down moments too, I can tell you, but not very often."

"Do you never think to yourself what's the meaning of it all—he meaning of life?" I affected this gloomy existentialism after Camus and would turn it on cheerful souls like Katie sometimes.

"Only God knows that," she said.

"You believe in God?"

"I like to think there's something out there that's more than us."

"So do I." I gave in easily; I didn't really want to be an atheist.. "Imagine you just live and die and that's it. What's the point?"

"You're a bundle of laughs tonight, wee lad!"

It was too uncomfortable to stay in that shelter any longer; we walked back down the hill, arms round each other, buffeted by the windy dark. What a wonderful feeling, you and your girl joined at the hip, the two of you as one now to face the cold streets, the lonely void of the world together.

"Are you coming to the dance? They don't hire out suits but m'Daddy'd lend you one of his ties. Don't think his other clothes would fit you. He's five-foot-four and as broad as he's long."

"Don't worry. I've been awake since five this morning and I'm dead on my feet. You go on and enjoy the dance with Helen and your family. I'll go back and have an early night with the lads and see you in the morning."

We kissed goodbye at the hotel. It was all lit up and the band was playing *Cherry Pink and Apple Blossom White.* There was an older crowd arriving, all dressed up: definitely not my sort of thing, even with Katie.

She was there with Helen at Forte's in the morning, fizzing with irrepressible life and fun, chatting away to the lads as if she'd known them all her life—but ignoring me, I felt, as any kind of special presence. How could this be when we'd felt so close the night before? Perhaps it was a kind of shyness, a defensiveness on her part, for all her seeming self-confidence, but I was taken aback and annoyed. So this was just a holiday weekend thing then after all, I told myself. Well alright. No doubt girls could be like that.

I was going with the lads on a morning train. When the time came I stood up with the others and we exited en masse. I didn't look back and Katie never came after me. The wind met us at the door, bracing and free. It was better to be your own man anyway.

Chapter 10

Summer Term 1964

I was all right. I was safe, just one of the lads again, all of us having a good laugh together in the fusty, ancient smoking compartment as the Belfast train licked along, putting Portrush and Katie Jane (as in Rupert Bear) behind me fast. I could feel good anyway because I'd really scored at the weekend. It meant I could do it again whenever I wanted. Love them and leave them, that was the way!

"She's a pretty wee thing, your Katie," said Malcolm, his words piercing me.

"Good court, you said?" Ronnie's glassy blue eyes registered vague lust.

"Oh, aye," I nodded, grinning them off. I just wished they'd all shut up now.

It hit me hard later on that day, when I was home, alone again in the gloomy quiet of my back bedroom: *I miss her!* The feeling lodged like a stone in my chest. I'd never felt such a profound loneliness. It was mixed with shame, as if I'd betrayed myself in some way—or worse than that, denied the very life force itself—and all out of pride, the sin of Satan. Anyway, she was gone, gone, gone. I didn't have her number or anything. And here I was back in my rat hole again, me and my dressing table mirror.

But when I phoned Stuarty that evening he told me Helen had been in touch with him already and she and Katie were meeting up with us all at his house on Sunday night. The news came like a reprieve. *She wanted to see me again!* My heart fairly leapt for joy. I knew now I didn't deserve her really. Maybe it was that "something out there" she'd spoken of, looking out for us!

It was meant to be! But as the time drew near I felt the return of the old debilitating butterflies, threatening everything. The slow, agonising quietude of Sunday stretched my nerves on its rack: the lie-in and the roast dinner, the *Sunday Express* with the old man by the fire, and at half-five the salad tea I scarcely touched. As I caught the 7.05 train the long spring evening had turned sunny. The light gilded the fields viewed from my carriage window and then the city streets, a rich, deep, luminous gold, thick as paint, transforming the facades of factory, shop and terrace and the figures on the pavements. I cringed away from the beauty and romance of it that seemed tied up with my feelings for Katie and too much to bear now I was actually on the way to meet my love. I shut my eyes in a kind of half-swoon and would gladly have died there and then on the bus that carried me up the Oldpark Road to Stuarty's.

Once inside the semi-detached suburban house I was quickly swallowed up in the crack going on in the front room. Stuarty's parents had gone out for the evening. The radiogram under the window was belting out *With the Animals*; clouds of fag-smoke hung in the shafts of mellow Sunday evening sunlight that penetrated the room. The piano against the wall supported framed childhood photos of Stuarty and Thelma, his much older married sister. We sat around in a wide, loose circle on the chairs and carpet. Katie was there at the centre of the banter and fun. She and Helen had brought their school chum Miriam. There was Stuarty, Hugh and myself. Even numbers. It was almost too good to be true.

When Katie asked after Malcolm and Ronnie, Stuarty said, "Guess who Malcolm's seeing tonight?"

"My wee Babs!" Hugh mimicked and added, "He's got it bad, that fella!"

"Och, that's nice!" said Helen in a dotey voice. "Romantic."

"Aye, in a pukey way," said Stuarty. "Like *the moon never beams without bringing him dreams..."*

"Of the beautiful Babs McCart-ney!" I volunteered.

"Rhymes an' everythin'," said Stuarty.

"And Ronnie's not allowed out," said Hugh. "He has to stay in and revise for his O-levels. His old man, the old Major, is awful strict. Ronnie has to have five Os for the Navy."

"O-levels!" Stuarty grimaced. "I've not even thought about them yet! *School the morra!"* He grabbed his head as if his brains were about to explode.

"Well, don't expect us to sympathise," said Helen. "We're working girls now, don't you know! Nine to five. Two weeks' holiday a year. Life of Riley being at school."

"What do you do, Miriam?"I asked the other girl who was sitting on the floor by the fireplace, next my chair. I saw she was attractive, dark and Jewish, small like Katie, with large brown eyes that blinked curiously as she gazed round her at the proceedings, missing nothing. Lots of teeth were revealed in a chipmunk grin that gave way readily to warm, uninhibited laughter. Now those big eyes, deep and dark, fixed me in a warm, glittery look and for a moment I had quite forgotten about Katie sitting on my other side being the life and soul of the party.

"I'm starting in a solicitor's office," Miriam answered me. "Friend of Mum's took me on although I'm not fifteen yet." I picked up a mid-Atlantic accent.

The way she held my eyes softly made me have to look away shyly. Katie and Stuarty were going at it hammer and tongs with the barbed Belfast wit and belly laughter.

"I'm tellin' ye now, wee doll!!"

"Dirty enough!"

"And that rhyme the wee lads used to chant after Audrey McQuitty in the street—*has awful big—!*"

"Stuarty, no! You're a naughty wee boy yourself!"

There was no alcohol, it being the "dry" Ulster Sunday, but it felt like we were all a bit drunk. Daylight faded in the room; Stuarty didn't turn on the electric light and the talk petered out in the deepening shadows. Then the girls were sitting on our knees: Katie and me, Helen with Stuarty and Miriam with Hugh. There was no awkwardness; it was just a natural progression. Then there was a parting, Stuarty and Helen, Katie and me up the stairs, leaving Hugh and Miriam the front room.

Katie and I had Stuarty's bedroom at the back; we lay on top of the covers on his double bed, kissing for a while. Then we talked softly in the darkness filling the room.

"You went off without even saying goodbye to me at Portrush," she said in a reproachful little voice.

"I didn't mean to, we were hurrying for the train."

The pale circle of her face framed in the long dark hair was mysterious and captivating in the dark bedroom. She was a different person on her own, away from the crowd, all sensitivity now. I preferred her like this.

"You're funny," she said.

"I can't help it."

"It's my own fault for pickin' a funny fella, s'pose?"

"Me too—I mean, you but not funny, that is."

"You were sweet over the sand dunes at Portrush, so gentle. Only I got a shock when you kissed me. You're supposed to open your mouth, you know."

I should have been mortified by her criticism but I realised that words just popped out of her mouth like that and she meant no harm, it was a Belfast thing. What did it matter anyway? There was no denying the real feeling of enchantment between us.

"'Mere and I'll show you. Like this," she said and demonstrated: jaw slack, mouth open wide, lips pressure applied with a firm clockwise motion. It wasn't difficult once you got the hang and practise soon made perfect!

I came away from that evening floating home on the top deck of the bus above the city streets, down the Oldpark Road, up York Street, and out on the last train along the Lough shore and over the dark fields to Loughside.

Time seemed to drop away and I was spirited across the miles in seconds, a magic carpet ride. Walking down deserted Station Road under the lamppost halos at quarter-past-eleven, I relished the hard rhythmical clatter of my Cuban-heeled boots on the pavement, waking up the people in the prim little houses. I wanted to let them know life had just begun. There was no more need for the Sunday night blues. Love had come and saved the world.

Back at school after the Easter break I couldn't stop thinking about her. Our gang, suddenly doubled in size with the addition of the three girls, was due to meet up again on the weekend. The only question was how to get through five days without seeing Katie. But lo and behold! As we walked through Donegall Square after school, there she was suddenly, right in front of me, as if she'd materialised out of my dreams. Her black leather coat flapped, her long hair blew and her cheeks glowed in the spring wind and sunshine. The smile she gave me stretched her shapely mouth ear to ear.

"What are you doin'?" I asked stupidly.

"They let me out to post some letters."

"Your first day at the Northern Asphalt Company. How's it been?"

She laughed when I said the firm's unglamorous name. "Oh, not bad," she said. "Look at you in your uniform, like a tin soldier!"

We stood there with the indifferent throng parting around us, a wee island of tentative, trembling new love in the concrete heart of the city. The lads had wandered on ahead discreetly. City Hall was on our left as we walked together, not touching but contained in a glow of mutual attraction, oblivious of the crowded square. It seemed to me more than a coincidence that we should just happen to walk into each other like this. Now every moment together was to be savoured. Words failed us; we just smiled foolishly at each other and she half-sang in a motherly way: *"Little tin soldier marching along!"*

I stopped at the narrow mouth of Wellington Street.

"Comin' to isibeal's?"

"Can't," she said. "I'll see you Friday, Miriam's place. You can ring me before that if you like."

I wrote her number in my school diary. "We're not on the phone," I said, "but there's a call box on the corner of the street."

"Hi, you're making me late back to the office!" she joked. She kissed me full on the lips, and then she had turned away in a clatter of stilettos, a swing of shiny chestnut hair and flapping black leather, her compact figure soon swallowed up in the crowd.

I turned away down the narrow canyon of the side street, so quiet and set apart there at the very pulse of the city. I savoured her kiss on my lips, grinning idiotically to myself. As I pushed through the heavy glass door into the cosy, coffee-smelling interior of Isibeal's, the lads cheered me from our usual corner table.

We roistered round Belfast city now in a glorious gang of boys and girls in the long spring evenings that lengthened and mellowed into summer. We went to isibeal's, the cinema, Stuarty's or Hugh's or Miriam's when their parents had gone out. In the houses we drank fizzy cider from the off-licence, chatted and played records. We always ended up necking on the sofas or beds in a cidery glow of passion.

Afterwards we kissed the girls goodnight at the bus stop in the mild blue summery dark and swooped away on lighted double-deckers to home and bed and school and no homework done that night again, no revision and *who cared?* We were living at last, not a little trio of monks any more. The weekend evening get-togethers soon extended into the week, Tuesday, Wednesday...

On a Wednesday evening we walked into town from Miriam's place on the Antrim Road: Stuarty and Hugh and me, Katie and Helen and Miriam, swinging along under the full green trees down Duncairn Gardens in the gold-paint summer evening sunshine. Showers had washed the sky clean and sweetened the air. We were laughing, carefree and jubilant, as if we owned the town.

I thought of the years I'd walked this road to the station from school, such a lonely boy and here I was now at the centre of everything with my mates and our vivacious, pretty girls. Tonight the streets were ours. North Queen Street, New Lodge Road. The ugly industrial streets that could seem dark and deformed and menacing, the architecture of nightmare, took on an exotic look in the blue and gold summer evening. The red brick walls of Gallaher's mill had mellowed to the glow of sandstone cliffs in the high horizontal rays of the evening sun.

Then as we emerged on to York Street a couple of wee millies shouted after the girls: *"Hi, what are yis laughin' at?"*

I was in front with Katie and Hugh. We looked back and heard Stuarty placating the millies: "I was making them laugh at me."

"You kape out of it, wee fella, Ah'm talkin' tae hur!" The millie, tough as a little bloke, squared up to Miriam.. "What's so huckin' funny?"

"Nothing." Miriam blinked defensively, standing her ground. Not for the first time I was aware that she had a tough side to her also.

"Think ye're *it* wi' yer wee pretty boy there and yer umbrella?" And so saying she snatched Miriam's umbrella out of her hand and poked her on the shin with it. "Well, ye're nat huckin' laughin' at me!" She threw the umbrella on the ground and swaggered away on with her mate.

The others were in stitches but I was horrified a girl could behave like that. You forgot what a tough city

Belfast could be behind the glossy façade of the central department stores and office blocks, restaurants and cinemas. Of course my city friends thought nothing of it; I was the naïve country boy. Within minutes the millie incident was completely forgotten by everyone else but it stayed with me disturbingly, a bad taste in the mouth.

The O-levels came and went in a blur of sleeplessness and adrenalin. I had left revision to the last minute. Reading that the young Tolstoy had passed his law exams by doing nothing all year then sitting up revising all night before them, I proceeded to emulate the great Russian (for I was a writer too!) I'd snatch a couple of hours' sleep before Mum woke me for school at seven.

It was the usual June exams' heatwave, everyone in their white shirts at the rows of single desks in the music room. I worked steadily through the papers with the conviction that I had become possessed of Tolstoyan intellectual powers. After Portrush it seemed I had broken through some barrier in my personal development and nothing could stop me now.

The weekend following the exams, on the Sunday night, I went to Katie's house to meet her parents for the first time. It was a five minute walk from the bus stop on Cavehill Road, down Sunningdale Park, a long, winding, silent road of redbrick suburban semis in the churchy stillness of a Sunday evening in June with the sun still shining warmly. Then as I turned up Sarajac Crescent a nasty little dog came flying down the garden path of the corner house and flung itself at the gate, barking madly after me. I continued, feeling a bit shaky.

Katie's house was halfway up the steep cul-de-sac. There was a drive to the garage at the side and steep steps going up through the rockery to the front door. The doorbell gave back a remote genteel chime—we'd only ever had knockers on our front doors. I saw the cute face at the ground floor bay window and then her small shadow on the door glass.

My heart was beating nervously as I entered the hallway. Katie had recently had her hair bobbed; it fitted like a helmet around her pretty face which wore a rather haughty expression, the queen of Sarajac here in her hilltop castle! Her plump legs were poured into blue denim jeans with big turn-ups like a tomboy and bare little feet on the grey hall carpet.

"I thought you'd got lost," she moaned. Mummy and Daddy materialised behind her like an inspectorate.

"So this is the famous Jim?" said Mummy, a forthright, glamorous woman with a round, pretty head like Katie, but paler skin and bubble-permed platinum hair.

Daddy was a wee fat bald man with glasses and a florid boozer's face, who laughed a sociable hoarse smoker's rattle straight from his big belly and exclaimed, "Hi, he looks like Paul out of the Beatles!"

"Aye, a good lookin' fella," Mummy appraised me. "Katie's been tellin' us all about you and we kept sayin' when are you going to bring him round to the house, is there something wrong with him?"

"I'm sorry, Mrs Burns, I've been preoccupied with O-levels," I said.

"I hope our Katie hasn't been distracting you?"

"Not one bit," I said truthfully for I had distracted myself.

"Well, make yourself at home here in the front room with our Katie. We're watching the *Palladium* next door. I'll bring you in a bite of supper."

It was an immaculate modern front room: discreet silvery wallpaper, grey wall-to-wall carpet and new-looking three-piece suite around a coffee table with a big cut glass ashtray facing an electric wall-fire. A blue record player was plugged in on the floor below a small collection of LPs and singles on a shelf in the corner. Not like the dusty junk shop of our front room at home; but no books, no piano here and if there were paintings on the wall I didn't register them.

"They're really nice, your parents," I said, though I was relieved to be on our own now.

"They approved of you, I could tell," she said. "You're only my second steady boyfriend."

"I'm glad if I've passed muster then."

Katie knelt down to the record player on the floor and put on a little stack of singles. It whirred, clicked and thumped and Peter, Paul and Mary sang *If I had a hammer.*

"Your mum's an attractive lady," I said.

"She used to be a singer in a dance band. Funny she chose m'Daddy!" Katie tittered. "She tells him *'Why did I have to marry an ugly wee runt like you, Albert?'*"

"He's a good personality maybe?"

"Aye, I like to think I take after her looks and his personality, not the other way round! Personality can be enough for a fella but not for a girl. Heard the one about the fella with the ugly new girlfriend but she'd a great personality? And he introduces her to his mates for the first time: *'Fellas, this is Elizabeth! Elizabeth—speak!'*"

We laughed wickedly together and cuddled on the sofa. It was nice being on our own for a change without the gang in tow. About half-eight Mrs Burns came in with a tray loaded up with tea, thin white bread sandwiches in triangles with the crusts cut off and a Peak Frean biscuit selection.

"Now don't for heaven's sake knock over the tray, Jim!" she said, putting it down on the low table. "Like Graham, Katie's first boyfriend—upset my best china all over the floor!"

"I nearly died!" said Katie. "Graham was such a clumsy big fella, long legs sticking out in the way and nervous, sweaty hands. But Mummy was dead decent about it, just made a joke of it."

"What else could I do? No point cryin' over spilt milk, literally! I couldn't very well kick him out there and then, could I?"

I approached the tray warily after that. I was always reassured when I hadn't done something as gauche as someone else. When Mrs Burns had gone I fairly devoured the sandwiches. "Mm, chicken—scrumptious!"

"You'd think you were half-starved, wee lad! And you're so thin. Lucky!"

"I keep forgettin' to eat since I met you!"

"Oh, aye? Tell us another one. Why are you going off to England and leaving me then?" she joked.

"You could come too!"

"How could I? I've a job here now. My career!"

"But there's no student jobs here for me, that's the trouble."

Suddenly the idea of going away from Katie sent a lonely shiver through my chest. I was conscious of the hands on the mantelpiece clock creeping towards ten, the slipping away of precious moments together. The Sunday night dark with its melancholy aura of the good times come to an end and Monday morning looming closed in at the window. It was time for some serious courting and we fairly clung to one another there on the sofa, boy and girl, in the brightly lit front room high on the hill above Belfast, as if we might stop time in its tracks.

"Don't miss your bus," she murmured out of a clinch at twenty-past-ten. "Stick your head in next door and say bye-bye to them before you go."

Mummy and Daddy were sitting in the dark, fag-smoke clouds hanging in the TV light in the back living room, the two figures remote from each other across the room in their separate armchairs. On the black and white screen the Sunday night Hollywood film was concluding in weepy melodrama.

"Goodnight, Mrs Burns and Mr Burns! Thank you very much for the supper!"

Katie held the front door open for me as I went on kissing her goodnight. "Go on, you'll be late!" she laughed and stood looking after me as I plunged down the steps and drive to the steep street. I looked back at the small figure framed in the hall light; a last wave and I took to my heels down the hill and round the corner, running for the bus.

It felt better running; a wild burst of energy swept me along with an effortless feeling under the streetlights along Sunningdale Park, my footfalls reverberating off the bedtime houses, like a fugitive in the suburban night. There was the mildness and promise of summer in the night air. The nameless apprehension I'd felt earlier with the two of us in that little room and the time ticking away remorselessly had lifted. I believed I could run forever like this—not running away from anything any more but towards life, to embrace it with open arms.

I was cutting it fine for the last bus to the last train but I wasn't worried, I knew I'd catch it all right *because I wanted to.* Nothing could defeat me in this mood. As I came out onto Cavehill Road I saw the bus waiting above at the terminus light up and move down the hill, perfect timing in my charmed life. A few more strides in my seven-league boots and I was at the bus stop across the road, sticking out my hand. I jumped on to the platform and clattered up the stairs, the only passenger on top, perched in the front window as the bus swooped down to Limestone Road. Turning a tight corner, we nosed along the narrow channel of North Queen Street, close to bedroom windows and I got down at Lower Canning Street for the final dash, flying over the cobbles like the highwayman, *riding, riding,* down the steep hill to the station. There were only a few days of school left and then we were off to England.

Chapter 11

Across the Water

There were five of us going from school: Stuarty, Hugh, Ronnie, Howie Irvine, and me. I'd arranged the trip, travel, digs and jobs. My brother and sister had been over before and knew the scene and the contacts; Dad helped me write the letters.

We kissed our girls goodbye there in the gloomy, cavernous cargo shed with its garbled Tannoy announcements and climbed the gangway to the Liverpool boat which was all lit up in the bright sunshine of a weekday evening in the second half of June.

The girls were waiting on the quay below when we emerged at the high deck rail and we waved and shouted to each other. Hugh's parents were there, his mum in tears, for he was their only child, going away from them for the first time. Our shouts were soon lost in the blast of the ship's siren and the mighty roar of the engines starting up. The gangway was rolled back; everything was vibrating madly and suddenly we were moving, pulling out on the dark oily water that lapped the harbour wall.

The quay slid away, the girls waved frantically, their figures diminishing rapidly as the ship gathered speed. In a minute they were gone from our sight and it was a queer exciting feeling watching our town slip away from us: the Victorian terraces, steeples of mill and church above them, all bathed in the rich crimson glow of the flat rays of lowering sun.

A flock of hungry gulls screeched in the ship's wake. I waited a long time at the deck rail watching the docks and wharves and shipyards go by and then the banks of the wide Lough were either side of us, the colour fading from the green hills in the lengthening shadows. I spotted the war memorial poking up against the flushed sky above Loughside, the ruled lines of the estate houses below the mountain, and thought of my parents there by the fireside and the telly before I turned away from the chill grey expanse of water into the sickly warmth of the saloon.

We travelled cheaply, steerage, no berths. It was midweek, just before the holiday season would get under way, so the boat was uncrowded. We settled down in upholstered seats in the bar area, though cups of tea were all we drank. Close by a card school was in progress, a group of Belfast workmen and a beatnik type with a cultured voice, like a mature student or an actor or artist, dressed in a scruffy jumper worn next his skin, faded grey flannels, gutties on his bare feet and a grubby white shorty mac over the back of his chair. His longhaired woman watched the game for a while before disappearing off to their cabin.

We stretched out on the seats to get some sleep. I dozed fitfully. The card school continued long into the night, the quiet, tense voices carrying as from a distance, monotonously, wordlessly to my dreams. Then around two in the morning I heard the beatnik say, "You will have to excuse me now, gentlemen, Judith awaits me in our cabin! Mustn't forget our duties to the ladies, eh?"

There were guffaws and when he'd gone one of the workmen said, "Your man's a quare gag! A character, right enough!"

"Got he's head screwed on alright, the same fella!" another one commented shrewdly. "I know I'm eighteen-and-six down to him!"

The lights dimmed and there was silence at last except for someone snoring. I had taken to the floor to get stretched out properly and felt the steady rolling of the ship under me. At last I had an hour or two of something resembling proper sleep.

We were woken by the jolting, juddering progress of the boat inching through the locks at Liverpool and we stood up stiffly and got some tea. Presently we stepped out on the deck for our first bleary-eyed glimpse of Beatle town, the massive commercial buildings of heavy dark stone looming out portentously in the still grey dawn.

The sun was shining brightly, promising a fine summer's day as we boarded the motor coach for the ten hour journey to the south coast. We sat down the back watching it fill up with old age pensioners. Finally the driver climbed in the cab, the engine started up with a shuddering roar and we were off, the long vehicle swinging out of the coach station and sliding through the morning rush hour streets with its giant's self-possession.

"Look, there's Ringo!" exclaimed Ronnie.

"Where? Nah, just looks like him!" said Stuarty but we all stared intently out the window now as if we might just spot one of the Beatles, the Searchers or the Fourmost waiting at a bus stop.

We put the city centre with its tall buildings behind us and were driving out past interminable redbrick terraced streets.

"Hi, we're back home in Belfast again!" somebody joked.

"Only bigger!"

At last we were clear of the city and out on the busy trunk road that sliced straight through the wide, open tract of countryside with its large flat fields. Half-slept, we started nodding off on the soft seats in the warm coach, head sliding down the window till you were jerked awake and then the process repeated itself. In my dreams I heard disjointed, disembodied voices and the queer insistent whining undertone of the engine rising and falling, punctuated by the hiss of the airbrakes. It got hotter under the blazing sun, like a glasshouse, and you had a strange burnt taste in your mouth. The hands on your watch seemed scarcely to have moved.

We made regular stops at service areas. As we got further south the people looked suntanned. We noticed the girls in their summer dress: *"Phoarrr! Lush!"*

Then there were the rockers hanging round the filling stations on their motorbikes, toughs with long straggling greasy hair, dressed like the young Brando, oily jeans and tight white T-shirt emphasising biceps.

"Where's all the wee mods on their scooters?" Stuarty wanted to know.

"Must be in the towns and cities in the east," someone suggested. The news had been full of pitched battles between gangs of mods and rockers in Brighton.

The roads grew narrower, the traffic lighter. We reached the West Country by early evening and the sun, big and fiery as ever, illuminated a storybook landscape of thatched villages, golden fields and green copses. Thomas Hardy country! We turned down the long sloping High Street of Dorchester. We'd just read *The Mayor of Casterbridge* for O-level and a thrill went through me as I recognised the green Roman amphitheatre on the edge of town where Farfrae and Elizabeth had met secretly.

On a hill overlooking Weymouth sands and Portland harbour we had our first view of the blue southern sea. Then there was another, final drive east along the coast to our destination, over heathland and in through the suburbs, bungalow land first, then large detached houses set back cool and dark among big pines. We went downhill into the busy town centre, the Square and the Gardens, and pulled up in the coach station with a conclusive piercing hiss of air brakes. We stepped down shakily on to terra firma at last, fetched our cases from the boot and shuffled off uncertainly in the direction of the Square and the town buses, blinking at the foreignness of the crowds and the buildings in the clear evening light.

"Look!" A gang of rockers on motorbikes roared past in a ragged formation round the Square, unkempt manes streaming behind them, a few pinch-faced dolls riding pillion. The Irish lads had never seen anything like it before.

"Attila and his Huns!"

"Shush, Stuarty, they'll stop and give us a diggin'!"

We located our bus stop across the Square, under a chestnut tree that spread out from the other side of the park railings. The cheerful yellow town buses converged

on the Square from every direction. The mellow warmth of the summer's evening, an intoxicating softness in the air, was continental—we'd done the school trip to Paris a year before. It was half-eight and the town full of life. We smelt Gitanes and heard a babble of European tongues—the students who came here to study English at summer school. When the bus came they jostled aboard, laughing and arrogant with their money and foreign insouciance.

"'Eah! Jest hang orn a minute, willya?" the little conductor exploded in a xenophobic fury. "Ever heard of a queue, you lot?"

"Vat ees theece? So we donna queue! Big deal! So ever'body must queue all ze time, huh-huh-huh!"

"Damn right, mate—this is England!" a little working man with a toothbrush moustache weighed in. Turning to me, he confided, "Bloomin' liberty, ennit, mate? Wait till our lads go round the town and dish out a damn good hiding to these foreign stoodents! Comin' over here and pushin' us round like we never won the war!"

I nodded sympathetically, siding instinctively with the locals. We settled on the noisy, crowded top deck and we were off round the Square and up a narrow curving street between tall shop buildings, out past the entrance to a wooded park and up to the roundabout by the redbrick clock tower of the technical college. We went out past hotels and leafy avenues where the foreign students got off, then we had the upper deck mostly to ourselves as the bus followed a long straight road of small shops with plain residential streets branching off. The conductor gave us the shout for Cleveland Road and we got down with our cases by the fish and chip shop.

"Hi, look at the prices!" Howie exclaimed in wonderment, examining the menu in the window. "Fourpence for a bag of chips! Tuppence cheaper than at home!"

"You could live on that: three meals, shillin' a day!"

"Aye, we needn't starve anyway, should we fall on hard times!"

We crossed over into Cleveland Road, a long ruled side street of brick semis with small front gardens. You felt the dusty net curtains watching your progress down the street. Our address was a longish way down near the railway bridge. It was one of the worst-looking houses in the street with a neglected front garden and flakey paintwork. The front door was at the side; I strode manfully up to it and gave the rusty knocker a good bang-bang. It was a scabby black door with kids screaming and wailing behind it, a telly blaring and a woman shrieking. The lads looked apprehensive but I was just glad we had somewhere to come to. Ned had stayed here the previous summer and it was cheap.

A plump youngish woman with long black hair answered the door.

"Pam? I'm Jim Mitchell."

"Edward's younger brother—I can see that!" she said. 'Five of you, isn't it? Now, I have a room for three of you here, and two of you can go to Elsie's three doors down. How's that?'

I took an immediate liking to this down-to-earth, homely woman with live and let live written all over her face.

Hugh and Ronnie were happy to go to the other house. Stuarty, Howie and I followed Pam in along a dark hallway, its dingy cramped space cluttered with bikes. A cat slithered against my trouser leg. Kids stuck their heads out of doorways to get a good gawp at us. The babbling TV set was turned up loud as a cinema in the sitting room. Pat showed us through to the dining room next door, a narrow space filled with a table and sideboard. "Sit down, boys, I have some tea ready for you."

Pam's eldest, Rosie, a pretty girl of ten with her mother's olive colouring, helped serve the meal of tongue salad, bread and butter and tea.

"Your brother still painting his nice pictures?" Pam asked.

"Yes, he had an exhibition in Belfast—street scenes mostly."

"Yi, he drew our street here on his little pad, our house. It was lawk a pho'ograph, only be'er."

Her husband Alvin came and introduced himself. He was easy-going like her, with a mild, crumpled face. "And wha' about yo'r brother's mate Fred?" he enquired. "Is he workin'?"

"Fred the Ted Harris? Been working as a barman, I hear."

"Oh, that'd suit Fred alright. Don't think he'll ever amount to much, will he?" said Alvin amiably.

We felt better after a meal. Pam showed us the kitchen where the self-service breakfast would be taken or we could make a cup of tea any time we wanted; then we carried our cases up the stairs after her to our room. It was at the front overlooking the street, a good-sized room filled with a double and a single bed. Not bad for twenty-five bob a week each, bed and breakfast. We had a key and could come and go as we pleased. Pam smiled tiredly and left us to our own devices.

"Bit of a through-other house," I said, "but that'll make staying here so much the easier and more relaxed." I was anxious the others shouldn't think I'd brought them to a slum.

We stretched out on our beds—I got the single—looking at the ceiling and talking. Replete and relaxed, we joked easily together. Outside the strange city spread itself around us but here we were self-contained and safe. The evening sun was fading from the room. The house had grown quiet, the kids packed off to bed. A car crept up the street with a low, growling, sinister sound, Al Capone's hit men looking for us. There was the rumble of a train under the railway bridge. We were conscious of the sound of our own voices, measured and strange, like actors in a play. We were centre stage in a drama of our own young lives, the adventure of strangers in a strange town, a long way from home, where anything could happen. The unreal feeling of being an actor in a play never quite left me all that summer.

"Hi, we're supposed to call for Hugh and Ronnie."

"I thought they were coming back for us."

"They've not gone to bed?"

"What, crying themselves to sleep?"

Immediately there had to be this rivalry between us and them just because they were in a separate house; it was a competitive thing with a faintly malicious edge to it.

Shadows filled the room. We lay there tired out but wide awake, as if paralysed. Finally, with a groan, Howie got up and snapped on the light and combed and patted his thickening fair hair in the mirror. "C'mon," he said, "I'm hungry again. Let's pick up the other two and go for some of those chips up the road then back for a cuppa char from Pam's kitchen."

We slipped out of the house and counted three doors down for the others. They came to the door full of excitement about their lodgings. "It's a really nice room, two single beds. Elsie fried us steaks and Sid gave us beer; we talked about everything under the sun. They're a really great couple."

"Got ye drunk, did they? Aye, wait till ye get the bill for the steaks and the beers!'" Howie teased. "Our room's good, isn't it, lads? We got so comfortable we could hardly move and Pam the landlady leaves you in peace."

We walked through the blue shadows back up the long foreign street, hearing our footfalls and breathing the warm, still evening air with its whiffs of cut gardens and overflowing bins. The town sounds carried strangely on the night air: dogs barking, a motorbike engine farting, shouts and indeterminate ululations that could have been animal or human or of another world. The oncoming warm southern night seemed charged with a peculiar menace. Because you were scared you felt more alive. The hot, greasy, mouth-watering smell of the chippy grew stronger as we approached the main road.

The yellow rectangle of light of the big shop window shone a warm welcome. Motorbikes were parked at the kerb and leathered greasers, both sexes, stood around eating parcels of chips and the other wondrous items on the menu in the window: cod, plaice, haddock, saveloy, pasty, chicken, steak and kidney pie. The five Irish lads sidled past the regulars into the bright, oven-hot, jostling interior. I hung back in a nervous sweat: the English voices walling me round sounded like some impenetrable foreign tongue and they wouldn't understand me either! But I took heart hearing Stuarty rap out his order manfully—"Portion of chips, please, with salt and vinegar!'—and nobody batting an eyelid.

"Same again, please!" I blurted.

Safely back in our room again—already it had acquired the feeling of home—we sat round on the beds and chairs eating the chip suppers from their wrappings and drinking the tea we'd brewed up in the kitchen.

"Midnight feast!' Hugh gloated. We felt that boyish sense of conspiracy, the dorm at Greyfriars, and the exhausted giddy state of our brains after the long day's travelling made us want to laugh helplessly at everything while trying not to wake up the rest of the house.

The knock at the door and Pam's half-seven "Wikey, wikey!" brought the shock of the real: here we were, in another country, *starting work.* It helped that we were all in it together. Howie was cheerful in the morning time with a debonair style he brought to simple routines, the towel slung from his neck, bare torso, his cheeky grin and cocky swagger as he went to his ablutions in the bathroom. Stuarty and I dressed fully, half-asleep, splashed our dials, combed our hair and were ready.

We clumped down the stairs to drink a cup of tea in Pam's kitchen, all the breakfast we could stomach.

"All set for your first day at work, boys? Where is it you're going?"

"Three of us to East Beach Cafe, two to the Pier Café."

"Yi, just walk through the Gardens and you'll come out opposite the Pier, then East Beach is to one side of it."

We left in good time, picking up Hugh and Ronnie and walking up Cleveland Road in the bright morning sun that shone hot already. A yellow bus came as we reached the stop on Holdenhurst Road. It was a fast, smooth run down to the Square. We took the path through the municipal gardens, under big trees down to the stream and the central area of lawn and colourful flower beds. There were few people around yet. The effect was cool and dewy, redolent of the scents of pine and flowers, a lovely walk to work. We passed the bandstand and came out at a crossroads: in one direction the ornamental pond and the steps going up to the redbrick Pavilion; ahead of us the promenade.

We exited through the gate, crossed the road and there was the sea with the Pier running out to the rotunda. The expanse of water was calm, palest blue with a bit of a mist burning off, little white sails and a grey battleship far out on the horizon under the clear blue sky. The waves washed up peacefully on the sandy beach that stretched away in a breathtaking long straight run below the cliffs till it faded in distant chalk headlands like some Valhalla.

The only people about were workers like ourselves, getting ready to service the holiday crowds. One of the attendants putting out deckchairs called out to me, "Fancy seeing you here, young Mitchell!" and I recognised Paddy Boyle of Derry, a Queen's student Ned had brought to our house, a Brendan Behan lookalike and the scruffiest, drunkest student on the campus. "Put me in the dirtiest bed you've got, Mrs Mitchell!" he'd told my mother. Now his shoulder-length raven hair had been shorn back to uneven black spikes, a concession to the hot weather.

I said, "Och hiya, Paddy!" weakly, taken aback to be greeted familiarly here so far from home and all I could think was to ask him the way to East Beach Café. He pointed past a pillared Bath stone Victorian shelter to the two storey white municipal building with its candystriped awnings and long rows of tall windows, almost opposite the Pier.

We said goodbye to Hugh and Ronnie at the Pier entrance and crossed the road to East Beach Café. A side door was open with an old fellow in a cow gown mopping the hall and stairs, muttering to himself like a head case.

"No-one here yet," he grumped and went on mopping, flicking us dirty looks. The smell of hot sudsy water commingled with yesterday's fried onions. Soon the staff began to arrive, middle-aged ladies who hurried in, grim-visaged, ignoring us. After a while the manageress came, Mrs Jenkins, a bustling, kindly older lady with white hair and winged blue-framed glasses who spoke to us in a warm, homely north of England voice.

"You must be my students?"

"Yes," I said, "I wrote to the Council."

"You're Scottish?"

"Irish."

"All the way from the Emerald Isle!" she enthused. "Well, I hope you'll be happy here with us for the summer!"

Mrs Jenkins directed Howie to the downstairs snack bar, Stuarty and me upstairs to the restaurant Wash Up. I was relieved to be working with my mate. Mrs Jenkins escorted us upstairs to the big airy restaurant with its tall windows overlooking the beach. The women, in pale green nylon gowns and paper hats, were busy with their preparations behind the long self-service counter. Past the frowning red-haired cashier balanced on her stool at the end—we named her "Rupert Bear's mother"—we entered the narrow dark doorway of the Wash Up.

Here we were to spend the greater part of our summer days, a dark poky hole with the daylight filtered through a high-up row of frosted small panes. The dishwasher machine with its convex aluminium hood occupied the centre of the floor; the sink unit was under the windows and there were shelves up the opposite wall stacked with clean white dishes.

"Arthur will be here any minute to show you the ropes, how to work the dishwasher and so on. But first you need your coats and hats." Mrs Jenkins fetched these for us, starchy white work gown and white paper hat, both bearing the council logo. "These must be worn at all times during working hours. Council hygiene regulations," she explained.

We hung round awkwardly in the uncomfortable stiff coats and pinching hats, waiting for Arthur. With nothing to do yet in the Wash Up we wandered through the restaurant to look out the window at the sea. There was a swishing and a clanking behind us followed by a parade ground bark, "Wot abaht doin' some work then, y'lizy blighters! Yo're not on yo'r holidays here, y'know!"

The voice made us start but it was only the eejit with the mop and we just stared coldly back into his bloodshot piggy eyes till he turned away to his work again.

It was a relief to find Arthur, when he came at nine, a gentle man, middle-aged and balding with a mild, adenoidal English voice and a gap in his teeth that gave a winning boyish effect.

The café opened at nine for breakfast and not long afterwards Jenny wheeled in the trolley-loads of dirty dishes. She was a little elderly lady with a round beaky face and round glasses, like an owl, white hair in a granny-bun. She'd puff out her red-veined cheeks comically and blow, as if pushing a great weight, and chirp her customary greeting to Stuarty and me: "'Allo, twins!"

We unloaded the trolley and sorted the dirty dishes into two piles, one that could go straight into the machine and the other coagulated grease and egg-stained plates that had to be hand-washed at the sink. The dishes went in at one end of the machine, packed into the big blue plastic tray, detergent added and the hood shut down on them. The indicator was set for the 3 minute wash cycle. The shake, rattle and roar of the machine drowned out any attempt at conversation. Afterwards we emptied the twinkling clean, warm, dry dishes out on to the shelves ready for transport through to the kitchen.

It grew hot in the cramped, steamy space and we sweated under our gowns and hats. Once we'd mastered the simple operation and got into a routine it was very monotonous and we grew conscious of the painfully slow passage of minutes, watching the wall clock for our morning break and lunch hour.

Arthur worked tirelessly at the sink. "I prefer the old method, by hand," he said. He was a gaunt figure with a long, lugubrious face, a wall eye and a high bald dome of forehead that wrinkled in perplexity. Under the work gown he wore a neat collar and tie, pressed twills and polished brown shoes. There was a kind of sad dignity about Arthur. Occasionally he'd pause in his labours, turning to talk to us with a glassy expression about his passion, cowboy books and films.

There was a staff dining area beyond the kitchen, in a corner of the still room where we took turns for tea breaks and lunch. Then Stuarty and I added in an unofficial fag break when we carried the Wash Up bin up steps out the back to the roof and the big bin on the cliff road. We stood there a few minutes in the bin stink puffing on our Cadets and squinting into the brilliant sunlight with a fiery dazzle on the sea and the bright holiday colours of the crowded sands: deckchair stripes, beach balls, plastic buckets and

rubber rings, inflatable dinghies and swimming costumes. Then it was back down the steps like rats into our dark hole.

I liked to go for the early lunch at twelve although it meant a longer afternoon, but I couldn't think that far ahead, I got so bored and hungry. The kitchen porter Vic served the staff meals. A short, stocky figure in his cow gown, with thick brown gipsy curls and striking sea-far blue eyes in his brown leathery face, like a pirate, he winked matily at me and said in a warm West Country voice, "'Ere'z one needs fattenin' up, fore you slip through a gratin',eh? You loike chips, Oi bet?" He shovelled them on to my plate. His powerful brown strangler's wrists were tattooed. "Extra sausage? Two enough? Go on! You'll eat a couple fried eggs, good for you. And here, there's tons of beans: good for the heart, the more you eats, the more—you know!"

I gaped at the small mountain of grub on my plate; I'd seen nothing like it since my Uncle Archie McQuillan used to feed me up like this.

"Wait for yor pudden. Eat a couple apple sloices? Custard? Ere, there's gallons of it. Oi tell you, mate, if we ate what them stingy buggers said, we'd starve! If yo're still hungry after eatin' that lot, you bring your plate back to Vic, okay mate?"

After the heavy meal I emerged at the front of the café into the fierce glare and heat of the midday sun, to face the dense crowds on the beach. I wasn't dressed for the occasion in my Irish hometown garb of brown tweed sports jacket, navy shirt and the lime green corduroy jeans I'd bought by mail order for 19s6d. I sat on my jacket on the sand and removed my shoes and socks. I felt distinctly out of it there, a pale drudge among all the liberated brown

holiday flesh. The smell of the Wash Up, of detergent and slop bins, clung to my pores. I felt heavy and sluggish and wondered how I could face the four hour afternoon shift. I lay back on my spread jacket with the sun on my eyelids. When I stood up to go I felt dizzy. It was a relief to go back inside to the darkness where I belonged, like a mole.

It was a long, long haul through the afternoon to five but then came the best time of day with work over and a blissful sense of release and sheer freedom. Outside the crowds had cleared. Paddy and the other attendants were stacking away the deckchairs, working at a frantic pace to get finished. We all met up on the steps down to the beach. We sat on there for a while just watching the sea and luxuriating in the evening soul-mellowness. Small blue and white waves tumbled in on the near-deserted sand, breaking with a tired but satisfied rhythm to match our mood.

Several hours of intoxicating golden light stretched ahead of us before bedtime. Our next stop was the parapet of the sea wall next the Pier to watch the beats' regular evening performance on the sand below. A small beatnik colony slept under the Pier. It included a Brian Jones lookalike but there was none of the Rolling Stones' musicality; the beats always sang the same song, the Irish navvy come-all-ye *Workin' On The Railway.* The one we called the King of the Beats, a stocky figure, bearded and horn-rimmed like Ginsberg, sang the verses and they all joined in the chorus. Afterwards the King came round with a hat.

"Do you dig Kerouac, man?" I asked him, half taking the mick.

But he looked me square in the eye and answered seriously, "Do I dig Kerouac, man!"

We walked through the Gardens to the Square for our evening meal at the Golden Griddle, a self-service basement restaurant where we dined invariably on egg and chips. Replete, we wandered back through the Gardens to the promenade. In a mindless sort of contentment, relaxing after our day's labours, we lounged by the sea wall, backs to the water, watching the holiday crowds stroll past in the peace of the evening. The cidery light mellowed and deepened to a red-gold suffusion while the scene took on a hypnotic clarity in which every passing individual stood out distinct and separate and unique and mysterious. Now we felt like contented old men who sit and stare, caring for nothing beyond the moment, accepting it might well be their last.

The uneasy feeling that girls were missing from the picture was pushed away to the back of our minds. We felt secure in a kind of male solidarity as we crowded onto a park bench in the failing blue light and sang *500 Miles* or *My singing bird, adieu!* Our voices rose strongly in sweet harmonies in the soft air fragrant with flowers. I felt the unique richness of these moments, the freedom and special magic of this summer place, our fresh young innocence out in the world for the first time.

We got back to the digs about quarter-to-ten, stopping off at the local chippie for our fourpenny bags we washed down with a cup of Pam's tea for supper. We were soon into our pyjamas, sitting up in bed reading Sartre and talking. Once we got into bed we seemed to acquire a new lease of life. Curtains drawn shutting out the night, we were self-contained in our own little bubble of light and companionship. The frowsty bedroom was home to

us, our retreat after the long day; a place where we could just be ourselves.

The strange heady exultation of the midnight hour combined with an underlying physical exhaustion to produce giddy anarchic bedtime humour. When you really thought about it, wasn't life funny? Wasn't it a crazy world? All we could do was lie back and laugh ourselves to tears at its absurdity. Each of us was a natural comic in his own way, so we fed off one another, keeping ourselves going into the small hours. It became a competition: who was the funniest, the wittiest? Howie had the advantage of being the new kid in town, the latest addition to the gang, so he had novelty value.

"I'm the boy to pl'ase yous!"he'd declare triumphantly. He had a likeable cockiness, a winning little boy mischievous grin. Maybe it was his genteel Jordanstown background but he could carry off sheer vulgarity in a way that was somehow inoffensive and even charming. His party piece was lighting a fart: lying back on the bed in his pyjama bottoms, knees drawn up wide apart, head erect looking down, cigarette lighter poised. *Click!* There was a muffled explosion and a disconcerting ball of flame that shot ceilingwards. It was a performance that never failed to impress and have us in stitches. Only once did he wince and find he'd singed his striped flannel bottoms.

Chapter 12

All Summer Long

After we'd talked till two getting up the next morning brought a grim reckoning, struggling out of bed with gummed-up eyes. We swallowed hot tea standing up at the kitchen table and hurried out for the bus. We were always ten minutes late for work, Stuarty and I dodging in the back door to the Wash Up.

We were inclined to tease our workmate Arthur a bit at first but we soon grew fond of this gentle and dignified soul. He told us he'd been injured in the War, falling into a dry dock in Portsmouth in the black-out. He'd never been the same after that; he'd led a solitary, itinerant existence, picking up casual work and living in men's hostels.

"Place I'm staying now is one of the worst I've been in," he complained in his slow, resigned voice. "Poles stayin' there got it in for me, see. Unplug me kettle when I'm tryin' to make cup tea, that sorta fing. I've spoken to them but it don't make no difference. They don't like me. I'll have to find another place, suppose. Don't seem fair, does it?"

He shook his head sadly and his brow convulsed in a tic, a mannerism that expressed perplexity and fatalism.

However Arthur didn't last long at the café. There was a tension between him and the ferocious flame-haired under-manageress Mrs Burchill, a personality clash, it seemed, as Arthur was a steady, conscientious worker. Mrs Burchill's very presence around the Wash Up was enough to shatter Arthur's normal patience and passivity. The blood surged to his face, he shook. Till one day the ill feeling between them erupted in an almighty row. It was impossible to hear what they were saying above the roar of the dishwasher machine but her tone was flat and deadly as a python's head, while Arthur's high, cracked voice might have shattered one of the newly-washed glasses on the shelves. He was close to tears as he threw off his work gown and hat, donned his gentlemanly brown suit-jacket and trilby, and stormed out of the restaurant never to be seen again.

"Reckon the Lone Ranger's rode off into the sunset for the last time," said Vic. "Hope he doesn't come back, colt 45s blazin', shootin' up the saloon."

Vic would come in the Wash Up and chat with us at quiet moments in the day. He showed us the cold store situated between the Wash Up and kitchen, conspiratorially beckoning one or other of us over. Inside the throbbing refrigerator-room he poured me a glass of milk from the tall aluminium pitcher.

"Drink up, mate, tis good for ee!"

I gulped down the chilled creamy liquid as fast as I could; its coldness made me gasp and my temple ache. The place gave me the creeps; I had an image of Mrs Burchill's corpse hung up with the sides of meat. Who dunit?

"What about some rump steak, take home for yo'r dinner?" said Vic, handling raw meat. "This is the stuff to put hairs on your chest!"

I declined the offer nervously. "We don't cook at the digs, thanks anyway."

"They owe it you, see, Jim. What they pay you—foiver a week?"

I looked over his shoulder nervously, in case Mrs Burchill should loom in the doorway.

Back outside, parting by the kitchen entrance, Vic said, "Oi tell ee, Jim, I'd be outta this place quick as a wink on the first boat I could find only I'm lookin' for somebody first."

He lowered his voice confidentially and looked round as if the somebody might have friends listening. Then the sea-far blue eyes in the brown leather face stared into mine. Now he was a character out of *Treasure Island.*

"'E was my best mate, see, Jim. S'posed to be, that is. Soon as me back was turned he ran off with me money. Jab we'd been on together. But that weren't all, Jim. He ran off with me bird too. Oi'd be happy with her now and money in the bank too if he hadn't done the dirty on me, Jim." He shook his head grimly. "But Oi'll catch up with the bastard one of these days, see. Don' matter how long it takes me, Jim. One day he'll feel the tap on his shoulder and he'll look round and old Vic'll be standin' there. God help him then, Jim."

I experienced a shiver of excitement despite the clichéd fictional ring of his story. I wanted to believe in adventures here.

Vic didn't last much longer than Arthur. One day he wasn't there any more.

"He was stealing from us," Mrs Jenkins explained sadly. Vic had certainly been less than discreet with his pilfering.

Two brothers, Nicky and Kim, came to help in the Wash Up. They were good looking, sociable public school boys who'd lived in Australia and liked a bet on the horses. Their auntie was the attractive actress who appeared in TV ads for Beefo stock cubes. They had us Irish boys round to their flat at Poole harbour for one of their mum's roast beef dinners—what else? She was the Beefo lady's sister and resembled her, a glamorous and charming housewife. I couldn't wait to tell everyone back home.

While a replacement for Vic was sought, I was sent to help in the kitchen. The hard, dirty work in the heat of the industrial ovens was revolting. There were mountains of dirty, burnt pots and pans to be scrubbed, some of them big enough to stand in. The sludge of washing up water with its spawn of grease and lumps of gristle and crusts floating was like the vile stew of Macbeth's black and midnight hags. It turned my stomach to have to immerse my arm to the elbow in it to clear the slops blocking the plughole. The big deep sink was over in a dark corner; you stood facing the blank, grimy, perspiring wall tiles above it, shrouded in steam, blinded by your own sweat. The burnt mucky stench of the job seemed to permeate your pores; I could still smell it on me in bed at night.

Tony the chef was a wiry, pale, fair young man, just eighteen but old before his time with dead blue eyes fixed in a surly, bony face. Sometimes I helped him at the ovens, fetching plates of food across to the serving hatch. Everything you touched burnt you and the heat was fierce as a jungle; no wonder he was often in a foul temper,

banging things about and swearing; but at least he didn't take it out directly on me.

"Don't worry if you drop one of them plates," he said. "Just scrape the fu'in food off the fu'in floor and stick it on another fu'in plate. Grockles won't know no fu'in difference!"

During a pause in our labours he farted casually, like his comment on the true meaning of life, and looking up at me said, "You could do with a haircut. Don't know how you can stand that growin' over your ears in this heat. You'll soon look like one of them hairy beatniks under the pier. That's the loife,eh? Lyin' on the beach all day. Birds bringin' them food and money, warmin' their sleeping bags for em too, I daresay. Birds seem to go for all that long hair. Reckon it makes them look viroile, loike a loi-in's mane, see."

He talked continuously like that, in one ceaseless moan; I listened politely but could never think of much to say, it was all so negative and one way. "You got verbal constipation?" he shot at me once, narrowing his eyes at me.

One day he came over to the sink and asked me, "You a virgin? Tell the truth."

"Technically, yes."

"If you really want it you gotta let your bird know you really mean business, see," he counselled me like a wicked uncle. "Keep on at her and don't take no for an answer," he explained grimly. It sounded like hard work. "Oi'm all right, Oi'm engaged, see. Here." He produced a grubby snap. "'Ave a butcher's at thik!"

I thought it must be a photo of his fiancée but he glanced furtively over his shoulder and hissed, "Stick it in your pocket quick! You and your mate can have a dekko when you do the bins."

Out in the reek of the big bins in the blazing sun Stuarty and I examined the creased black and white photo. It was like a puzzle, holding it this way and that till gradually you identified the contours of nude figures, men and women, piled on top of each other, all joined up in a bewildering confusion of arms, legs and bits, their eyes blacked out to conceal their identities. Stuarty and I shook our heads and laughed. The effect was queerly repellent, as if the aim was to make the sex act as impersonal, ugly and unfeeling as possible, or else a branch of gymnastics. My whole being cringed away from it. I thrust the picture away in my pocket; I just wanted to be rid of it.

The new kitchen porter Barney was a fellow Ulsterman, middle-aged, a short, powerfully-built hunchback, with a round bald head, pallid skin and elfish features. He was another gentle dishwasher who brought a professional sort of dedication to the job

"Ah was workin' in Pontin's before," he told me in a crakey country voice that was good to hear again. "Gude money but wild hard ould graft. Ye're from B'lfast? Derry, me. Been over here workin' the kitchens this thirty years. Ach, it's all right. Sure it's a livin' and there's damn all work at home."

The English schools had broken up and there was an influx of school students working in the café. Christine and Jackie were waitresses, serving behind the counter and clearing tables.

"Aoh, knickers!" Christine exclaimed as she manoeuvred the overloaded trolley awkwardly through the narrow Wash Up door. She was a chattering, ingenuous

gingerhead with a freckled, beaky little face. She came straight out with, "Oy Stuarty, when are you an' Jim gonna ask me an' Jackie out?"

"Tonight?" said Stuarty.

"Meet you at the Pier entrance at seven," said Christine.

Jackie was a sulky brunette, olive skin, back-combed hair, attractive in the Helen Shapiro mould.

"I know!" said Stuarty. "Let's take them out in a rowing boat."

"That would be romantic," I agreed. "Can you row?"

"Aye, sure anybody can."

The girls were there at seven and we set out along the prom to the boat hire, Stuarty and Christine walking in front, chatting away, while Jackie and I followed in silence.

"You finished school for good now?" I asked her for something to say.

"Yi."

"You plan to stay in catering?" I enquired stiltedly.

"Dunno,"she shrugged. "Might work in a shop."

"What kind of shop?" I persisted desperately; it was getting like *Twenty Questions.*

Shrug. "Any kind."

It was a relief to have an activity planned. The girls giggled together as we clambered aboard the rowing boat, feeling it rock precariously under our feet. Stuarty and I took an oar each; it was a heady, masterful feeling.

I had learned to row some years before once, on holiday in Bangor, County Down. I knew Stuarty had been a Boy Scout. We dipped our oars, pulled on them, got into a sort of rhythm together moving out over the water.

Christine cheered, "Yiy!" and Jackie nearly smiled. They'd be dying for a court after this.

But the feeling of jubilation was short-lived. The waves were building up, coming at us with a hostile intent, and we were struggling to stay on course.

"We're goin' round in a circle!" Stuarty bleated. "Pull harder on your side, Mitch!"

A wave whacked the side of the boat and the girls squealed as the flung spray lashed us. We kept going round in circles hopelessly, rocking dangerously under the onslaught of the waves. Water jabbled on the floor of the boat.

"Aoh shi', we're sinkin'!" Christine yelped.

"Just sit tight!" Stuarty commanded grimly, the Boy Scout again, though he'd gone a whiter shade of pale. "We're gettin' on track! Head for the shore, Mitch!"

We fought on manfully then next thing the girls were moaning and being sick over the sides of the boat.

"Hang on, we're nearly there!" I tried to reassure them against the terrified pounding of my heart.

But they weren't waiting; they jumped overboard into the water, up to their thighs and waded desperately for the shore, carrying their shoes aloft.

Christine and Jackie had gone when we finally landed. "Well, bugger that for a romantic outing!" snorted Stuarty.

"I don't blame the girls," I said. "I thought we were all sent for!"

But we had to laugh as we walked back along the prom on rubber legs.

After that Christine and Jackie pointedly ignored us.

We got a shock when we returned to the digs one night to find Vic the fired kitchen porter there. Vic and—I really thought it for a minute—Sean Connery were sitting under the dingy light at the kitchen table drinking tea. Sean jumped up and pumped our hands. He had the Scots accent and everything but on closer examination he was a lighter, younger version of the amiable actor and he introduced himself as Jock.

"I work at Alum Chine restaurant with Ronnie and Hugh. Good to meet you, Howie, Stuarty and Jim! I've been hearing all about you!" Jock's natural personable charm bowled you right over. "You're already acquainted with m' unemployed friend here, I believe!"

Vic sat there looking completely at home in Pam's kitchen, his brown, muscular, tattooed arms displayed in a white T-shirt. His curly brown hair had grown shaggier, like a dog's coat, and his teeth and blue eyes gleamed in his swarthy face, more like a pirate than ever as he grinned and gave us his gentle, matey wink.

"Yeh, we'm old shipmates, ain't we, boys?" the soft voice drawled.

"We've moved into the wee back bedroom," Jock explained. "Ronnie arranged it with Pam. We've been living in our sleeping bags in the Chine. I didn't mind, the weather's been so good, but ye start to miss the home comforts and ye can be done for vagrancy of course!"

I couldn't quite work out the connection between Jock and Vic. They seemed so utterly different, how had they ever come to be together? I would find out in due course.

"You're the chef, aren't you?' said Stuarty. "We've been hearing about you."

"Aye, so-called chef. It's no' exactly haute cuisine, a thousand fish 'n' chips a day for the grockles but Ah'm no' complainin', it's a job, which is more than Vic has."

"They've blacklisted me, the bastards," said Vic mildly. "Oi'll be lucky to ever work in this town again. But where the hell else can I go with no money, eh boys?"

Jock laughed, "References! I tell them I was a chef in the army but I trained as a butcher doing my national service. After the army I was a kitchen porter in the Russell Hotel in London, helping Pierre Cochon the famous chef, picking up a few cookery tips along the way. I like good food and I can cook anything once I set my mind to it."

I said, "You keep Hugh and Ronnie entertained with your singing too, in the kitchen. I hear you do a fine rendition of *Kevin Barry!"*

"Aye, m' name's no' Murphy for nothing. Ah can sing the rebel songs okay, Jimmy, but Sinatra is more my style really. "

"Songs for Swingin' Lovers," said Stuarty, 'with the Nelson Riddle orchestra. Now that is groovy!"

"Aye, magic!" Jock's face lit up."Ye cannae beat ole blue eyes!"

We moved upstairs, Vic to the back room to bed while Jock joined us in our room for more crack, sitting on the side of the double bed with his long legs crossed in smart tan corduroy jeans, offering his tin of rolling tobacco round and talking, talking.

Dark and good looking with an easy sense of style about him, he combined the Scots homeliness with an aura of cosmopolitan sophistication, an intellectual curiosity and a simple enthusiasm for living. I at once felt more alive in this man's company.

As Jock talked, a self-portrait emerged: Gorbals tenement childhood, but a musical education as a Roman Catholic cathedral choirboy, and in the army a stint as a batman. "M' first experience of the good life, how the officer class lives."

Since National Service he'd been a semi-professional singer performing on the club circuit, highly praised but no real breaks. He was trying the local clubs here; casual work as a chef kept him going. It was to be a little while before we learned there was a significant omission from this c.v., that would also explain the connection with a man like Vic.

"What'll you do when you finish school then, men?" he asked us.

Howie was the only one who could answer that question with any certainty. "The bank. My uncle's a manager, he'll fix me up."

Stuart shrugged. "Maybe teacher training."

"I want to be a writer," I said, knowing I could tell Jock this.

"Oh aye?" Jock's interest pricked up. "Tell us, what writers d'ye like, Jimmy?"

"The kitchen sink school: Storey, Sillitoe, Braine, Barstow and then American writers mostly: Salinger, Carson McCullers, Tennessee Williams and Kerouac."

"Ah, Kerouac's ma favourite! *Maggie Cassidy,* the Irish girl, his first love. The mill town in the snow, the Catholic background. It could have been my own life I was reading about!"

"I loved the whole atmosphere of that book," I said. It wasn't hard to see Jock as a character out of *On The Road* either. I said, "My favourite's *The Town and the City,* his first and best, I reckon."

Now I was sure Jock and I would be friends.

Hugh and Ronnie, Howie, Stuarty and I sat on the grass in the public gardens in the warm dusk singing in harmony, keeping our voices low, songs with a nostalgic Celtic flavour, *The Wild Rover*, *Rosin the Bow.* The passers-by turned their heads appreciatively, some smiling. Some girls came and sat next us on the grass.

"Are you a group?" one of them enquired.

"Yeah," said Stuarty, "but anybody can join in. What songs do you like?"

"Beatles."

"We love the Beatles! D'you know *You can't do that?* C'mon then!"

We all sang together, the girls keeping up with us the best in their sweet, lighter voices, unself-conscious and natural. With the ice broken we sat on chatting together as darkness fell and the lampposts and coloured light bulbs shone out under the trees. A little way off spotlights illuminated the ornamental pond and rockery below the Pavilion like a scene of faery.

"Fancy a game of bowls?" the girls suggested and we all trooped up the path together, out into the lights of the Square. As we turned up the dark back street to the bowling alley some people shouted at us from a slowing car, *"Mods! Mods!"* then getting a closer look at us, changed their minds and shouted, *"Mids! Mids!"* Whatever we were, it was exciting being out in the streets in a big group of boys and girls, all just getting to know each other.

The bowling alley was a welcoming large clean modern space with areas of light and dark and the background rumble and clatter of the bowls down the long wooden alleys. The activity of a game saved us from inane conversation and united us as a group, as the singing in the park had done. I was warmly conscious of Carol the lively little blonde and felt the buzz coming back off her as we passed or stood close to one another. When the girls were leaving after the game and a drink of Coke at half-ten, I walked with Carol to the door. When she gave me a pathetic look and said "Bye," in a tiny voice I bent down and kissed her on the lips. She closed her eyes responsively then blinked at me dreamily before she turned away and was gone with the rest of her gang, swallowed up in the night.

I was restless at work the next morning, my thoughts swinging back obsessively to the girl I'd kissed the night before. For once I had no interest in the staff lunch; I went straight out at noon through the Gardens and up the town in mad desperate hopes of finding Carol. The midday sun blazed mercilessly down on me; its dazzle and the streaming holiday crowds made me dizzy, disorientated after the gloomy seclusion of the Wash Up. Blonde female heads bobbed all around; I was short-sighted but had left my glasses in Ireland, so I looked searchingly into the faces of these females, like a predator. Besides, I couldn't call up a picture of Carol's face at all in my mind's eye and could only hope I'd recognise her when I saw her again. All I had was this tender, longing sense of her that I cherished to myself. I looked in the record shop, the bookshop, a couple of women's boutiques—looking as if I was searching for my steady girlfriend, hopefully and not appearing to be either a voyeur or a transvestite shopping—and finally a cafe where younger girls were gathered drinking Coke and espresso coffee. What would I say then if I saw her, anyway? I wasn't thinking straight!

"Jim!" she exclaimed softly, as if to herself more than me.

She was looking in a jeweller's window. If she hadn't spoken first I could have missed her. Her features weren't at all familiar to me although I knew it was her from a general impression that had remained with me. Of course this was her daylight face, more schoolgirlish now, with her fair hair tied back, a cute snub nose and wide-set eyes that in the brilliant noon sunlight were an aquamarine borrowed from the ocean below. These eyes scooped me up now in smiling surprise and she blinked and shook her head as if to convince herself I was really standing there in front of her.

"What are you doing up this end?" she cried. She had that effervescence I got on best with in girls; I couldn't be doing with the flat types like Christine.

It would have been so romantic, such a good line to have retorted, "Why, looking for you!" but I never felt confident being as direct and Romeoish with girls as that, so I just said dully, "I'm on my lunch hour."

"Doing some shopping?"

"Just browsing records and books. Are you buying some jewellery?"

"Just looking. See that jade necklace and earrings?"

"Aye, it'd suit you—match your eyes," I said and gulped at the extravagance of my words.

But she gave a wee smile and said, "That's a nice thing to say." She went on, "I'm going to sit in the Gardens and eat my roll. You coming?" Those two simple words fell like a blessing on me.

"Aye, I've got till one, another half-hour."

We walked together through the crowds down to the Square and into the Gardens. It felt so good to be with a

girl; everything looked different, no longer hostile. And just finding her like that in the crowd was surely a little miracle in itself. Not for the first time in affairs of the heart, I felt Cupid's arrows at work in crucial timings and coincidences—*fate wanted you to be together!*

The sunken park with its flashing stream, green turf and gay blooms was a bowl of hot sunshine. The brass band blared out from the bandstand, pensioners watching from the rows of deckchairs below. Carol and I found a space on the grass; I spread my brown tweed jacket for us to sit on and she dug in her handbag for her lunch, a paper bag containing a roll, and the ubiquitous bottle of Coke.

"Cheese salad okay?" she said, breaking it in half.

"Have you got enough?" I said. "I forgot to eat any lunch today."

"Eat up then," she said, solicitous as a little mother. I loved the way a girl looked after you at first.

It tasted extra good because she was feeding me. Half an hour ago I was this desperate solitary figure hunting through the lonely crowd; now here I was with Carol, sharing her lunch, the two of us on my coat on the grass as if we were going steady already. We chewed on our half-rolls and took gassy slugs from the sweet dark bottle, our saliva commingling romantically. The stupefying heat and the band trumpeting out *Standing on the Corner* blotted out conversation but there was no need to talk anyway.

I kept sneaking sideways looks at my holiday girl. She wore pink flip-flops and her toenails and fingernails were varnished pink. Her blue jeans were turned up to her calves. It was her nape entranced me, however, milky white and ineffably smooth and delicate under her bunches of corn-coloured hair.

"Do you have to go back?" she enquired naively, brushing away crumbs from her lap and hugging her knees under her chin. She consulted her tiny gold watch with the pink strap. "It's nearly two."

"Oh!" I scrambled up groggily, muttering a light curse, like a man shaken from a trance.

She said, "I'll walk over to the beach with you. I've got my bathing costume on."

I silently cursed the Wash Up, to think I could be on the beach with Carol instead! Maybe I should become a beat!

As if reading my thoughts she said, "Never mind, I'll come and meet you out of work. Trish and the others should be round too."

"The lads will all be there after five, at the steps opposite East Beach."

***

Sid and Elsie went off for a week's holiday leaving Hugh and Ronnie in charge of the house. The first thing we did was throw a party.

Carol and the girls were coming and we invited the two foreign students from Queen's in Belfast, who had a room in the house, and Jock and Vic of course. The African students loaned us their record player and jazz records. Jock had gone avidly through their LP record collection, speaking with such enthusiasm and authority on the merits of Miles and Trane, Basie and Ellington, Charlie, Dizzy and Monk, that the two big, solid, dignified black men had to laugh in amazement at him.

We moved the furniture back against the wall in the sitting room and put out a few bottles of cider and saucers of peanuts and potato crisps. The jazz playing in the background helped create an atmosphere of sophistication and excitement as the girls rolled in: Carol, Trish, Franny, Voot and Mandy. The older male guests put in a polite appearance and left early and as dusk filled the room the party turned into a teenage courting session.

The honeyed crooning of Johnny Mathis's *Misty* filled the darkening room. The cider bottles were emptying rapidly and we were in the "happy" stage of intoxication. I was cuddling with Carol on the carpet, our backs against the wall. The blonde head sank weakly, submissively down on my shoulder and I turned my head and kissed the white centre-parting. She lifted her face to me blindly, half in fear—I thought she mustn't have kissed many boys before, but her lips were eager to get busy now.

Vic never found another job. At first he spent all his days in the tiny back bedroom he shared with Jock. Sometimes he'd call out to one of us to come in. He lay there stretched out on the narrow bed against the wall in his stocking soles, T-shirt and jeans, hands clasped behind his head, the sea-far pirate's blue eyes dreaming of hidden treasure. He had no reading matter, not as much as a deck of cards to pass the time. The bottom of the sash window was propped open on the warm summer's day. A train rumbled past in the cutting beyond the tangle of blackberry bushes at the bottom of the garden. It took a minute for the slow, glassy blue eyes to register the visitor; the tentative, shy grin crept over the mild brown face and he spoke softly, "How's it goin' then, Jimmy boy? Siddown and tell us how the world's bin treatin' ee! Got any snout? Oi'll buy ee a packet when my dole comes through. They lil uns you smoke, coupla puffs and they'm gone! Don' mind if I take off the cork tip? Oi smokes Capstan Full Strength—ever

tried 'm? You know you'm smokin' a fag wi' one of them buggers, Oi'm tellin' ee, Jim!"

Vic's dole was a long time coming. Jock brought him leftovers from the restaurant kitchen. Pam let him do her garden in part-payment of rent arrears. It was working in the garden that he got to know the woman next door, attractive and single, at home looking after her invalid mother. Soon Vic was doing their garden too and odd jobs about their place, then Jock and the woman became lovers.

"Sandra's a real woman, Oi'm tellin' ee, Jim. Matoor loike. Her's got class, boy, the genuin' article. You should see the stuff they got in their house, Jim: heirlooms, antiques. Father died when Sandy was jus a lil gurl, see. Mother had to sell the family home in Christchurch and move down here. Then after Sandra finished school the ole lady took bad with her rheumatics and Sandra's had to look after her ever since, no life to call her own."

I sat on Jock's neatly made bed, my knees almost touching Vic's as he leant forward confidentially, the blue eyes misting over sentimentally as he continued, "But now her's got me. She were a virgin when Oi met her, Jim. Thirty years old. Never had the chance to lead a normal life for a young woman. She croied when she tole me, Jim. She says, 'Don' hurt me, Vic, please!' Oi tole her, Vic'll look after you moi pet, don' you worry! She loves me now, Jim an' OI love her."

My eyes were misting over too. Yet I was never sure how much to believe anything Vic told me. I felt that the dividing line in his mind between fantasy and reality was blurred.

The next thing was the burglary of our room after Pam, Alvin and the kids had gone off for their week at Butlin's.

We came back one evening and Howie found his locked travel bag slit open and the ten pounds gone which his insurance broker father had given him to set aside in case of an emergency. When Vic came back and we told him what had happened he was all outraged decency.

"If there's one fing Oi can't stand it's the sorta bugger what fieves from or'nary workinclass people!" he fumed. "'Foi get holda the bastard what done this to moi friend Oi'll break his legs!"

Vic proceeded to carry out a Sherlock Holmes hunt for clues. There was a window open in the kitchen. "Musta got in here! Lemme fink: Oi went in next door at nine. What toime ju get back? Arf-past!" He rolled his eyes up at the ceiling and lowered his voice melodramatically. "You know what, boys? He's still here in the house! Reckon you disturbed'm when you came in an' he's hoidin' in the loft waitin' for us to go to bed. Oi'll sort the bugger!"

Vic got the bread knife from the kitchen drawer. "Oi'm gonna be waitin' when ee comes down! Don' care if Oi gotta sit up all noight!"

He crept upstairs and placed a hard chair on the landing under the loft hatch. We went off to bed leaving him sitting there in the dark, clutching the bread knife and staring up at the hatch. Perhaps his seafaring days, the long watches, had given him this ability to sit and stare for extraordinarily long periods of time. And of course he believed absolutely in his schizophrenic, farcical performance.

Worse than that, *we believed it*, at least while it was happening. We were such nice, naïve middle class boys; we liked our mate Vic and didn't want to believe what was clear as the light of day, that he was broke and hanging round the place all day, and had already been sacked from his job in the café for kleptomania. The penny dropped afterwards, when it was too late to do anything about it.

We wondered if the girlfriend next door was another fantasy but not long after the farce of the burglary Ronnie and Hugh saw Vic downtown with her. She was blonde and attractive and Vic was wearing a suit and tie. He told us afterwards they'd been to get the engagement ring.

"With my bloody money, no doubt!" said Howie.

Jock posed a similar enigma, only in a different way. At the end of the day I could take Vic or leave him but I desperately wanted to believe in Jock. Everything seemed so much more alive and meaningful in his company. It was a sort of hero-worship on my part, I suppose. He was an older man who had time for me; he was handsome and "cool" and articulate and knew literature and jazz, like a character out of Kerouac, lonesome traveller, beat.

With all that there was his homely Scots warmth and kindliness. Like waking me up on my day off work waving a bag of chips under my nose and planting a steaming mug of tea on the bedside table. My day off in that week—we worked weekends—happened to be Jock's too. I'd not even heard the other lads go out at eight that morning. Jock pulled the curtains letting the midday sunshine flood the frowsty bedroom. He sat on the side of the double bed vacated by the lads, sipping his tea, smiling and chatting, really matey and homely, working up the unstoppable enthusiasm he felt for each new day.

I sat up on my elbow with the lovely refreshed feeling in my limbs that you got after the long deathlike sleep of a weekly lie-in. I loved the idea of chips for breakfast! Well, why not? I was a beatnik now too! They were the fat brown smoky chips from our local chippy; the slugs of sweet strong red-brown tea I washed them down with tasted delicious too, like nectar, I thought—not that I'd ever tasted it.

"Ah thought ye'd be gettin' hungry, Jimmy," said Jock. "D'ye fancy a run down the town? We could look in at the bookshop and the record shop."

"I'd love to." The idea of a whole day with Jock all to myself seemed perfection, as if I had walked into the pages of Kerouac. I imagined the two of us drawing together in close friendship like Sal and Dean.

"Ye're not seeing Blondie then?"

"She's gone away for a few days with her family."

In half an hour I'd dressed, washed my face and combed my hair, and we were out in the glaring street of high noon, walking to the bus stop. Jock donned a pair of sunglasses which gave him the mysterious, distinguished look of a film star. I felt glamorous just being in his company. Every moment with just the two of us like this felt privileged and precious, charged with deep meaning. All the precious free hours of the summer day stretched ahead of us, the bustling sea-town awaiting our pleasure.

The bus came on cue and we sat upstairs at the front with the wind in our hair as we were hurtled Route 66 style downtown. In ten minutes we alighted in the dazzle and crowds of the town centre and entered the gloomy quiet cool of the bookshop. The new paperbacks were on the ground floor; a sign directed us upstairs to the second-hand department. It was a cavernous dusty attic with creaking floorboards and long high shelves stuffed with old books. There were few other customers and no staff present. I found a row of old Shakespeare pocket editions with maroon and gold-tooled soft leather covers, the kind of slender volumes that beg to be pocketed.

"Shove a few of them down your shirt, Jimmy, I would," Jock whispered, as if reading my mind.

I undid my shirt buttons; my heart was pounding in there in my skinny chest. A final glance over my shoulder, only Jock looking on in calm encouragement, nodding, man to man, and I slipped *Sonnets* and *Coriolanus* in, cold and hard against my skin and buttoned up my shirt and the middle button of my jacket. It was done! I had entered upon my life of crime.

"No rush now," Jock counselled me. "C'mon, we'll ha'e a look downstairs. Cool as ye please.'

I felt weak and shaky with the enormity of what I'd done, but also a sense of empowerment now as we descended the stairs and wandered down among the walls of paperbacks on the busier ground floor. It was the heady feeling that I could have anything I wanted now, it was all there for the taking!. The weight of William Shakespeare resting on my belt gave me a satisfaction only tinged with the fear that he might at any moment come bursting out of my shirt and I would stand there helplessly in the full glare of the public eye, exposed as a book thief.

What I couldn't do was just walk straight out the door like this; such a course could arouse suspicion. To cover my tracks now I would buy a paperback. I chose Franz Kafka *America* and took it to the till. My newfound audacity shocked me. What a brilliant touch: of course nobody would suspect a paying customer and I could walk calmly out the door without fear of pursuit.

But as I handed over my silver and received my small change from the woman assistant I saw her face darken and sour horribly. Was it my sports jacket with the middle button fastened on one of the hottest days of the year? Could she see my bump? Did I exude a guilty criminality?

It wouldn't be the first time in my life I'd given the game away by emanating the wrong psychic vibrations. But the assistant placed the Kafka in a paper bag and handed it over to me. Worryingly there was no "Thank you," no half-smile. Was she ready to sound the alarm? I moved away steadily, staunchly out the door though I was ready for the hand on my shoulder.

Once outside the shop I took to my heels, weaving through the holiday crowds down the bright, curving, narrow street, keeping going until my breath came harshly and I ducked in a shop doorway to wait for Jock. It was the record shop blasting out the great rock hit of that summer *The House of the Rising Sun*, an old folk-blues tale of prostitution, gambling and general low-life down in New Orleans. I was "sent" as the Hammond organ broke away in a terrific rift, building to a frenzied, jabbering, emotional climax that synchronised with the wild beating of my heart and swept me away on an exultant tide of outlaw liberation. I'd got away with my first crime and entered the self-same shady, shameful but exuberant underworld that the song celebrated.

Jock caught me up, smiling his approval, relaxed as ever and I fell in beside him in the anonymous, innocent flow of pedestrians. We walked down to the Square and through the Gardens to the promenade. Only when we'd found a space on the crowded beach did Jock comment, "Ye did well there, Jimmy, three for the price of one."

We sat on the sand, browsing.

"Kafka's another one had problems with his father," said Jock. "Like me—twenty-seven years old and still afraid of my da! Can you believe it?"

"Do you ever go back to Glasgow ?"

Jock shivered and quoted from *The Wild Rover:* "No, nae, never!"

We took off our shoes and socks and sat on our jackets. We were near the Pier, in front of East Beach Cafe amongst all the sun-worshipping flesh. We were the workers, set apart from all that self-indulgent vacuity.

"They call him Mr Beach." Jock nodded towards the thick-set, foreign-looking man who was a daily fixture here on the beach, always in the company of glamorous women. It was a scene that put me in mind of the newspaper ads for men: *You Too Can Have a Body Like Mine,* with the drawing of a big muscular grinning man on a beach, a swimsuited lovely under each arm, kicking in delighted protest. The dream of every eight stone weakling who'd ever had sand kicked in his face.

Not that Mr Beach ever smiled: the dark, pocked, brutal face with its Zapata moustache was set in a snarl. His black body hair was like a pelt and he waddled on bandy, muscle-bound legs and dangled his long powerful arms, half-ape. His scantily-clad Continental women were gorgeous after the jet-set fashion of glossy magazines.

"What do they see in him, Jimmy?" Jock asked, scratching his head, genuinely perplexed.

"Animal magnetism?" I trotted out the expression memorised from a film magazine, about Brando, I thought. "Or something—maybe just plain loaded."

"Aye, that's more like it." Jock heaved a sigh. "That's the only real difference between Mr Beach and you or me."

Towards five o'clock the holiday crowds were thinning out on the beach although the day was glaring and hot as ever. We were well into August now and it seemed the perfect summer weather would never end. Jock and I went and sat on the steps opposite the café to wait for the others coming from work.

Howie came first from the ground floor snack-bar with his jaunty, half-bashful swagger, gangster-fag wagging in the corner of his full lips, crooked wee-boy grin and blue-eyed twinkle as he hailed us cheerily. Winningly short, he always looked cool and stylish, this evening his stocky, athletic figure moulded into faded denim shirt and jeans, with tan moccasins. His ripe wheat-coloured hair grew thickly over his collar. His job frying burgers had brought his face out in sore-looking acne.

Stuarty came soon after, down the stairs from the restaurant, advancing with a cocky stride that was somehow Belfast through and through, recognisable throughout the world. Like me he had lost weight on this working holiday, both of us down to eight and a half stone; his face was all hazel eyes under the heavy dark Beatle fringe and his clothes hung limply on him. We were often mistaken for one another.

"You and Stuart are black Irish like me," Jock had remarked. "The others all have a touch of the Viking."

Stuarty flopped down spread-eagled on the sand, like a tramp in a ditch.

Ronnie was next, over from the Chine, approaching with his quick, stiff, rather gangling walk, Adam's apple bobbing in his long neck. Obsessive sunbathing between shifts at the cafe had bleached his fair hair and tanned his long thin face a golden hue that emphasised the pale round glassy stare of his blue eyes.

Hugh arrived Paddy-last as usual with his dawdling cowboy gait, all the time in the world. You'd spot him a mile away with the longish yellow hair resting on his eyebrows and collar, flowery shirt open to the navel, yellow slacks and white plastic beach shoes. Here at least nobody wolf-whistled after him or called him "Fruit!" which he wasn't.

"Did yous manage without me at the restaurant today, Hugh?" Jock enquired.

"Just about! Till round lunchtime there was a big commotion from the kitchen, a lot of shouting and swearing and then a scream and an almighty crash followed by a terrible silence as if someone had been murdered. One of the waitresses had a row with Mike the kitchen porter and threw some plates at him but he survived. I think they'll be glad to see you back in the morning."

We lounged on the steps for a while, leaning back on our elbows, mesmerised by the quietly persistent advance of the tide, the pale blue water unfurling creamily, until the last of the deckchairs had been cleared and the beach had a forlorn look about it, with the evening breeze picking up, everyone gone to tea.

Jock walked us to a different restaurant he'd discovered, a little way out of the town centre. He was eye-catching in his new red blouson with a big C (for campus?) on the breast pocket. The Manrico Restaurant was larger, quieter, darker and cooler than the Golden Griddle and offered table service and an extensive menu. It was almost empty. Jock charmed the waitress with his apparent sophistication and talked throughout our dinner about his love of good food. The meal took on the quality of a ritual, of "lordly offices" and the food tasted better somehow, though in truth it was fairly indistinguishable from the Golden Griddle's offerings.

"You never truly appreciate the pleasures of eating until you've starved," said Jock philosophically. Then he trotted out one of his strange-but-true facts: "Do you know, boys, Colman's who made this mustard got to be millionaires from what people leave on their plates."

He collected up a tip to leave for the waitress. It was all a bit of an occasion.

We strolled back down the hill into town, replete in the peaceful, mellow evening sunshine. Along a short cut behind some tall houses, the sound of a jazz trumpet, throaty and soulful, drifted out from a high open window, down through the soft evening air.

"Listen!" said Jock. "That's no' a record! I'm telling you, whoever's blowing that horn *knows Miles."*

Back in our room that night Howie was being cynical about Jock. "All that palaver about leaving a tip for the waitress when it said 'service included' on the menu! And then the trumpeter who *knows Miles*, man. Jock's a bit of a bullshitter if you ask me."

Howie's sentiments rang true enough but there is a truth that enlightens and a truth that kills. I so wanted to believe in Jock and found myself springing to his defence.

"He just gets a kick out of the sort of little things that make life more interesting. It doesn't harm anyone. Jock's not afraid to dream, that's all."

We'd soon become aware that Jock had a criminal record. He never talked about it directly; it just slowly emerged from oblique references he made. It explained his connection with Vic, with whom he had nothing else in common. As with Vic it was hard to know what to believe about Jock; where did the fiction end and the truth begin? I wanted to believe whatever was different and exciting. I wanted holiday adventures. If Jock was a criminal at least he was an intelligent one, a nice one, not the sort who'd ever hurt anybody, so that was okay with me. Then suddenly it all began to happen.

Ronnie had gone out to a nightclub with Jock and ended up going to London with him. Previously a non-smoker, Ronnie sat on the side of his bed the following evening, puffing inexpertly on a State Express with a shaky hand and looking as if he'd seen a ghost. He was stylishly dressed in the new clothes he'd bought in Oxford Street: a matelot top and bell-bottom jeans; he sported a gold identity bracelet. I felt jealous as he described his adventures of the last twenty-four hours.

Seventeen and tallish, in his jacket and a borrowed tie, he'd passed muster at the nightclub door with Jock. Inside they spotted Mr Beach and his entourage at a table. Ronnie felt it the height of sophistication as he sat there sipping Scotch on the rocks. Jock got up and sang a couple of Sinatra numbers with the band.

"He was brilliant," Ronnie enthused, "went down really well with the audience in the club. Another Matt Monro, you might say." We'd spotted Matt, the singing bus driver, a short, relaxed figure walking on the prom one afternoon; he was on at the Pavilion. I was relieved to hear that Jock truly was a singer as he'd claimed and a good one at that. My faith in him was restored.

Later on Jock bought drinks for a couple of women. It was all going well chatting them up till a drunken ex-boyfriend turned up and there was a fight. Jock floored the ex with a single clean right hook and he and Ronnie had to get out of there fast as they could. It was two o'clock as they walked back through the deserted town centre.

Jock said something about doing a job. He picked up a milk bottle from a doorstep. At the TV and Radio shop he used the bottle, wrapped in his hankie, to smash a hole in the window. Reaching inside he snatched out the new portable radios, passing them to Ronnie then filling his own arms with them.

"It was all over before you could blink," said Ronnie. "Cradling the stolen goods, we ran up a back street and into the churchyard. We hid the radios there behind the bushes."

They were back at six in the morning, filling their suitcases with the radios and catching the early train to London. A few hours later they were breakfasting at Maltese George the Axeman's café in Bethnal Green.

"Then Jock took the cases and went off to see the fence. He told me to wait there, he wouldn't be long. But two hours passed and I began to lose my nerve. I sort of lost my self-control. I asked Maltese George and the other people in the café if they knew where Jock had gone. You should have seen the looks they gave me, like I was a squealer or something. I expect they shoot people for that kind of thing. At that point Jock finally arrived back. He was none too pleased with the rumpus I was creating in the café and hurried me away, up the West End."

Ronnie got his cut of the money from the fence. It was only a fraction of the retail value of the radios but enough to splash out shopping in Oxford Street and going to the cinema to see Hitchcock's new film *Marni* before catching the evening train back.

"So you're a wanted man, Ronnie?" said Hugh chillingly, fixing his friend with scary tunnel eyes. This was Hitchcock for real.

"Aye, that's bad enough," said Ronnie, "but if my da could see me smoking now as well, he'd kill me."

The radio shop robbery was duly reported in the *Echo*, a column inch that gave us all a thrill, reading it and knowing we were all implicated—on the wrong side of the law now.

After the London trip Jock went a bit funny, strange moods of abstraction alternating with impulsive, eccentric behaviour. As we were dandering up through the town one evening he hissed at us, "Keep walking!" and disappeared over a low wall into some shrubbery. When he caught us up afterwards he explained he'd seen his father coming.

"Now he's in town I'm going to have to watch my back. Most likely my sister and her kids are with him too."

Jock took to wearing his sunglasses in the street all the time, sometimes along with his new herringbone tweed winter overcoat purchased on Oxford Street, which of course only singled him out in the continuing heatwave. There was a self-parodying, surreal touch about his behaviour which was expressive and amusing, like an art form.

Jock drew ever closer to Stuarty and me, taking us into his confidence increasingly. He made it clear that he no longer had any time for Ronnie as a partner-in-crime after his performance at Maltese George's and he'd be coming to us for assistance with his next job. That was okay with us; we wanted to get our hands on some of that easy money too. We wanted excitement. We were just waiting for the nod; nothing much had to be spoken. He took us to look in various jewellers' windows in the busy daytime, calculating the value of the glittery goods on display and surreptitiously testing the thickness of the plate-glass windows with the edge of a half-crown piece. In the end he settled for the jeweller's in the Arcade.

"Five thousand nicker," he totted up their window display. Later he explained, "That's five hundred quid from the fence. A hundred each for you. You've only got to watch the far end of the Arcade. I can do the shop end myself. Once I hit the glass you beat your feet the hell out of it. Two minutes and it's done. How's that for a night's work?"

We nodded emphatically, our eyes glinting with greed. A hundred quid each! It was a huge sum of money; It'd take twenty weeks to earn that working in the café! It would buy us luxuries—leather jackets and Polaroid cameras—and we'd return to Belfast loaded, showing off to our girls. Most of all perhaps there was the kudos of it, the suspense and thrills like starring in our very own black and white British B-movie. *Smash and Grab*, with Sean Connery as Jock Murphy. Introducing James Mitchell. From the novel by James Girvan Mitchell. I could just see it all!

We met Jock at the bowling alley at ten and hung round there till late, emerging on to the dark, deserted streets after midnight. Jock went one side of the Arcade, Stuarty and I the other, reconnoitring around the block and meeting up again in the Square. Something delayed Jock.

When he appeared he said, "C'mon, lads, hame! Not tonight, Josephine."

As we walked back he explained he'd been stopped by a bogey and asked to account for himself. Jock had his new winter overcoat on, a milk bottle inside a woollen sock in one of the deep pockets, ready for the smash 'n' grab.

"The bogey was taking a close look at me under the lamppost. They have our mugshots stuck up in all the nicks. I told him I was a commercial traveller in Harris Tweed, doon frae bonie Scotland. Of course I looked the part in my coat. And the bogey says, 'Oh, excuse me, sir, we can't be too careful in these days of rising crime statistics.' And I says, 'Not at all, Constable, I commend you for your vigilance!' I commented that we could be doing with more of his sort back in Glasgow with the razor gangs and he tipped his helmet and said, 'Sorry to bother you, sir, goodnight!' Real old school Dixon of Dock Green he was."

We left it till later in the week to let Jock's encounter with Dixon blow over, and then started at a later time, waiting in the bowling alley till one a.m. before we ventured out on the streets. A bogey on a bike—"It's okay, it's not Dixon!"—came up the street past the Arcade at half-one, not bothering with as much as a glance in our direction.

"He won't be back for an hour now," said Jock. But there were taxis queued at the rank in the Square overlooking the jeweller's end of the Arcade. "We're still too early," said Jock. "By the time the cabs have cleared off the bogey on the bike will be back."

By the third night Stuarty and I were getting used to it, like turning out regular for the night shift. The teeth-chattering suspense had gone out of it; the dark empty streets acquired a reassuring familiarity. On the lookout for any figure, any movement, every detail of those streets had imprinted itself on my mind's eye. The night streets belonged to us; it was an empowering feeling. To kill time after the bowling alley had closed we reconnoitred a wide circle around the town centre, Stuarty going one way while Jock and I went the other. Jock, a light smoker normally, chain-smoked his liquorice paper roll-ups as we walked, hunched in his big coat with the milk bottle in the pocket while he talked and talked nervously, winding himself up to the act.

"The thing is, Jimmy, I need a new wardrobe and I'm not going to get it working at the beach cafe. A singer needs to look the part. It doesn't matter how good you sound in the end if you don't look the part. Look at the young Sinatra, the clothes he wore.

"And that's not all, Jimmy. I'll go crazy if I have to stay in that wee room much longer looking at that daft bugger Legg lying on the other bed, the pair of us scratching our flea-bites from Pam's mogs. At least Legg's got the blonde next door. How could I ever bring a bird back to that box room? Anyway, you need dosh to pull the right kind of bird. I want a nice flat of my own with a sea view, a record player and a shelf full of good albums—I'd sit there and listen to Basie and Brubeck and read Kerouac and Ginsberg.

"I'd have a cocktail bar and when Ava Gardner or someone who looked just like her came by in the evening we'd drink our g-and-tees together, hold hands and watch the moon come up over the ocean and Ava would turn and look in my eyes and say simply, 'I love you, Jock!'

"And after tonight you and Stuarty can do whatever you want, lie on the beach all day if you feel like it. And you'll go back home to Ireland with some real dough in your pockets.

"And of course, Jimmy, if you're going to write you'll have the experience of this night to look back on. I tell you what, when this is over and we're loaded I'll take you and Stuarty camping in the New Forest. How about that?"

The soft, obsessional voice hypnotised me; I could have walked the streets all night listening to it. During these moments I was entirely in Jock's confidence, completely at one with my hero. I'd stopped feeling nervous at all.

It was half-two in the morning. Jock was positioned down the jeweller's end of the Arcade. On the other side of the block Stuarty and I observed the ploddingly pedalling figure of the bogey on his bike go past at half-two, creaking, labouring up the hill, as we slunk downhill in the shadows. We timed the action for fifteen minutes after that, calculating that the bogey would by then be at the far side of the town. The taxicabs had gone from the stand; the town centre was utterly dead at last, nothing moving but scraps of litter stirring in the night breeze; only the figures of the mannequins frozen in their elegant poses in the shop windows—and us. Our time had come. The hands of the clock on the department store jerked to three. A last long look up and down the street and we whistled the agreed all clear signal, *Mack the Knife,* as we drew level with the Arcade.

Our whistling seemed to lose itself in the echoey length of the Arcade but Jock had heard us alright; we had a glimpse of the tall figure in the long coat lunging at the big plate-glass window, hurling himself bodily at it. The frenzied thunderous *boom-boom-boom* of the milk bottle in its sock against the jeweller's window reverberated down the Arcade and out between the tall buildings in the street, chasing us down the hill in a blind panic, past the startled mannequins in the window of the department store. Now it was really happening the fevered terror of nightmare took hold. The banging died away behind us and there was just the pounding of our feet on the pavement keeping time with our heartbeats. You were fully alive now in these moments, that was for sure.

We ran across the Square and up the hill on the far side to put as much distance as we could between us and the scene of the crime. Run out of breath, we stopped in a small recessed public rest area with shrubs, flowerbeds and benches overlooking the Square and Gardens below, all peaceful and innocent there, watched over by the man in the moon.

"It's alright, we're safe!" I gasped triumphantly, but immediately gave a start as I suddenly became aware of the still figure watching us from the bench. With relief I saw it was only an old tramp, traditional unkempt beard and rags, half the brain eaten away by alcohol.

"Oh, hello there!" I blabbed in a false matiness, hearing my Irish accent—incriminating evidence maybe? "Isn't that a lovely moon up there?"

The tramp just stared back suspiciously at us. In the bright moonlight he was clear as a woodcut illustration in an old book. Mute, inscrutable—*witness for the prosecution?*

We edged away and cut along unfamiliar side streets, circumnavigating the town centre until we emerged under the clock tower of the tech, the hands of the big clock at half-three, and turned up Holdenhurst Road.

Safely on our way home now, our fear gave way to jubilation and we seemed to float past the long rows of shut-up small shops under the light of the friendly moon, sailing among white clouds, trailing us all the way. We were free and we were rich; it was a fact!

We got to bed around four. Up again at half-seven, half-dead but it was worth it.

We weren't rich; it was a fact.

"Specially reinforced glass," Jock explained when we saw him that evening after work. "I just bounced off it. It'll take a pick to shift it."

The only consolation was no longer being haunted by images of the desecrated jeweller's window, the news reports and the police investigation.

"I'll find a road works where I can get a pick," said Jock but we'd all lost our enthusiasm for the project. Then Jock disappeared, quitting the cafe and the digs without notice. It was soon after we'd seen him talking to the strange man in the street: heavy-framed glasses, neat sweptback dark hair, bull neck and broad shoulders; he looked like Clark Kent. Jock didn't hail us and introduce his friend to us; we guessed they were talking serious business of the unlawful kind. We were right and would read all about it in due course, in the *Daily Mirror*.

When Jock vanished like that without as much as a goodbye, leaving the jeweller's window still intact, we wondered if the police were on to him and whether they'd be round to the house soon asking questions. That put the wind up us, especially Ronnie and we sat in our room one night drinking cider and winding each other up in our paranoia, waiting for the knock on the door, the clever probing of the detective with his questions and notebook as the beating of the tell-tale heart grew louder, louder...

We kept our heads down after that, working overtime at the café.

On a mid-August evening of our last week in England, we caught a bus out to the funfair on the common at the edge of town. The carnival thump and blare of the amusements carrying on the evening air and the sight of the Ferris wheel turning in the pale sky level with the dark green treetops filled us with childish excitement and hurried our footsteps as we walked from the bus stop.

The attractions were laid out in long straight rows either side of the trampled grass track. We ambled through surveying the garish stalls and the rides painted up like sets from a horror film. Generators throbbed, the powerful machinery thundered to frenzied life, youngsters screamed. Pulsing waves of deafening pop music, different tunes overlapping, washed over us. The odours of machine oil and scorched rubber mingled with the sour, greasy fumes of hot dogs and chips, the sweetness of toffee apples and candyfloss.

There were all the usual mad whirligig transports that built to a smooth blur of sickening speed; it made me queasy just looking at them. The fair folk urged us to try our skills on the rifle range, coconut shy, hoop-la: win a teddy bear for the girl in your life. The scary painted hoardings of the ghost train brought smiling childhood memories of its cavernous, dark, squealing thrills. Something to take a girl on now, feeling her wee face burrowing against your shoulder in fright, your protective arm encircling her. As always I was drawn to the mystic romance of the fortune teller's gipsy caravan, yet too shy to venture within.

We started simply with the hall of funny mirrors, easy, instant great crack, pointing and laughing ourselves hoarse at the gross caricatures of our distorted reflections, the gang of us like big kids.

But what was this?

Striptease!

Knowing nobody who mattered would see us here and our mums could never get to hear of it, we queued up with the biker louts and sad older men. Inside the muggy tent we stood in a crowd on the grass looking up at the wooden stage. A bald, pointy-headed man, stripped to the waist revealing bulging muscles and tattoos, was swallowing fire. As he bowed out a scratchy old record of *The Stripper* blared out and a hardchaw peroxide blonde sashayed forth in a skimpy red frock, making half-hearted, contemptuous movements to the music while she chewed and blew bubbles of pink gum dopily, drooping her eyelids meanly at us.

When she'd peeled down to bra and panties the record cut off abruptly and the fire-eater reappeared, a drum slung from his neck, beating a crescendo of drumrolls, while the stripper stood facing the audience squarely. The drumming stopped, the bra fell away and she stood there stock-still, diddies exposed like some shocking mammal fact. She glared defiantly down at us, with something like a look of pure hatred, as the curtain was quickly drawn to by Pointy-Head.

It was a bit of an anti-climax; there was a brief stunned silence, a ripple of indignation that it was all over so soon and we all shuffled off back outside with a seedy frustrated feeling, blinking in the evening light.

Then who should we bump into but Carol and her gang. I felt my heart lift—what a difference it made to an evening just having some girls around.

"We thought you'd gone back to Ireland!"

We'd lost touch while we were tied up with Jock but it didn't seem to matter; Carol fell in naturally beside me, my summer girl.

"We've been doing overtime," I said, which wasn't untrue in itself.

"You can take us for a ride then with all that money you've been hoarding!"

"We want to go on the Rotor Barrel!" said Mandy.

A few minutes later we were standing inside the gigantic black barrel, backs to the wall, looking up nervously at the sheer sides. Faces viewed us curiously from the gallery above as if we were specimens in a jar.

"I'm scared!" Carol whispered, squeezing my hand. I felt braver then.

The girls squealed as the machinery roared to life and the barrel began to turn, the noise building deafeningly as we spun, faster and faster, the centrifugal force pinning us to the wall.

Just as it seemed we couldn't go any faster without taking off into outer space, the floor dropped away mechanically beneath our feet, leaving us stuck there helplessly, high on the wall, like insects. Opposite me a lady's skirt had blown over her face, exposing her suspender belt. To one side of her a leathered greaser struggled into a standing position somehow, defying gravity, and in a remarkable feat of strength began walking on the wall in big slow motion steps, like Spider-Man.

Just attempting to raise my head to look around, I felt a sickening wrench as if my neck was breaking. I resolved to stick out the torture, shutting my eyes against the fantastic whirling horror of the infernal machine and hanging on to Carol's sweaty little hand for dear life. Turning my head sufficiently I had a glimpse of her, blonde hair flattened in a sunburst against the wall, peaky little face like the heart of a flower.

After what felt like an eternity on the rack the barrel began to slow down. The wall slackened its iron grip on our shoulder blades and we began to slide down it, jeans yanked up tight into crotches as the floor rose to meet our feet again. We went staggering off, dizzy, with the queasy, grateful feeling of survivors.

Stuarty and Mandy, Carol and I, took leave of the fair and walked to the digs, back through the purlieus in the fading

August evening light. The big trees we passed under down the long suburban avenues gathered the twilight under their dense, heavy dark green foliage. The breeze ran in the leaves above our heads, rising and falling like the dying breaths of summer. We felt insubstantial, wraithlike in the slowly failing mauve light with its garden scents, and I wanted to walk like this forever with my girl, buoyed along on her pure spirit, light and free and warm as the English summer.

At the digs we crept upstairs with the girls and lay on top of the bedcovers, courting in the darkening room. Half an hour later we were walking the girls to the bus stop. Their carefree girlish laughter rang out in the quiet street as bedroom lights came on in the houses. Mandy's tranny crackled out Luxembourg in the blue dusk-light and oh what a song it was coming out of the tinny little box in her hand like teenage magic—*I Get Around,* the numinous Californian harmonies like the quintessence of youth and summer, fixing that moment in time in my memory forever.

Chapter 13

Home

The blazing English summer weather of 1964 saw us through to the end; there was only one showery day in the whole two months. We finished work at the end of the third week in August and had our last day in the town off, spending our back-pay shopping for presents to take home and mod fashions to go with our long hair so we could arrive home in style. On the Liverpool coach early the next morning we occupied the long back seat and sang our harmonies as the day-long journey began.

"Are you a group?" a youth off the coach enquired at a services stop.

"Not officially," I said. "We just enjoy singing!" It had become a habit with us that summer, bursting into song at every opportunity. I wondered if it was a kind of Irish thing we'd inherited, something in the blood, a good way of smoothing over the day's long labours.

"I heard you singing and wondered," said our fan. "You look like a group." Of course that pleased us no end,

We ate the beetroot sandwiches Pam had provided us with and stared out the window at the expanse of ripe English meadowland sizzling golden in the hot sun. We were happy enough, however, to be going home. *Back to school!* Our O-level results had come: we'd all failed nearly everything. It was a glorious, Holden Caulfield kind of failure that made us fall about in stitches in our room at the digs. Of course we could resit the exams in the sixth form. One thing was certain now: school was an easier option than working for a living.

There was the long haul on the coach back up the length of England to Liverpool and the Belfast boat. The Liverpool docks, the Liver Bird receded in a violet dusk; it was a calm crossing and not a bad night's sleep sitting up in the steerage. We were awake with everyone else at 4.30 a.m. drinking tea served from an early hatch. It wasn't long then till we were ploughing up the Lough between green fields in the bright, fresh morning. I thought of Mum and Dad waking up under the mountain as we passed Loughside. And lo and behold, Belfast was still there at the foot of the Lough! Shipyard, dock, church and factory steeple, cosy terraced streets materialising out of the blue-white morning haze. There was the familiar smoky tang of coal burning in the chill morning air. We felt the thrill of returning conquerors as the Customs House clock hove into view and the ship docked at Donegall Quay.

The mist was lifting; lemony sunshine flooded the High Street. The red double decker bus took Howie and me to York Street station, the opposite direction to the commuter hordes pressing in to work. We had a compartment of the train to ourselves, lounging, feet up, full of our own significance. We were back in our own land, the small green diesel train whisking us out along the Lough shore and burrowing inland between the green embankments, under the grey stone bridges. There was Whiteabbey station, Bleach Green halt and the Valley of Death; all so familiar, yet fresh and wonderful now in a way that nowhere else in the world, however exotic, could ever be.

Howie got down at Jordanstown. As the train pulled out my compartment window overtook the ambling, stocky figure at the end of the platform near the ticket barrier, his thick golden hair grown over the collar of his pink shirt, and he turned his face to me and raised his hand in a farewell salute. What a friendship we shared now, all us lads, after the long summer's adventures together.

The train went over the level crossing. Alone now, I sat staring intently out the window at the small green hedged fields between the mountain and the Lough, as if I'd never seen them before. The thrill of homecoming beat up joyfully in my chest.

The house in Coolmore Green was a shining wonder of cleanliness and comfort after our English digs. I soaked in a warm bath, my first since leaving home in June; dried myself with a big clean soft towel, combed my wet black long hair in the tiny mirror on the cabinet door over the wash-hand basin. Then I got out Dad's shaving soap and brush and razor, inserted a new blade and carefully shaved the two months' fuzz from my upper lip. My slight body was white as ever but my face had picked up a tan. My hair, long as a girl's, lent an androgynous quality to my features—Shelley-like, I told myself.

I put on clean clothes, comfortable old rags retrieved from the back of my wardrobe: faded blue jeans and a frayed-collared blue and black pinstriped shirt, and hurried downstairs. The bacon smell of breakfast cooking mingled with the fragrance of house polish and the scent of sweet pea, colourful in a vase on the hall table. A self-satisfied grin fixed itself on my face as I entered the living room.

A fire burned in the grate against the morning chill, Dad in his armchair reading the *News Letter*, head back, nose wrinkled and arms extended, peering down his bifocals at the small print. He looked up smilingly, softly and folded the newspaper away, exclaiming in his soft Meath accents, “Ah, Seamus! It’s a new man you must feel like now entirely!”

“Aye, Pam’s bath was always full of washing. We got a bath whenever we went in for a swim.”

“That was a through-other place your brother sent you to! You’re very thin—half-starved, I suppose?”

“We got plenty to eat working in a café but then we sweated it off in the Wash Up. You’re lookin’ well anyway, Dad!”

The old man sat straight-backed in his chair to one side of the hearth, long legs crossed and his asthmatic “whiffy” at the ready in one hand. He was well-dressed, as ever, for a man about the house: black pinstriped suit-jacket and grey flannels, collar and tie. His soft, wavy crown of hair was snowy white now and summer in the garden had given him a film star tan. He’d been on “the sick” ever since his accident in the shower and was due to retire in a year when he was sixty-five; he had no real intention of ever going back to Railway Accounts.

“Oh not too bad all summer with the nice weather,” he said. “Just the odd wheezy night and these angina pains in my arms if I walk too far.”

I exclaimed appreciatively when I saw the big Ulster fry Mum brought through from the kitchen and placed on the table under the window. There was bacon, sausage, liver, a small steak, black pudding, egg, tomatoes, beans, soda and wheaten farls, pancake and potato bread. The late morning sun clearing the tiled roof of the block of flats at the back slanted in on the green linen table cloth. As I tucked into the grub, Mum bustled attentively to and from the scullery, replenishing the teapot, fetching me another fried egg and for afters her own freshly baked soda bread and a saucer of Kitty's gooseberry jam—"goosegab" as Dad called it.

"Your mother got a bit worried when we didn't hear from you for four weeks," said Dad. "I looked up the Reas' number and spoke on the phone to Mrs Rea who'd heard nothing from Stuart either. We both agreed that maybe no news was good news. We had a bit of a yarn and put one another's minds at rest. A very nice woman. So tell me this and tell me no more, Jim, how did you get on over there in England? I used to go and stay with my Uncle Billy McComb at *'I-stings.'* There were a lot of small Englishmen, I remarked. Uncle Billy took me to Chipperfield's Circus; I always remember the ringmaster teasing the clown: *'Yo've neveh seen an ossie's tile before?'"*

I'd heard this same affectionate mimicry of the southern English accent, the "horse's tail" many times before, the words of that long-ago circus performer in Hastings imprinted on Dad's aural memory. It was a limited yet very accurate impersonation that somehow encapsulated the character of the English or an aspect of it, their phlegmatism and practicality perhaps.

"I loved it in England, where we were," I said. "Nobody bothers you. Maybe it's the larger population and no-one cares that much. It's a sense of freedom."

On my third cup of the hot sweet tea I began to pour out an account of our summer adventures in a rapid, excitable voice, employing a subtle censorship of course, while still conveying a sense of the liberation we'd experienced. The old man listened attentively, nodding man to man, putting in the odd interested question or remark. It was as if I'd come back a grown man, our relationship changed to one of equals, at least for the time being.

"Well, you stuck out the hardship of it, son, all of you, and that is to your credit. The six day week in the Corporation restaurant. The digs with no bath. Cat fleas biting the shins off you. And you say those two drifters in the back room were crooks? Well, well, you live and learn! There are bigger crooks on the Stock Exchange in the City of London if the truth were known! As long as those fellows behaved decently towards you, that's all that matters. We half-expected you'd all be back home here by the end of July with your tails between your legs."

We sat out in the sunshine on the deckchairs on the back lawn for morning coffee made with boiled milk. Dorothy was there, back on a visit from London where she was teaching now.

"I can't take my eyes off that long hair of Jim's!" she exclaimed at one point.

Later I walked up the road and phoned Katie at work. I'd sent her a postcard after we arrived in England, and had one back from Port-na-Blagh where she and Helen and Miriam had taken a caravan for a week. I'd not been in touch since then and felt a little nervous as I walked to the phone box on the corner and dialled her work number. A lot could happen in two months. She could have met someone else.

"NACO. Good afternoon.'" She was on the switch-board.

"Is that the Girl from NACO?' It was one of our jokes, a parody of the TV programme *The Man from Uncle*.

There was a full-hearted burst of appreciative laughter from the other end of the phone. "You're back!" She sounded bright as ever, no hint of reproach from her for my lengthy, uncommunicative absence.

I got down from the bus in Royal Avenue in the golden evening light. I was going to meet my girl and my friends, back in the heart of my home town and I'd never felt so happy, such exultation. I was conscious of the distraction my long hair provided to people in the street. One old pensioner stopped in his tracks and glared incredulously after me. I ignored their reactions; I enjoyed shocking them all a bit.

I crossed busy Donegall Square and ducked down the shady, quiet lane of Wellington Street. I smelt the Espresso coffee and observed Hugh's relaxed presence, blond hair and white cotton poloneck, looking out on the street from his table in the big window. I pushed through the door, a clean dive into warm, familiar waters.

"Here we are again!" Hugh sang, conducting, as I pulled up a chair.

"You're early for once, Boydo,' I said. "What's wrong?"

We were the first evening customers in the intimate little coffee bar-restaurant with its dark polished wood and green cottagey upholstery. Joy, the easy-going South African manageress, was busy at the steaming Espresso machine.

"Oh, got bored hangin' about the house with Greba fussin' over me. Who'd be an only child? Though God love her, she means well, me poor ould Ma."

I knew he was keen to see Miriam again too.

Maurice the waiter approached with his soundless mincing step and hovered, biro poised above bill-pad.

"What can I do yous for?'" he enquired in his camp nasal drawl . He was a short, portly middle-aged figure, always immaculate in white jacket and shirt, black dickie-bow and trousers, with the mannerisms of an irascible woman.

Stylishly we ordered "Coffee." We'd come back with a few extra bob in our pockets.

"Where's your girls?" Maurice demanded, cornflower blue eyes twinkling wickedly in the round florid face under corn-coloured hair. He was something of a national treasure in a local way.

"On their way," I said. "Late as usual. You know the weemin, Maurice!"

"Aye, but they'll be glad to see yous back. Been dead here all summer with the students away."

At that moment the girls breezed in the door in a gust of laughter and clatter of heels, instantly transforming the shadowy quiet of the place. Katie, Miriam and Helen: their appearance had changed significantly, marking a passage of time. The schoolgirl natural look had been left far behind and they were each of them every inch the glamorous secretary now: bobbed hair that fitted like a hat, heavy dark eye make up and false eyelashes, dangly globular earrings. Irrepressible, they seemed to fill the small restaurant like a crowd. I realised Hugh and I had been talking in something close to whispers. Then Stuarty arrived sporting his big wavy bush of black hair, to whoops of welcome from the girls.

Maurice scribbled our orders busily on his pad, getting flustered and sharp. The conversation took off; in the background the Espresso machine roared, hissed and gurgled as Joy got busy. Maurice bore the steaming beverages to our table on a tray above his head, in an ostentatious display of professionalism. We stirred in brown sugar. Hugh passed round his *Piccadilly Filter*.

"Ronnie's not comin'," said Stuarty. "He phoned, told me his da, the old major, had sent him straight out for a haircut: 'Ask for a short back and sides, they'll know what that means! Good grief, I thought it was a son I raised not a daughter!' Gave him a proper parade ground rollicking. And now Ronnie's refusing to step outside the door till his hair grows again."

"Aw, all that lovely blond hair!" said Katie.

"And guess what?" said Stuarty. "Howie's got a girl in Jordanstown now. Already! Must be the long hair!"

Miriam reached over and stroked my long locks. "And what did your ma have to say about all this?' she enquired softly, her big black, fun-filled eyes teasing me.

"There was no comment," I said. "Think they were too pleased to see me back safe and sound. Anyway, Mum's a fan of the Beatles and m'da always said haircuts give you the cold."

The talk turned to our working holiday and the girls listened eagerly as, with much comic mimicry of English and Scots accents, we regaled them with our tales of the cafes and the digs and Jock and Vic—though not our venture into crime which would remain a well-guarded secret. It all gained something in the retelling, a coruscating world of magical, humorous experiences ever unfolding. The boredom and drudgery that is always the greater part of human experience, the monotonous work, the pointless hanging around, were left out and forgotten.

Apart from the wet week in a caravan In Donegal, the girls had worked away in their city offices throughout the summer. There was lunchtime dancing at the Plaza, evenings at the Jazz Club, and of course by now they knew everybody in Belfast who was worth knowing, all the latest local pop groups and the best looking boys.

We spent an hour or so in Isibeal's then caught the bus out to Miriam's. Her mother was away on business in Liverpool and Katie was staying with Miriam. We sat with our arms round our girls on the top of the bus and surveyed the streets of our city opening out cleanly, calmly below us in the clear evening light. On the Antrim Road where we got down, we sent Hugh into the off-licence for the cider. Soon we were trooping up Miriam's secluded side road under the big trees heavy with their late summer foliage, past the popping of balls and polite cries from the tennis courts.

It was a posh-looking detached older house set back across an expanse of lawn; the Golds occupied the ground floor flat. The large, high-ceilinged rooms were comfortably furnished. We sat round easily, chatting and drinking the cider and listening to Miriam's Rolling Stones and Beatles records as the evening shadows filled the living room. Miriam turned on a large table lamp and drew the long heavy curtains on the tall bays. In the soft, shadowy light and a creeping warm rosy mist of cider the courting commenced.

Hugh and Stuarty went for the last bus, with Helen walking back to Sunningdale. Miriam had offered Katie and me her bed while she slept on the sofa. Katie and I were the serious, going-steady couple, though I hasten to add, this was 1964 in Ireland, she was fifteen and the lovemaking

was confined by mutual agreement to petting and cuddling before sleep. Indeed, that was daring enough.

When I opened my eyes in the morning light Katie was sitting up beside me in the narrow bed we shared, her hand propping her chin, staring at me with a sort of affectionate, amused indulgence, rather as a mother might dote over her sleeping infant. Her flushed cheeks, tousled soft hair and smudged eye make-up, like a panda, were endearing. She was wearing a pink Baby Doll nightie. I reached out for her but she said, "Oh look at the time! It's eight o'clock and I have to get to work!"

I lay there watching Katie get ready, her back to me and her little face reflected in the dressing table mirror as she applied her make-up. She was telling me all about some fellow who'd been mad about her over the summer. She told him she had a steady boyfriend but he went on plaguing her with love notes and phone calls asking her out.

"Till it really got on my nerves and I says look, Derek, just go away and leave me alone, will ye! Anyway, not long after after that I walked right into him outside the Athletic Stores. I felt a bit sorry for the poor fella after speaking to him like that so I says hello, Derek, and do you know what, he just stood there in front of me with the tears rolling down his face, cryin' like a baby!"

She smiled to herself in the mirror, applying eyeliner generously, as she imparted the final sad detail of this tale of unrequited love: "Then before I could say another word he turned away and disappeared into the crowd!"

With the war paint freshly applied and her hair blow-dried, enclosing her face solid as a helmet, she was ready to do battle for another working day. She bent down to

kiss my lips and then she was off. I heard her call out to Miriam and then the front door bang.

I lazed back on the pillows, lordly, hands clasped behind my head, admiring the moulded plaster collar around the high ceiling light, dreaming I lived here in this fine old place. Ah Lord, here I was now, only sixteen and I'd spent a whole night in bed with a girl! Pretty, personality-plus Katie who had fellas in tears, dying for her in the streets of Belfast! But it was I Jim Mitchell that she wanted. The warmth of last night had left me in no doubt about that. Could it be she was the One already, and we would always be together now? My life just kept getting better, it seemed. What had happened to the lonely boy of less than six months ago—lonely and blue?

There was a tap at the bedroom door and Miriam entered bearing two steaming mugs. "Caw-fee?" she said in that mid-Atlantic accent and came over and set them on the bedside table and sat down close to me on the side of the bed.

With a quickening of my heartbeat I was conscious that I had nothing more than my underpants on under the bedclothes. Miriam wore a slinky dressing gown and when she crossed her legs the folds of it fell away revealing lengths of slim, shapely leg, smooth olive skin and the lacy trimming on the pale green panties of her Baby Doll nightie.

"I'm going in later to the office today. Sleep well?" Her voice softened as she fixed me with the big dark pools of her eyes—whirlpools, I mused, that could draw you down to your fate.

Two lovely girls wanting me at the same time! There could be no doubt I was leading a charmed life. But I couldn't do the dirty on Katie, as my parents called it, could

I? Yet there was no denying the attraction I felt for Miriam too. Where Katie was all girlish freshness and sweetness, a crisp rosy apple, Miriam was already woman—darkness and sensuality, like black grapes. But did I really want that darkness, her heaviness? It could only lead to pain. Katie's sweet ingenuousness and vivacity made light of the hours of the day. I needed a friend as well as—the other.

A wee, sleekit half-smile tugged at the sides of Miriam's mouth. "I'm tired now!" she sighed and put her face down in my pillow.

Her feet were still on the floor, the curve of her hip pronounced under the silky dressing gown. The dark head on my pillow cried out to be touched. And oh my God, my trembling hand was moving as with an unwilling life of its own, then my fingers were stroking the thick black hair. Oh, that blackness! My heart was thumping unpleasantly. I felt myself sinking into a dark marsh of erotic nausea.

"Miriam always fancies Katie's boyfriends!" Helen's words came back to me. And I could hear the voice of reason, the old spoilsport: "*So what happens once you're* not *Katie's boyfriend any more, after you've become Miriam's? Presumably Miriam won't really fancy you any more? So you'll have no girlfriend then. Imagine losing Katie for—what? Nothin' it'd be then, you'd be on your own again, back to square one!*"

My hand retracted itself. Miriam lay there a minute then turned her head expectantly. "You've stopped?"

"I'd better get ready," I said.

"But that was nice," she grinned.

Now I'd recovered my senses it seemed the right moment to stop, while we were all still friends. I pulled on clothes hurriedly and headed for the bathroom.

"Have some breakfast before you go," said Miriam and we had more coffee with toast in the living room. She was still in her dressing gown. It was nice here in her luxury flat, being looked after by her, her mother far away across the sea. I could have this all the time if she was my girl. I couldn't help a last yearning look at her smooth, marbly kneecaps below the dressing gown; we sat on her warm bedclothes on the sofa where she'd slept. Who knows? I found myself musing—there was always another day and I was free to choose. *Living with a woman*—now that would really be something!

It was gone ten when I left Miriam's, turning down the silent, curving old street to the Antrim Road in the sunny morning. The leaves on the trees shook a dapple on the pavement around my feet, like the gold coins of my good fortune. The tennis balls were popping in the courts and through the hedge I could glimpse the lissom leapings of the girls in their short white frocks. And once more I had that tremendous feeling of going from strength to strength, my life opening out before me in marvellous adventures and the love of women! Whatever had happened to the tragic adolescent quality of my existence? That was the old dead life now. The only problem these days was which girl to choose!

Before it was time to start school again Katie took me to one of the new clubs springing up around town to hear Wal Madigan. It was out of the town centre, up one of those long suburban roads on the east side, a first floor premises over shops with the entrance up a fire escape at the back.

We queued in the industrial evening sunlight. It looked like every longhaired youth in Belfast had come this evening, all fifty of us plus the girls, a very small youthful conspiracy. Gathered together here we were a force for a new aesthetic of some sort, not anything directly political. Ned had been a beatnik in the fifties, dropping out of art college. By the summer of 64 the day of the hippy hadn't quite arrived; this was something in between and more salubrious than either of those youthful trends. Our washed clean shiny long hair, nice as a girl's, flowed over the collars of pink or blue denim tab-collared shirts or light grey knitted crewnecks. Bell-bottoms swung fetchingly about our ankles. It was about the male identity; the girls just looked gorgeous as ever.

Katie was uncharacteristically serious; going to see Wal was a reverential business. The atmosphere in the queue was solemn, as if we were entering a church. This was no regular dancehall crowd. Listening to the music was everything here. That suited me.

"Oh you must hear Wal!" Katie had raved about him from the day I got off the boat. Naturally she and Miriam knew him personally, following the nineteen-year-old East Belfast man's rise through the Plaza ballroom lunchtime sessions and the Jazz Club that summer. "He's a livin' flippin' legend!"

She'd slip into an impromptu impersonation of Wal growling out the surly blues: *"Ah'm a man, m-a-n!"*

Inside we packed the dark, windowless, low-ceilinged space. Katie pulled me after her to the front of the crowd, facing the centre of the small stage area level with the rest of the floor. The group with shiny electric guitars, keyboards and drums, standing between the stacked black speakers, was striking up *Green Onions.* The musicians, close enough for us to touch, were mild, studious-looking young men with long hair like their audience. Billy had a neat beard, Sammy wore heavy black-framed glasses. They'd eschewed the showband uniforms of Ireland at that time for the kind of everyday fashion boutique casual clothes the audience was wearing—nothing to separate them from us in any way.

Wal emerged from the shadows like a kind of force to sing *Hoochie-Coochie Man,* growling into the microphone and blowing banshee-wails on a harmonica. Katie and I were standing immediately in front of him in the dense crowd pressing about the stage. Nobody was dancing or talking or courting; everyone was listening, concentrating.

It was the first time I'd laid eyes on Wal but he already seemed familiar from Katie's eager talk of him: an orange-shirted, short, stocky figure, with a heavy, pale, scowling visage under a gingery bush of hair. He had a strong poetic presence together with an aura of earthy physical density and power. Every inch of his squat bulk was poured into the music. He was the solid driving force at the heart of the band. Katie indicated his girlfriend Maureen watching from the side of the stage, a petite figure in a long dress, red-gold hair in a headband, noble little face, like Pocahontas.

Wal was pacing to and fro like a caged lion now, snarling and roaring*, j-j-just a- walkin'* , thrusting his fingers between his lips to give a piercing dog whistle. He went straight from one song into the next, scarcely pausing to catch breath. The more you listened you became aware of a powerful undercurrent flowing through the music and beyond it, a cumulative effect, building, building to sudden amazing passages like dazzling revelations.

Now Wal had ceased to be an individual. Eyes closed, body swaying trancelike, he was a medium through which the music communicated itself from some mystic universal source, putting the strong voice, like a black man's, through the gamut of human emotions: rich with the sense of beauty, dark with passion, heavy with pathos, gravelly with irony, tripping and breathy with excitement, babbling and incoherent with intensity and the pleasure it took in itself like a musical instrument.

He sang till I'd lost all track of time. Despite the sweaty discomfort of the airless, jammed space I could have listened forever. It was the brilliant swan song for that joyful summer of liberation in my life.

A few days later I had my hair shorn for going back to school. I didn't like seeing my ears again, but we wouldn't have got past the school gates with our Rolling Stones mops. The sunny spell passed and I felt the first breath of autumn on the back of my shaven neck.

Then it was September: the very name spoke of a closing in and melancholy. Blobby raindrops shone in a pale watery sunlight on my bedroom window as I dressed for the first day of the new school term. My school uniform was well-worn, faded, the blazer a bit small with leather patches on the elbows, shiny-seated grey flannels. I'd reached my full height of five feet-nine and a half inches at fifteen and then got thinner, so my clothes had lasted, with the comfort of familiarity. I looked forward to going back to school, seeing the gang every day.

Chapter 14

Winter Fires

My sixth form timetable was light and pleasant. I was allowed to drop the sciences. PT and Sport were no longer compulsory. I missed the English classes; I'd gained distinctions in Language and Literature, but I'd botched the Art paper, knocking a jamjar of water over my composition. Stuarty and Hugh were in a similar position, so we had all afternoon from lunchtime in Patrick Gough's art class, mucking away with charcoal or watercolour at the back of the big light airy comfortable room, permitted to talk quietly among ourselves while we worked.

Patrick was okay as long as you were getting on with something; any carry-on would bring the gaunt, emaciated figure in black corduroy bearing swiftly down on you. Deadly pale blue eyes bulged in a cadaverous yellow face under crimped, wavy jet-black hair. He exerted a vicelike grip and wielded particularly bony knuckles. It was funny, this paradoxical sadistic side to arty types—my brother Ned was the same.

At ten to three when we finished classes we caught the bus down town to isibeal's where we would happily sit till the cows came home. Two or three nights in the week we stayed in and did homework; in my case that was more likely to mean fiddling about on my guitar and the piano in the front room, then bed with Luxembourg on the tranny and a good novel to read.

On the other nights we met up with Katie, Miriam and Helen. Miriam's flat remained the focus of our social life for a time, with her mother frequently away on business. The Golds kept a well-stocked fridge—a favourite snack was mazzos and salami—and an eclectic record collection: Beatles and Stones of course, The Ram-Jam Band, *West Side Story,* Frank Sinatra's *Songs for Swingin' Lovers.*

I enjoyed the sense of sophistication at Miriam's, but as the winter set in she started to tire of us and the welcome there ran out. She told Katie we were too young for them and soon she was going out with some sleazy older bloke from the Bone district. Katie found another girl for Hugh from her office, wee Nan, a sweet, pale little pixie-girl from Sandy Row, and we met up at his place on Crumlin Road or Stuarty's on the Oldpark Road. There was a nice collective spirit in our little group of boys and girls, and, after the innocent fashion of the times, under the influence of fizzy cider, there were good-humoured five minute girl swaps—or were they boy swaps?

"Stuarty's a real good kisser!" Katie enthused yet I felt no jealousy; it was a technique not an emotion that she was talking about. That's how light-hearted it all was. I never thought for one moment that Katie could ever be serious about anyone else but me.

The Sunday nights at Katie's continued, just the two of us courting on the sofa in the front room while Mummy and Daddy watched *Sunday Night at the London Palladium.* We wriggled around on the sofa in various contortions or Katie knelt on the floor with her back to the electric wall fire, looking up at me.

"What long legs you've got!" she exclaimed, like Little Red Riding Hood, running her hands up the outsides of my black "elephant" corduroys.

"C'mere, Boo-boo Bear!" I commanded, pulling her up on my knee. She had rolled-up jeans and bare feet. "Hey, Katie, did I ever tell you you've got prehensile feet?"

I had of course told her many times and it always made her laugh—she liked the sound of the word.

"Ah'm an ape-girl, am Ah?" She shoved her hands up my jumper, tickling my ribs.

"Och, you'll stretch m'poloneck!" I protested.

"*Och muh poloneck!*" she mimicked. *"Don't stretch muh poloneck whatever you do!"*

I let out a bray of helpless laughter.

"You're wild ticklish, wee lad!"

She ran her fingers through my Beatle mop.

"M'hair! Och, stop, you're mussin' it, so ye are!"

"*Oh, m'hur! Don't muss m'hur!*"

We kissed, closing our eyes then opening them close up, like staring into each other's souls, then we burst out laughing.

She showed me how to inflict a love-bite, fastening her mouth on my neck and hanging on like a leech. Afterwards I examined the bruise on my flesh in the mirror over the fireplace. I suppose it was a kind of badge declaring your desirability to the waiting world.

"Now you give me one!" she commanded.

"Well, I'll try," I said. I fastened on her soft white throat like a vampire. But however hard I tried, when I pulled back and viewed my handiwork the pink blotch I'd raised faded pathetically to nothing and I felt my obvious inadequacy as a boyfriend.

"You're hopeless!" she laughed, frowning at my efforts in the mantelpiece mirror.

"I can't even jive, can I?" I reminded her mock-bitterly. The jiving lessons in the front room had had to be abandoned. I liked jumping around freely to music; jiving was too mechanical, like puppetry, and I'd go all stiff and awkward like an oaf, while Katie bobbed and twirled effortlessly.

"You've no sense of rhythm!" she informed me cruelly. There were so many things a fella did wrong.

We sat up straight and civilised on the couch, smoothing our clothing as Mummy entered at nine bearing the supper tray of tea, sandwiches, cake and biscuits. Mrs Burns had an outgoing personality with a disarming forthright Belfast manner. Sometimes she'd stop a minute and listen to a record we were playing. She'd sung in a dance band in the forties. Remarkably she approved of my Bob Dylan records—the general opinion at the time was that Dylan couldn't sing.

"He has a great voice, that fella!" she pronounced.

She'd married wee Albert when she was just seventeen and by all accounts it had not been a happy marriage. At one point she'd gone on a protracted visit to her sister in California, leaving Katie and Annie at their grandparents' in York Street. She got out the album one evening and showed me a photo of her linking arms with a tall man.

"That was my big American fella out there." Her blunt words shocked the clergyman's grandson in me. Her favourite song, she said, was *I left my heart in San Francisco.* A bittersweet comment on her life, I supposed.

"We thought she wasn't coming back," said Katie.

After supper Katie and I went quiet, courting seriously on the sofa. The 45rpm record stack played out and we didn't get up to change it. Faintly through the partition wall there carried the gabbling, harsh movie-voices and melodramatic theme music of the Sunday night film. The cold, deathly dark of Sunday night pressed its monster lips about the window of our warm, lighted haven on the hill. The seconds ticked away on the mantelpiece clock as we kissed ever more desperately. When we could put it off no longer and it was time to go I could have blubbered like a baby on Katie's bosom. It'd be two long days till we were together again! I'd marry that girl, I told myself. She'd be sixteen in January. We'd both be old enough then!

Christmas Day came round, a white one, perfection after a heavy fall of snow in the night. I woke in the magical trance state that had stayed with me potent as ever from childhood Christmases. I dressed in the snow light in the dingy back bedroom with its electric fire and went out into the whiteness, the crisp, bracing air and weak silvery sunshine, to meet Katie off the midday train from Belfast.

She looked radiant in the snow, beaming her Christmas smile. We went straight down Station Road to the Gibsons' party, an annual event that ran from midday till late. We passed kids sledging down the hill, building snowmen in front gardens. Some wee boys were having a snowball fight; one of them, about ten years old, paused to wolf-whistle after Katie.

The tall Douglas firs behind the Church of Ireland were majestically robed in snow, bringing memories of campfires under them in the dark churchyard in winter after school, spuds baking and a Woodbine fag passed round. And the Christmas services in the church with my parents and Dorothy; the church decked out for the big day, the carols and Reverend Jacko looking so happy, glorious in his vestments when he stood up to lead the service. A shaft of special magic Christmas sunshine straight from heaven penetrated a window, lighting up his wavy gold hair and glasses like a myopic saint.

We turned down the lane to the Gibsons'. The hedge had sprouted white blossoms of snow. Holly berries glowed like a brazier. The young married couple had moved here from their flat on the estate after Leila got pregnant. A muddle of fresh footprints ran before us in the snow and Katie indicated big pointy ones, exclaiming, "Those must be Fred the Ted's!" This was to be a gathering of living Belfast legends.

The rented older redbrick house stood on its own at the end of the unmade lane. Beyond the garden the pristine snow-carpeted fairy fields stretched away unbroken to Carrickfergus. In the window Christmas tree lights glowed warm and rich like jewels in a cave and an open fire waved a welcome. This was Christmas magic, all the crack and booze just waiting for us. Every moment was special and I wanted this day to never end.

Michael Gibson greeted us at the door, expansive in a new, Christmas box shirt and tie and stylish red braces and smoking a small cigar. The warm savoury blast of the bird cooking came up the hallway to greet us.

"Michael, this is Katie," I proudly introduced my girl.

"So Katie, you're the reason we hardly ever see Jim any more?" said Michael in mock indignation. He ushered us down the hall to take our coats and Leila came out of the kitchen, a tall, slender woman with long straight blonde hair, cheekbones curving in a gentle smile, emanating an easy, familiar warmth.

"Hello, Katie," she said. "We wondered when he was going to bring you along to meet us. He's a dark horse, is Jim!" Her candid blue eyes widened humorously

"You used to teach him?" said Katie. "Bet he was a mischiev-ious wee boy!"

"Aye, he was in my music class," said Leila. "He and two other lads formed a group and sang in front of the class: *Dream Lover,* the Bobby Darin number one at the time, 1959. Jim had every verse off pat and the two other boys on backing vocals. They'd rehearsed it for weeks. The class loved it!"

Her words brought back the richness of childhood, my happy time in the village school. I counted Leila a friend now, an equal, but I'd always think of her as the young music teacher out of Stranmillis College, of that happy eleven-plus year.

"We've observed Jim growing up," said Michael. "I can hardly believe he's standing here now with a charming young lady of his own. It seems no time since he was a round, chubby boy going off from here to the grammar school in his first pair of long flannel trousers—voluminous bags to accommodate his rather large posterior!" Michael released a gust of his wicked belly laughter that had no hint of malice in it. "Though you'd never believe it seeing the slim, handsome figure he cuts nowadays in the fashionable clothes he favours, imported from Carnaby Street!"

Michael had retained something of his youthful devilment, but he was a father now, his soft, wavy fair hair silvering at the temples and his speech more pensive, enunciated with a measured pedagogical precision, his light blue eyes glazing over in abstraction as he struggled for the *mot juste.*

We were In the small, dark back sitting room where the table was laid for the buffet, decorated with Christmas crackers and Michael poured us drinks, vodka and orange for Katie, Scotch and ginger ale for me. Ah, heaven! Armed with our glasses we moved through to where the celebrities had gathered in the front room with its Christmas tree, snow light and log-flicker and the contemporary navy three piece suite they'd brought from Kenbane Crescent.

Ned was there proclaiming in the mournfully rejoicing tones of a Belfast street evangelist: "I looked out my window this morning and saw the Lord Jesus Christ walkin' on the fields!"

He'd his English girl Gail over for Christmas; they were sleeping here at the Gibsons'. There was Fred the Ted, Paddy Boyle, the crowd who drank in Lavery's "Cobbles" up by Queen's University. I felt we had entered a charmed circle. Like Ned himself they were all larger than life characters, legends in their own time.

Ned's voice continued to dominate the company, his own voice now—booming and anglicised, sardonic, it had been cultivated amongst the intellectual washers-up of Colin Wilson's Soho and honed in the new brutalism of the Angry Young Men. He was telling a very Belfast yarn now, a bit un-PC as we would say nowadays, about "some poor wee darkie student backed into the corner of Smokey Joe's University Cafe, the wee fella's eyeballs rolling in his head in terror, and only meself between him and a kicking from these mad Sandy Row Teds.

"Anyway, I had to think on my feet. Says I, 'Hang on, lads, this is George—named after one of our monarchs and do yous not know George is a good Presbyterian?

Aye, and not just that, he's a good Orangeman too—the Grand Orange Lodge of Togo in West Africa where he comes from. Aren't ye, George? There is no colour bar for Orangemen, I'm tellin' ye, lads!'

"Of course when they heard that, the Teddy boys were all over the wee fella, apologising, 'Och, you're all right, George mate, sure you're one of us! 'Mon up the Row with us and we'll buy ye a drink!'"

Noticing I'd come in the room, he dropped his voice conspiratorially and said, "Careful now, everybody, what you say! He keeps a notebook, you know, records your conversations. Not wearing your plimsolls today? They're best for note taking."

It was a family in-joke likening me to Clinton Williams in the James Leo Herlihy novel *All Fall Down.* Clinton bore an uncanny resemblance to my earlier, fourteen year old self, a lonely boy scribbling compulsively in notebooks. I'd loved that novel and taken to cultivating my Clinton persona right down to the sneakers. Uncannily the wild older brother figure in the book, Berry-berry Williams, was a bit like Ned.

Ned in his trademark brown corduroy jacket was sunk down on the long, low sofa nursing a glass of the black Irish stout with its clerical collar. Beneath the head of curls he liked to think of as Byronic, his face was hollow-cheeked with an alcoholic flush, the consumptive-artist-in-a-garret. His girl Gail, over from England for Christmas, sat beside him, beat girl with dyed-black hair and black eye-shadow, black clothes, looking fashionably detached and bored.

"Where's Beryl?" Ned enquired. It was a family nickname for Dorothy after the Peril in the Beano.

I said, "She was in the front room with Tony when I left. Reading."

"Reading!" he snorted. "That's a new word for it!"

Katie got chatting with Fred; they had a mutual friend, an older girl who drank in the Cobbles. Katie prided herself in knowing everybody who was anybody in Belfast, or failing that, knowing somebody who knew them.

Fred hunched forward in an armchair, James Dean style, pouring himself another stout, his long legs stretched to the fire in old greenish tweed suit-trousers and gnarled, worn-shiny suede shoes. A heavy-knit salt-and-pepper poloneck sweater enclosed his chin. The gaunt head topped by rumpled brown-fair hair seemed carved in wood. He wasn't really a Ted—perhaps he had been at one time or maybe it was an ability to "handle himself" that showed in the pugnacious set of the jawline, cleft chin and full lips or now, as I looked at him, the blue eyes that sank and burned icily in his skull like a killer's.

He'd come out of the Merchant Navy in his late teens into the university boxing clubs and student drinking dens, becoming indistinguishable from the students. I'd first encountered his name on a letter Ned asked me to post, addressed to Fred Harris at Purdysburn asylum. He'd swallowed a bottle of Aspirin or cut his wrists or something. I pictured some psychotic yob Ned had taken under his wing; Dad had always said, "You can't keep Ned away from the gutties." So I was pleasantly surprised to meet a sensitive, cultured soul when Ned brought him to the house after he came out of the asylum. Incredible feats of heavy drinking, learned in the Merchant Navy, seemed to be the problem; Ned's more respectable friends shunned Fred as "amoral". There was a kleptomaniac tendency there, probably another consequence of the drink. Of

course that entire crowd drank too much and were never out of scrapes.

Fred was rolling another cigarette, keeping a permanent fag going and speaking in his warm, deep, gravelly voice with its student pub-intellectual honing, telling us about his Christmas stocking: "Ten Park Drive and a pair of Y-fronts. When I shook my head in disbelief my old lady started into me, 'Never look a gift horse in the mouth, son. You're lucky to get a present with us struggling now on your da's wee bit of pension and you drinkin' your buroo money the day you get it and borrowing off us the rest of the week. Lyin' in bed till four in the afternoon then out to the pub all evening with the student bowsey set—you never see the light of day. And your big sister a schoolmistress now. We always thought you'd grow up and get a half-decent job with your intelligence and be a help till us in our old age.'

"Och, quit yappin', Ma, says I, sure you know I tried working once and couldn't thole it interfering with my drinking. Only jokin', Ma! So I gave her a wee hug and managed to scrounge the train fare down here. Don't think they wanted me hangin' round all Christmas Day anyway."

Fred turned his attention to the small rotund figure of Paddy Boyle in the corner supping his stout. "Look at Boyle guzzlin' away there, the wee pig!" he exclaimed with deep affection. "Just gettin' quietly pished out of his wee head as usual, eh, Paddy?"

The Derry man smiled back with his touching boyish shyness. With greasy black hair down to his shoulders again and the nondescript rags he wore, he could have been a tramp who'd wandered in to warm himself by the Gibsons' fire. He spoke a few modest words, with an

endearing slight nervous stammer. "Me p-pished, Fred? You know fine rightly it's against my re-religion."

"You wouldn't think it just lookin' at him," Fred continued in the same warm, teasing, affectionate vein, "but he's got a fan club of wee fresher girls who sit round him in the Cobbles hangin' on to his every word, thinking this is it, the true intellectual bohemian life they dreamed about back in Muckmacross. Then one evening he's drunk so much, *whoosh!* the stout comes back up again, gushing out of him like oil from a geyser, all down his front and all the wee girls are backing off, turning white, ready to sick up themselves. But Boyle just sits there wiping his shirt-front down with a disgusting lookin' hankie that's been in his trousers' pocket since his ma put it there when he left home and 'Righto, girls,' says he, 'whose round is it anyway?'

"Later we carried him back to his flat, ran in a bath and dropped him in it with all his clothes on! "

I sat there quietly myself, keeping count of the number of glasses of Scotch I drank, one, two, three, but aware that I was losing track of time. The Christmas buffet was served. The sitting room filled up with more guests. Daylight faded at the window till Leila drew the curtains, shutting out the murk and freeze and any suggestion of reality outside the crack in the warm, bright, crowded room.

Now the proceedings took on the quality of a pageant. There were all kinds gathered here at the Gibsons'. One was a scruffy, undernourished student type, the revolutionary sort that was emerging—actually he'd been sent down from Queen's after one drunken episode too many involving a broken off-licence window and his arrest by the police—a Trotskyite they said, with fiery red hair to match his politics: Eamonn from Derry who was speaking in a rapid, articulate, incisive, persuasive voice while he gestured meaningfully with his palms.

He was debating the Coming Revolution with one of the workers, Billy Davison from the estate, a shop steward at Courtauld's, reputed to be a Communist troublemaker but even worse than that, a "Fenian-lovin' Commie." He looked a harmless, thoughtful man now, listening attentively to the revolutionary ex-student—Billy sucking ruminatively on his pipe and nodding conditionally or shaking his head neutrally. There seemed to be some agreement on certain basic Marxist principles, but less so on tactics: Eamonn was for direct action now, Billy for building a mass movement.

Their dialogue with its heady overtones of revolution that seemed to go with the snow outside, like Trotsky's Russia, was the last bit of rational conversation, comparatively speaking, I can recall that day. From that point on there was a complete degeneration into booze-fuelled surrealistic farce. Wee Rory, the Gibsons' solemn, bespectacled three-year-old was going round the room begging sips of stout out of the men's glasses. Fred the Ted was in a circular argument with an obstinate workman from the estate who insisted that "Jesus was exactly six feet tall—the only man that was iver exactly six feet, nat a fraction more or less!"

"Well, I'm six-four, so I must have been exactly six feet tall at one point," Fred was challenging him. I would have agreed with the tipsy man just to be rid of him.

"Well, that just goes to prove it then, doesn't it?" the man insisted. "Ye never stayed at six feet, did ye? See, ye can be over 't or under't or passin' through but niver exactly six feet tall! No other mon in the whole of human history was exactly six feet..."

There was an icy blast of air from the hall as Michael greeted another guest. The front door shut and he appeared at the inner door escorting a figure who looked somewhat uncertain on his feet. It took a few seconds till I recognised Mouse McTaig. A quick mental calculation told me Mouse couldn't be more than twenty-one now but already he sported a beer gut, his mouse-brown hair, still slicked back Fifties style, was thinning noticeably and his features, once sharp and rodent-like, were blurred with fat and corrupted to a crafty reptilian malevolence, what we called *sleekit lookin'*.

Yet it was still the same Mouse McTaig there before my eyes, a vision from my long ago-seeming childhood. I knew Mouse had followed in his hero Elvis's footsteps into the army in Germany and in Mouse's case out again with a drink problem and into a mix of dole and unskilled labouring jobs and marriage to some equally tough girl, with tough kids now and all of them sharing his parents' council house down the bottom of Station Road.

Mouse would turn up periodically, always the worse for drink, at Michael's, the one authority figure who'd ever shown any interest in him. This evening he was put in a low armchair next to me, his knees sticking up, slitty red eyes dully registering the crowded, jabbering room.

"Do you remember me, Dennis?" I enquired in drunken bonhomie, using his given name.

"Aye, the wee lod from the estate." His prompt response surprised me. I was quite a bit older, taller and thinner than the wee lad of five years ago, but I'd done an unforgettable Elvis impersonation in those days for Mouse and the other Teds, ingratiating myself with them for life, I'd hoped.

I watched Mouse going through the Gibsons' record collection on the carpet by the record player till he came to *Elvis's Golden Hits* with pictures of Elvis in his gold lame suit raining on the cover.

"The King!" Mouse grunted reverently. "He's still the King! Putt it on there, wee lod, wud ye?"

So I was still the "wee lad". Well at least Mouse liked me; I was safe.

Teddy Bear crackled out sultrily.

"Louder!" Mouse commanded. "He's still the King!" He hung his eyelids and twitched his upper lip in unconscious imitation of his idol. But his eyes were closing, while his lips continued to move as if in prayer, "The King..."

In a minute his snores were competing with the rich bass voice of the King of Rock and we were doing our best to ignore him when suddenly he lurched to his feet, eyes wide shut and reached for his flies.

"Look out, look out!" Michael shot over and rushed Mouse outside. Michael reappeared ten minutes later on his own. "You nearly had your boots filled then!" He laughed his warm devilish roar. "I packed him off home! He's stotious again!"

I'd kept count, or thought I had, of the number of whiskey and gingers I'd swallowed: fourteen, a record. It was over a six hour period, with food, and I was congratulating myself on how good I felt until I got up to go to the toilet and couldn't manage the stairs. Katie came and helped me and I had to go and lie on a bed afterwards. Far gone herself on the vodka, she joined me and we got under the bedclothes to keep warm. I didn't know how long we'd slept when Michael stuck his head in the door and said, "Katie, do I need to phone your parents and tell them you won't be back tonight?" We agreed that'd be the best thing.

The crack continued below with the party sounds of talk, laughter and the chink of glass, only more subdued now as the numbers had shrunk. It was nine o'clock. I had nothing worse than a thick head and a parched mouth and accepted Michael's offer of hair of old dog. Now the whiskey tasted like poison. I appreciated the quieter, less crowded atmosphere, only an inner circle of the close friends remaining.

Now each person present had acquired an individual clarity about them, like the realistic figures in a classical painting, vivid, luminous against the shadowy backdrop of the room. Paddy Boyle had passed out in an armchair, sprawled agape, empty bottle of stout in hand, like a study of the young Behan. Gail had nodded off in her corner of the sofa but Ned and Fred were still drinking steadily and talking in hard, determined, men of the world voices.

Fred seemed entirely unaffected by nine hours of steady drinking but Ned's face flared violently and he was talking too loud and repeating himself in the precise actorly tones he favoured, in a long, looping soliloquy peppered with the b word, the b and k consonants landing like blows. I have omitted the repetitious harsh expletive here in deference to the sensibilities of my readers.

"...So I had a word with Smith and O'Kelly," he was saying. "I says, look men, there's this smart b— over there lookin' a b— diggin', only he's got his cronies round him and I don't want to have to take on half the b— from the Rugby club on me own, so can I depend on you two to back me up if needs be?

"Well, ha, ha, you should have seen the pair of dossers panicking at the prospect of a real fight! Then O'Kelly says, 'Hang on a minute, Ned, I know him, so I do! That's Maurice Canavan, I went to St Mary's with him!' Says I,

'Your b— arse, O'Kelly, ye're yellah!' And he says, 'No, Ned, honest, he's a frena mine, so he is. Mon I'll introduce yous!'

"*B— off*, O'Kelly! says I. "I don't want to be introduced to the b—! Did you hear what I said a minute ago? I want to kick his b— melt in and I'm asking you to b—well help me do it, for b—sake!"

It never did come to a fight, as far as I remember—the intention was everything in this story—though we were all waiting with baited breath for a suitably dramatic bloody resolution.

Katie and I left at half-ten, floating back through the white night mystic stillness to Coolmore Green. The strange potent Christmas magic seemed to hover palpably in the starless night sky. The long hours of gladness and celebration, the booze and the crack, a rare sense of community, and being with my girl—it was all part of the magic.

Our hall light was left on for me, the key in the front door, everyone gone to bed. The living room fire was snoring under its night time blanket of slack behind the wiremesh guard. The ceiling listened. My mother came downstairs in her dressing gown with a pile of bedding for Katie to sleep on the chair cushions on the hearthrug and when that was laid out Mum and I said goodnight to her and went up to bed.

I got into my pyjamas and into bed and lay there with my ears straining in the silence until I was sure everyone must be asleep. Then I slipped soundlessly downstairs. Katie knelt up on the bedding by the fire in her Baby Doll nightie, arms open to receive me, all softness and giving.

"Jim!" my mother's voice came sternly from above.

Then my father weighed in, "Jim! Come on to your bed now!"

Katie laughed softly, "Go on then!"

It was a painful wrenching away from all my young male instincts but that was that!

Chapter 15

When I Was Seventeen

Travelling up to Belfast on the packed rush hour diesel on fine spring mornings, I'd slip into the first class compartment at the rear of the train and ensconce myself in the backwards-facing window seat where I could view the receding panorama of patchwork green fields spread out before me like a quilt, filling the whole range of my vision.

I lounged back lordly in the illicit first class comfort. With my back to the rest of the train I might as well have had it all to myself. Contentedly I surveyed my own green land, all dewy fresh and glittering from the slopes of Knockagh to the silver Lough, till I could feel it inside me, my self dissolving into it. The track feeding out under my feet focused me in a kind of meditation. All the strands of my life at sixteen seemed to come together in a satisfying sense of integration and wholeness.

The express train gathered speed, flashing heedlessly through the stations along the way, into the cutting, to emerge in the pale sea-light past bleak Greencastle halt. For the fifteen minutes of that journey I was suspended in time, with no sense of before or after, beginning or end. I could have sat there forever; the journey was everything.

The good feeling stayed with me as I came out of Belfast station, detaching myself from the crowds streaming to the city centre buses. I crossed at the traffic lights and entered Lower Canning Street. How often had I walked this way in six years of school? Yet I never lost the feeling these Victorian side streets gave me of stepping back in time, and the sense of secrecy and conspiracy suggested by their maze, *Odd Man Out* with its doomed fugitive patriot fleeing down alleyways, hiding in a disused air raid shelter. Putting the busy thoroughfare of York Street behind me and falling into a walking rhythm, I was off on another meditation, absorbing the quiet back street world in the mild air and clear light with its first intimations of summer approaching.

How can this be? I had to ask myself at times. My life had become a marvellous succession of happy lived days. It was like looking at a different life altogether whenever I cast my mind back just three years to my sickening fear of Cheyenne and maths and the sense of an overwhelming existential loneliness I'd carried around like a rock on my young shoulders.

Such alienation was unthinkable now. The long magic English summer had completed the growing up process. My close friendships were sealed. Katie and I had been going steady for a year now. *My girl*: what two words could compare to those? What a sweetness and beauty there was in them, that mocked all the loneliness and pain in the world. I gave little thought to school work, or the next round of exams, or my future prospects. Life was right here now in the palm of my hand and it was good. Nothing could spoil that.

Crossing into Upper Canning Street I caught a glimpse of Howie and Steve away ahead of me, their fair heads and school blazers near the top of the hill and the junction with Halliday's Road. The Jordanstown train got them in five minutes earlier. I went briskly, cutting through the long alley and catching up with the lads at the shop on Duncairn Gardens. The shop ran a sort of smokers' club for our school. Howie and Steve were over by the pulp magazine stand finishing their butts. I didn't fancy a fag so early in the day—they were both already heavily addicted—but I enjoyed the sense of bad boy conspiracy with them.

We walked on to school together, along Hillman Street and across the Antrim Road at The Phoenix. We had late passes because we came on the train; the rest of the school was already in morning assembly. Steve, fair and muscular, with debonair good looks, was on the edge of our inner social circle. More of an individualist, he was preoccupied with his girl Jennifer, a willowy, pretty blonde, the daughter of a Duncairn Gardens butcher.

"So when are we getting the group together, Jim?" enquired Steve who played guitar and wrote his own songs, forty of them to date, he told us. His idol was Buddy Holly.

"After the exams—after the summer now?" I said, excited by the prospect. The idea of the group, a proper group, had been dreamt up in the long, lazy afternoons at the back of the Art class.

"Stuarty on lead, me on rhythm," said Steve. "You 'n' me sharing lead vocals, Jim. Can you play bass? Never mind, I'll show you. Hugh or Malcolm on drums."

"What about Howie? Can't leave him out!"

"Sure. We'll fit you in on bongos or maracas, old son."

As we strolled leisurely in that easy, close companionship, up the avenue of newly green trees in the fresh spring morning, past the red sandstone wall to the school gates, feeling so young and free and all our adult lives in front of us, I fantasised that we might soon be appearing on *Ready, Steady, Go,* like the Yardbirds. Could I learn to blow a harp too, like Keith? For a moment at least, anything seemed possible. I already had a name for our group: *Shades of Blue.*

The rest of the school day continued in the easy mode established in that first hour or two. The first class of the day was History, the small resit group taken by Mark Moriarty, the head of the department, in the glass box of a room that extended from a corner of the Johnston Wing. Most of my friends, past and present, were in this failures' class: Hugh, Stuarty, Howie, Roy Campbell.

Moriarty, tall and angular, grey-suited under the black gown, scholarly stoop, would arrive in a bad mood. He must have seen us as the slackers and n'er-do-wells, and teaching us as an onerous added duty. We sat there, the small group in the small room, quiet as mice while Moriarty fumed through the typed notes he issued us with.

Yet once he'd got into his stride I found him impressive, like a stage actor, with his hawk profile and the longish grey hair swept back in a clump on the egg-shaped cranium. I was fascinated by the incredibly scrubbed, cutthroat razor-shaven pink flesh of his throat and jaw against the spotless celluloid collar. In full face the grey eyes glittered fierily, close-set to the hatchet nose. He might have been a character out of his own history notes; in appearance a Wolfe Tone perhaps. He brought these characters—Davitt and Parnell, Gladstone and Disraeli, Rasputin and Churchill—vividly to life with his detailed descriptions of them. Enthralled, I watched them parade before our eyes there in the little classroom in the costumes of their day, larger than life aristocrats of the soul: extravagant personalities, colourful, incredible men.

The modern history course began with the French Revolution, the struggle for democracy spreading to America and our own little country of Ireland, successful in the first two, ending in slaughter here once more, of insurgent Presbyterians and Catholics alike, who had joined in common cause.

Then we were into the nineteenth century with hard won British parliamentary and industrial reforms. In Ireland the Great Famine halved the population. Afterwards there was the Land League and the Home Rule movement, and as desperation for change grew, the Fenians and the rise of Sinn Fein.

Our own twentieth century brought the unprecedented slaughter of the First World War. In Ireland there was the Easter Rising of 1916 leading to the war of independence, ending unpromisingly in partition and civil war. After the Great War there was depression and the new movements and governments of Communism and Fascism.

We concluded this sad and sorry tale of human folly known as modern history with the Second World War that had ended just three years before we were born. Hitler and the Nazis seemed to be the culmination of all the brutal imperialism of history—victims themselves it was true, like most psychopaths, freakish, twisted men believing in their racial superiority and fired up with the "worst passions that ever corroded the human breast" as Churchill put it.

Churchill—statesman, writer, artist, one of the giants of the century—died that sixth form year of 1965 and Moriarty, an admirer, exhibited his *History of the English Speaking Peoples* and other volumes on a table in the corridor outside the little history room.

Random quotations resounded down through the years, rolling off Moriarty's actorly tonsils: *"Heavy swells with whiskers lounged in late and left early"*—the unreformed Civil Service. In some respects life sounded more romantic and fun before all the worthy commissions and reforms and the growth of the state. Moriarty, a Trinity man from the south of Ireland, had a cultured voice with little trace of an Irish accent, yet it wasn't an English voice either.

Churchill aside, Ireland had the best speeches. My favourite spine-shiverer was Pearse's oration at the graveside of the Fenian leader O'Donovan Rossa (that all sounded like a poem in itself):

"They think that they have pacified Ireland. They think that they have purchased half of us and intimidated the other half. They think that they have foreseen everything, think that they have provided against everything; but the fools, the fools, the fools!—they have left us our Fenian dead, and while Ireland holds these graves, Ireland unfree shall never be at peace."

Whatever the grim reality, it was the romantic side of Irish history that got you in the end. Somewhat less romantically there was *"Ulster will fight and Ulster will be right!"*—Randolph Churchill stoking up the fires of sectarian division against Home Rule. Irish history had a special resonance for us of course, sitting there in Belfast. I knew all about "Ulster" being "right" but I had to confess

the other side, the nationalists—most of their leaders Protestants anyway—sounded a lot more interesting.

History in general, all of it, was one big bloodbath with the taps left running. It should have served as a warning to us that we lived in a wild and dangerous world, yet studying it there in that boxy little schoolroom in the peaceful morning quiet it felt more like a Grimms' fairy tale, gruesome but cosy because we were safe and sound in here and it had all been and gone somewhere out there—or so we fondly imagined.

In reality history was like some fantastic, never-ending Tolstoyan novel unfolding, but with unbelievable characters and anarchic, cataclysmic turns of events that the purely human imagination could never have conceived of. To prove a point, I don't think anyone could have imagined the troubles still to come to us in Ireland, just a few years down the line; yet the clues, the cause and effect, it was all written down there in the history books, century upon century.

The summer term settled in bringing the first hot weather of the year. Sunshine flooded in the tall windows of the art room where we slouched over our pictures at the back, drawing, painting, chatting desultorily in soft voices in the somnolent postprandial quietude, belching discreetly, liver and onions, mash and gravy. I felt I could have remained forever like this, just painting. Perhaps I should be an artist like my brother? But for me painting could never be more than a simple pleasure, a form of meditation and relaxation, never a passion the way writing was to me. Now I was no longer studying English I missed the thrill of the Saturday afternoon composition written in the quiet of our front room and reading it aloud to Miss

Brown's top set in the week, after I had been awarded the highest mark.

Music, my other interest, was fun, that was all. If you enjoyed listening to it and singing along, then why not have a go yourself? There was much eager planning of our group. We argued self-indulgently over what kind of music we should play. Steve still clung to a fading era of simple, old-fashioned rock; the songs he wrote were in that style, rock ballads he crooned to us in a Cliff Richard voice. However, Steve was the one with real musical talent, who would drive the group. Stuarty and I had put our Everly Brothers' harmonies behind us and moved on to the current blues revival, which Steve was a little contemptuous of as a pseudo-intellectual fad. However there was agreement on the music of the Beatles, Stones, Kinks and other groups in the charts.

As April turned to May and I had turned seventeen, I was conscious that my schooldays were numbered. I had become so comfortable in the familiar, secure, easy routine of it, the free periods, being with my mates, daydreaming in the back of classrooms, the supreme contentment of afternoons in the art room, that I didn't dare think what might lie ahead. With the exception of Steve who was going on to A-levels and university to study civil engineering, all my friends were leaving; and although I'd an eye to teaching now—how else could a writer use his skills to earn a living?—it was out of the question that I should hang on here without them—my friends were what school was all about to me.

At the end of the school day we headed for the city centre with its bright, open, summery bustle and our refuge of the blessed dim cool of Isibeal's. We occupied our usual big window table with talk and crack over cups of tea. Sometimes Wal Madigan and his Soul Men would be there, sitting mutely over in a gloomy corner. Nobody had ever heard Wal speak, though Katie claimed to have, once at the Plaza sessions. "Awfully well spoken," she said.

Wal and the group cleaned windows in the daytime for ready cash. "Such quiet boys!" was Joy's comment. "Do you know Maurice wouldn't let Wal in with his long hair at first and he used to hide it under a cap!"

Howie bought the *Daily Mirror* every day and flicked through it, reading out any funny bits. Then one day there was a small photo of Jock in there and another man, vaguely familiar with his sweptback hair and thick glasses. The headline was:

Battling Buckleys Beat Post Office Burglars.

The postmaster of a Hampshire sub-post office and his family, the Buckleys, had tackled the two burglars who'd broken into the post office in the middle of the night. In the course of the ensuing struggle Kenneth Luckhurst had stabbed Mr Buckley. The determined efforts of the Buckleys, with even the Buckley kids, Tim and Priscilla, joining in, had detained the robbers long enough for the police to arrive and make arrests. Mr Buckley had survived the stabbing. Luckhurst, 34, and Andrew Murphy, 28, both with prison records, had been sentenced to 12 years. We recognised Luckhurst as "Clark Kent," the man we'd seen Jock talking to shortly before he disappeared.

There was the usual five or six of us always there for the crack in isibeal's, plus the odd persons who'd drop by for a chat, some more welcome than others. Fat Grose was unwelcome everywhere so that didn't bother him, rather he thrived on it. He was nineteen and still trying to get his O-levels; his extra years and weight meant he could dominate younger lads like us to some extent. His father was a judge and they lived in a big house on the Antrim Road. Hugh had known him since much younger days at Saturday horse riding lessons in Glengormley.

"Ridin' school was right, Cuey,eh?" The heavy, swart face creased in a vulpine leer. Hugh's cordial detestation of him only seemed to encourage Grose's vulgar excesses.

"Mind you and Avril Ardill in the stables?" Grose persisted. "Don't tell us ye've forgotten that now, Cuey?"

Hugh's face reddened; it was strange the impotent fury that Grose never failed to arouse in Hugh's mild-mannered person.

"Cuey's doin' a roast!"

"Don't call me that!" was all Hugh could manage to say, though clearly the needling went back a long way and ran to something deeper than a nickname.

"Cuey? How about Cue-ges then—that better?"

"Grose by name, Grose by nature!" Hugh spat.

"Ach, not that ould one again, Cue! Can ye not come up with somethin' original?"

"There's nothin' original about you, Grose, apart from original sin! You fat…!" Hugh spluttered with rage, words failing him. Nothing could erase the foxy grin splitting Grose's face from ear to ear. Although he was hefty, the "Fat" tag was more a hangover from the junior years when he'd been a genuine fat freak, an incredible pneumatic figure that could barely squeeze into a school desk.

"I hear ye're startin' a group," he said, tired of baiting Hugh. "My ould lad says he'll buy me a drum kit if I get me O-levels. I could be your drummer. I look like Dave Clarke!" He grinned cheesily under the acne-concealing fringe. "See?"

"We've already got two, thanks: Hugh and Malcolm," said Stuarty.

Grose turned on Malcolm sharply. "I never knew you played the drums, Malc? The dark horse there! The quiet one with the Buddy Holly specs, hidin' away behind his drum kit."

But Malcolm's dark reserve deterred even Grose who moved on swiftly. "Not like Stuarty there. He'll be up front wavin' his guitar around, showin' off to all the wee-girls."

"And Mitch here, the pseudo-intellect, he'll be takin' it all very seriously of course. The protest singer—doesn't matter what, he'll protest about it anyway, isn't that right, Jim? Look at his wee hands! How do you get those round the neck of a guitar?"

His words had no effect on me; we were so different that I took his insults as compliments.

"Your flannels are awful smart!" I said. "Do you press them yourself? Only you've got railway lines down the crease."

It was hardly much of a needle but it hit the spot and Grose lashed back, *'Ha!Ha!Ha!'*, yellow fangs bared, his face darkening in a murderous seizure. I didn't turn a hair; he was big and ugly, it was true, but so was a pile of manure in the road—you didn't stop to play with it, after all; you pinched your nostrils and walked round it.

Predictably the heatwave came with the exams at the end of May. We worked in our shirt sleeves, blazers over the back of our chairs, crouched over the exam papers in long rows of single desks. There was silence except for the tapping of nibs, shuffle of paper, the creak of the invigilators' shoes as they glided wraithlike up and down the aisles. Blue sky filled the big windows which were open at the top, admitting the odd insect-buzz of traffic from the avenue and tantalising summery fragrances like the sweet smell of freedom itself.

We were let out of the school grounds in the extended lunch break between the sessions and everybody headed for the waterworks behind the school, down one back street then another to the oasis of tree-shaded grass banks and shiny water under a blue sky, the girls there too, sunning themselves. Separate playgrounds and dinner tables kept us apart normally outside class. There was little interaction here either but it was a bit of excitement just seeing them there on the grass, unsupervised.

Books were open on laps or on the grass but I don't think much revision ever got done at the waterworks. We lounged and joked and revelled in the last hours of camaraderie—all those years growing up together, coming to an end now. Cause for relief or regret? We weren't sure. Even the bad times seemed good.

On the way back through the quiet wee artisan streets to the afternoon exams we stopped off for a quick puff up an alley. I treasured these last moments, poised between schoolboy conspiracy and the freedoms of the adult world. There was a supreme happiness being one of our little gang up a Belfast alley. I found myself looking round deeply, affectionately into my friends' faces, each with his distinctive mannerisms, a look, a laugh, a turn of phrase, all so familiar to me, so endearing. How well we all knew one another; what a lot we shared. It seemed unlikely I would ever know this kind of friendship again. We were going to Guernsey on a working holiday that summer; after August we'd be back in Belfast, scattered to different jobs or courses.

The adult world waiting beyond the school seemed a lonely place, businesslike and cold. The great friendships of life belonged to youth. You were expected to grow up and grow out of all that.

But that is another story and so I take my leave of you there, dear reader, in the shady cool of the alley up by the Belfast waterworks, that sunny afternoon in May in the year of our Lord 1965.